PRAISE FOR BRIAN LEUNG'S
TAKE ME HOME

"Heartfelt. . . . Leung's writing is so clear and lovely and his characters are so well-realized . . . the character of Wing speaks eloquently for thousands of Chinese miners whose voices are lost to history." —*Dallas Morning News*

"The coal mine culture of Wyoming comes alive in this story of forbidden friendship." —*Lambda Literary*

"This beautiful novel is about forbidden friendships, secrets kept, and one woman's quest to stay alive." —*Pittsburgh Tribune-Review*

"Leung wisely narrows his plot into a tightly woven and unusual love story. . . . [His] writing, in fact, has a train-like rhythm that will keep any reader turning the page to see what the journey home looks like." —*Kentucky Monthly*

"*Take Me Home* is a riveting novel of two heroic people attempting to transcend the prejudices of their time and place. Through Leung's skillful artistry and empathy, we see the worst aspects of humanity, but we also see the best." —Ron Rash, author of *Burning Bright* and *Serena*

"Brian Leung's exquisitely crafted novel *Take Me Home* is a story of the Old West for investigative readers, a necessary and cautionary tale spun from the lessons of real history. . . . [His] lyric gifts as a novelist bring the deftly plotted story alive." —*Louisville* magazine

that offers an important window into the West and therefore the American story."　　　　　　　　　—Percival Everett, author of
Wounded and *I Am Not Sidney Poitier*

"Brian Leung takes us to a time when it was difficult to be a strong woman, to be Asian, and, at times, to be simply human. And yet in his graceful, lyrical, empathic hands, *Take Me Home* is very much about humanity—very much about our *need* to love, no matter how forbidden. Lovers of history and heroines will want to devour this book."　　—Nami Mun, author of *Miles from Nowhere*

"Brian Leung's *Take Me Home* is powerfully imagined. He vividly and precisely renders pioneer life, the racial tensions against the immigrant Chinese men employed by the railroad and the impossibility of friendships. Leung's pristine prose recounts a time of tough women dealing with the loneliness of the Wyoming plains and the unforgiving landscape of an 1880s coal-mining town, a time when we were all immigrants in search of a place we could call home."　　　　　　—Helena María Viramontes, author of
Their Dogs Came with Them and *Under the Feet of Jesus*

TAKE ME HOME

A Novel

BRIAN LEUNG

HARPER PERENNIAL

NEW YORK • LONDON • TORONTO • SYDNEY • NEW DELHI • AUCKLAND

HARPER ⬤ PERENNIAL

A hardcover edition of this book was published in 2010 by HarperCollins Publishers.

HarperCollins books may be purchased for educational, business, or
sales promotional use. For information please write: Special Markets Department,
HarperCollins Publishers, 10 East 53rd Street, New York, NY 10022.

FIRST HARPER PERENNIAL EDITION PUBLISHED 2011.

Designed by Jennifer Ann Daddio / Bookmark Design & Media Inc.

The Library of Congress has catalogued the hardcover edition as follows:
Leung, Brian.
    Take me home : a novel / Brian Leung.—1st ed.
      p.   cm.
    ISBN 978-0-06-176907-8
    1. Rock Springs Massacre, Rock Springs, Wyo., 1885—Fiction. 2. Chinese—
Wyoming—Rock Springs—History—19th century—Fiction. 3. Coal miners—
Fiction. I. Title.
PS3612.E92T35   2010
813'.6—dc22

2009052254

ISBN 978-0-06-176909-2 (pbk.)

11 12 13 14 15   OV/RRD   10 9 8 7 6 5 4 3 2 1

For my father, Yee-shing Leung—

And for Tom Alvarez who is forever the genius-genius-genius
of the world.

The years seemed to stretch before her like the land: spring, summer, autumn, winter, spring; always the same patient fields, the patient little trees, the patient lives; always the same yearning; the same pulling at the chain—until the instinct to live had torn itself and bled and weakened for the last time, until the chain secured a dead woman, who might cautiously be released.

—WILLA CATHER, O PIONEERS!

If heaven and earth will endure,
Our reunion will come as surely as our parting.
The dust of my carriage has obliterated the interminable road,
But the road is interminable: how can I forget?

—T'AN SSU-T'UNG, FROM *"Parting Chant"*
(TIMOTHY C. WONG, TRANSLATOR)

Their happiness was to be together; they radiated something of their calm amongst others, and could take their place in society.

—E. M. FORSTER, MAURICE

"I thought you'd be taller."

"I am," Addie said without looking at her chaperone. "Much."

She waited, then smiled. They stood at the open end of the observation car, steep gray rock rising on both sides, track receding behind them as if the train was the tab of an endless zipper, which seemed right to her. That's the way the world was going, from buttons to zippers. She looked at her companion, Buckley Orner, the unfortunate young man who'd been tasked with getting her from California to Wyoming. She'd known his father, disliked him, but didn't bring it up. She was more surprised that after all these years somebody at the Union Pacific thought she was important enough for the fuss. She would have preferred to make her own way, but they wouldn't listen. Too many connecting routes—Las Vegas, Salt Lake, Ogden, Green River. A woman traveling alone needed help on a trip like this, they insisted. And their version of help was this poor young fellow who seemed to her just out of the cradle, more than tender. Buckley wore an immaculate gray suit, white shirt, and a tie so orange it seemed a gleaming flame rising out of his vest. The excess of 1927, she thought, the very reason she avoided going into the city itself back home in Los Angeles. "You ever wear the same clothes twice?" she asked. She'd known him three days and not seen evidence to the contrary.

"If I can help it, ma'am, no," he said proudly. By far he'd certainly brought more luggage than she, had purchased a number of things in Los Angeles. But then, who could blame him? He lived in Wyoming. It had been over forty years since she'd been there, but if it was anything like she remembered, he had a right to raid every department store and haberdashery on the West Coast.

"What's it feel like, ma'am, to be a lady heroine marching back into town?" Buckley was leaning on the cast iron guardrail, the stony mountainside rushing behind him, the train itself sounding like a thousand women on washboards, scrubbing in unison.

Addie laughed, grateful they were the only two on the platform, grateful for the fact there weren't others around to hear her referred to as "ma'am" time after time. "Don't know what stories are filling your head, but I'm no hero."

"Really?" Buckley stood upright. "I heard all different kinds of things about you rescuing men from a mine collapse, that you were friends with the Chinamen, some say you helped run them out of town—"

Addie raised the hand in which she held her cane. "Me running Chinamen out of town?" She shook her head. "Son, that don't make sense. The UP spent all this money dragging me back to Dire Draw to say farewell to an old friend, a *Chinese* friend, and you think I'm one of them run 'em out?" She caught her voice, which was much louder than it needed to be, even with the noise from the train, and she hated the thought that she was playing any part in the rising cacophony of modern life. What she wouldn't give to hear again the timber-muffled world of her childhood.

Buckley looked into his chest, rocked with the movement of the car. The part in his dark brown hair was white as a streak of chalk. Maybe she'd been a bit too firm, she thought, but she had a right to be sensitive on the matter. There wasn't a day that passed when she didn't think about Wing Lee and the circumstances that forced her out of Wyoming without a word to her husband. It was a time when it seemed her only option was to run, and she never felt right about it. She'd agreed to come back, but now she worried about how many folks might be coloring her up the same as Buckley, as if there was another Addie Maine, a ghost who'd stayed around Dire warping the truth about what happened.

Sometimes that earlier version of herself seemed like a ghost even to her. She had been so young that day of the riots when she took off from Dire, rode hot and hard in the saddle toward Rock Springs. She recalled the smallness she hadn't felt since the first months she arrived in Wyoming Territory, riding the hours toward Rock Springs over land so flat and broad it was as if God had spread it out with a table knife. There had been a lot of bad days, but she knew then that September 2, 1885, was likely to be her worst. By the time Addie was a mile outside town it was near dusk, the distance marked by columns of black smoke bleeding into the sky. She reined her ride, Racer, to a stop at the sight of a man limping through the sage, looking wholly dazed as he approached. When he was nearer, Addie saw that he was Chinese, and one side of his face was beaten raw. She slid off Racer and completed the distance between them, startling him into rigidness when she grabbed him by the shoulders. "What happened?" He didn't speak. From the looks of it, he'd been attacked by more than one person.

Addie led the man back to Racer, wishing she'd thought to bring water with her. "Let me ride you into town and get you to a doctor," she offered, unsure if he even spoke English.

The man slumped to the ground and pulled on his shoulder where his sleeve was torn. "No," he said hoarsely. "I don't go back."

Kneeling, she could barely look at him directly. He was wheezing, and up close it looked like someone had gone at his face with a hay rake. "Who did this to you?"

"All," the man said. He was out of breath. "They chase us. They shoot." He pointed to his pant leg, which was damp with blood, the color nearly black against the blue cloth.

Addie guessed if he'd been shot he was merely grazed, or he wouldn't be walking. She asked if he knew Wing, but he shook his head. "You can't wander out in the middle of nowhere," she said, though she understood his limited options. The black smoke was certainly a kind of flag, warning him away from the white fists beneath it. What gets into folks, she asked herself, turning into savages? Practically from the moment she arrived in the Territory she'd heard Chinamen called all manner of things, had been warned that they were like animals. Just a year earlier she'd never seen one in her life, but by the time she got off the train she had been convinced they were practically kin to wolves. And now look at who the animals turned out to be. Even her husband, Muuk, who'd once seemed so even-tempered, had turned. It wasn't two weeks earlier he was bragging about beaming a Chinese miner in the back of the head with a rock and getting away with it. "Blood came," he'd said, smiling.

She stood and got her bearings, pointing in the distance to the straight line running through the valley. There she saw other forms; from that distance they looked like dark blue beetles on the run. "Best thing for you is to get near the tracks." It was a sad reality that this man and those in the distance more or less belonged to the UP, and she was certain the men who ran it would find a way to round up their property. With Addie's help, he pulled himself to his feet, but refused to let her put him on Racer. He stared straight ahead at the tracks where Addie directed, then moved forward at a slow, stumbling pace. She wondered if this looked like the kind of failure vultures catch from the corners of their eyes.

It wasn't a thought she lingered on long, because keeping Wing alive was her priority, and in that moment she made a decision. When she got to Rock Springs, when she found Wing, she would throw him on the back of Racer and they would ride out. Ride to California, or maybe up to the territories in the Northwest, but she would take him as far as necessary to get him to safety. She was never so sure about anything in her life as at that moment, even if it meant, eventually, waving good-bye to him from a dock as he went back to his homeland. Maybe that was the best thing. Maybe it was near impossible, but it was the only way.

Addie wondered if Wing was in similar shape as the man she had just met, or if he was still in Rock Springs. If it was the former, he might be all right, but if it was the latter, he needed her help. And since she was the one who made him leave Dire for Rock Springs, it would be her fault if he got hurt, she thought. She wouldn't let it happen.

Buckley hadn't yet gotten the nerve to look Addie in the eyes. Inside the observation car, well-dressed men and women lounged in straight-backed red velvet chairs, peered out the windows at rock and pine trees, read newspapers. She didn't know any of them, but she could stand where she was and make up a pretty good story for each. And wasn't that the way of history? Strangers looking at strangers from afar, telling what was knowable, filling in the rest with interesting guesses. Suddenly she found her face reflected in the window glass, or it found her. It struck Addie that the effect was much kinder than if she'd peered into a mirror. Here she was a suggestion of herself, outlines really, concealing the fact that her hair was going white fast, taking thirty years off both her complexion and the lines around eyes that spent decades squinting under the California sun. She wasn't sure which Addie folks in Dire were expecting, but then again, it didn't matter, she wasn't going for them; she was going for Ah Cheong, she told herself, and if she could manage it, she'd avoid her husband Muuk altogether. "I just hope there's no fuss over me," Addie said, partly to her reflection, partly to Buckley.

"Well, Miss Addie, ma'am," Buckley said, finally looking up, "forty years is a long time to be away. I don't live in Dire myself, but I know people are curious. Maybe you should see this." He pulled a large billfold from his coat pocket, removing a neatly folded rectangle of newsprint, which he held out to her.

In her hands, the not-quite-white paper with black print had little weight, but Buckley's shy tone made her understand that the contents were more consequential than she'd want. She undid the first fold, then once more, the broadening paper now flapping in the train's draft. The masthead read "The Draw," and below it, a medium-size headline: "Dire Heroine to Return."

She looked at Buckley before stepping inside. It was a newspaper all those years ago, she recalled, that was handed to her on her sickbed and forecast the troubles to come. "You take in the view while I sit down and read this."

Aside from the missing rush of air, the observation car wasn't much quieter. She found a seat across from a sleeping man, gray fedora pulled low on his forehead, chin in his chest. Outside, the landscape passed more slowly as the train took a steeper incline. She looked again at the article, undid its remaining folds and read. "Adele Muukkonen, formerly Adele Maine, and wife of former Dire miner Atso Muukkonen, will return from California. Old-timers knew her as Miss Addie, the woman whose glorious heroism saved the lives of two men in a mine collapse." She cringed, as if she'd been pinched. The first sentences were correct, but to see her married name in print pained her. At home, she rarely used it, had gone back to Addie Maine. The story was contained in a long, thin column on a half sheet of newsprint the color of which brought to mind the shade of well-used dice.

She read the column through to the end. It reported that after the riots at Rock Springs, Adele Muukkonen had taken leave to California, where she grew oranges. The memory of her as a feisty, independent woman stayed in Dire, such that a lot of the younger miners wondered if she ever really existed. But it was true. She had sold game meat to make a living, had plunged into a collapsed mine when the miners themselves wouldn't go. She'd had an entire floorless house presented to her, lifted over her head and set down around her. And then there was her charge to Rock Springs on the day of the riots, which was done, the article said, out of her respect for the Chinese miners when such consideration was more than frowned upon. Now the retiring Ah Cheong had requested her return before he left for China, and the benevolent UP was making it happen. She would be there for his farewell luncheon. "And what a bonus for the old-timers," the story exclaimed, "to see Mr. and Mrs. Atso Muukkonen standing side by side after all these years!"

There it was again, her married name, and her first obliterated. It wasn't a pleasant thought, but she was going to have to see Muuk after all. And no mention of her dear brother Tommy, and certainly not Wing, unfortunate proof that the secret she and Wing shared along with Muuk remained just so. The omissions were a shame, she thought, because she lived long enough now to look back and see that of all the people she'd known, Tommy had loved her most, and Wing had transformed her life. It wasn't for Ah Cheong, she understood, but for them that she agreed to this journey to Dire. But Ah Cheong was important. She had something for him to take back to China.

Refolding the article, Addie granted that its thrust was accurate, but it also made her sound like something out of Buffalo Bill's Wild West Show. She chuckled. That hadn't been around for decades. No, it was moving pictures people thought of now, gobbed-up westerns that bore no resemblance to the life she'd lived. There had been no Elinor Flairs in Dire, that was for sure.

After a few minutes Buckley entered the car and approached. For the life of her she couldn't imagine how such a tender thing as him could survive in Wyoming. Things must have really changed. "What do you think, ma'am?" he asked, pointing at the folded article still in her hands.

"They left some things out."

The train plugged forward, and Buckley gripped the back of a seat to keep his balance. "Like what?"

"Well," Addie said, "people, for one thing. Important people. And the reason I left Dire in the first place." She wished she hadn't said the last part. Buckley took a seat next to her, waiting for an explanation. "I was shot, is all."

"Shot? By who?"

"Can't count the number of times over the last forty years I run that question through my head. The sheriff never brought up charges on anyone."

"Maybe," Buckley said, leaning in, "it was a Chinese, ma'am."

Addie scoffed at the remark with a huff. She'd known Ignorance, and here was its grandchild. "No, son, it wasn't a Chinese. It came from the crowd, and that's the thing. There had to be witnesses, and not one person spoke up."

"Then the shooter might still be alive."

"And waiting to finish the job." She'd meant it as a joke, but she was surprised to find herself suddenly overcome, so much so that Buckley put his hand on her shoulder. It wasn't that she hadn't thought about that night, because she had, and more times than was healthy, she sometimes told herself. She just hadn't thought she might someday be face to face with the one who shot her. "The truth is," she continued, "my husband knew who did it, I'm certain. Never got the chance to ask him directly." She decided not to let on just how certain she was because it was really nobody's business but her own.

Buckley sat upright, went wide-eyed. "Ma'am, you got your chance now," he said, pointing to the newspaper article. He was right, she guessed. Muuk was alive, and she was bound to see him whether she wanted to or not, and when she did, she told herself, she'd do it. She'd put the question to him. She might have done it back when, but that was a time when she thought she had to run. Addie's own mother had abandoned the family, a fact that even now sat in Addie's heart like a cold stone. For the longest time she hoped she'd see her mother again, if only briefly, long enough to ask "Why didn't you take me with you?"

Now it was a different question she was bound to ask. Forty years spent wondering who shot her, adding things up. "Never thought I wanted to see him again," she said to Buckley, "but I'm going to look him straight in the eye and get my answer." She was surprised not by the question, but by the sudden urgency for finality.

"Boy," Buckley said, "that write-up about your homecoming sure missed the mark."

"No," Addie sighed, "I suppose what they wrote is true." She was thinking of two men she wanted to see again more than anything, and the one she'd have to face. "But they got it all wrong."

EPISODE ONE

It was forty years earlier that Addie first asked the question. When she came to that morning, she knew things weren't right. She remembered the previous night and how the riot was going full force when she rode in. There was the awful sound of Chinatown burning, angry faces, and a woman who was so proud to have thrashed a Chinese miner. She remembered the Chinese man she'd encountered outside Rock Springs, beaten to a pulp, who refused her help, and the pair she'd sent off on Racer's back. And she remembered she'd not managed to reach Wing; she prayed now that he'd made it out of town. Addie's head was clear, though throbbing. What she had no recollection of was how she'd arrived in the bed in which she lay, nor why her midsection was wrapped in bandages.

Across the room a lace-curtained window was filled with the pink light of dawn. When she tried to raise herself she found her body full of ache, and she was thirsty, so thirsty she thought she could polish off a barrel full of rainwater. She felt the bandages. "Oh, hell," she said. "I was shot."

Then she recalled the sight of Muuk standing behind a wagon when she was carried off. It had happened so fast, but now she held him in her mind, unmoving as a daguerreotype. He was tight-lipped and glaring, standing with his arms crossed. No matter what their marriage was like, she did not want to believe her own husband would shoot her. By all rights he should be the last one on her mind, but so much had transpired between them, her mind kept returning to Muuk's angry stance. He had a right to resent Wing, she supposed, but not so much that he'd take part in the riot, not so much that he could see her standing on that bridge and pick her off like she was a squirrel on a woodpile. One thing worked against his innocence. Whoever shot her had missed the mark, which was typical of Muuk's aim. For his sake, she hoped it wasn't true.

And where was she now? Addie wondered. On either side of her was an empty bed with a bare mattress. Below the window was a small white cabinet, fronted by crooked drawers, a pitcher and washbasin sitting on top. The door to the room was shut. At first Addie thought she'd wait until whoever was caring for her entered, but the more her thirst came on, the more she convinced herself they'd want to know she was awake. "Hello," she called softly, and then, clearing the morning from her throat, called again louder. She listened. From below came a creak of wood and then, "Up in a minute." It was a man, and she didn't recognize his voice.

"I'm awake is all."

"Up in a minute," the voice repeated.

It was an odd sensation, waiting for someone to help her, needing it. She stared at a painting on the wall. It was a mountain landscape foregrounded by dark green trees. Trees, she thought, a simple thing to miss, but she hadn't touched one, a real honest-to-goodness tree, since she arrived in Dire. They were what made the meadows so peaceful, she thought, the ones she loved as a child, wide pools of grass hugged by oak and maple and ash. That was what Wing always brought her, a core of calm security. But she'd given that up, let him down, and for all she knew, it may have cost his life. On that point she renewed a promise she'd made to herself the day before. He had to be alive, and she would find him. She would take him out of Wyoming, westbound by train if she could, on horseback if she had to. It was not only right. It was what she wanted.

Almost a minute on the dot, she guessed, when she heard someone approach the door and offer a gentle tap of permission to enter. The face that peeked in was smaller than she expected, and from an older man. "Dr. Bemmer," he said, stepping in. He was short and bald except for a pair of hairy ears and a patch around the back of his head, the skin of his pate red and spotty. She guessed he wasn't one to wear hats. He'd had a shave not too long ago, she could tell, and as he approached the bed he showed a distinct limp, his right leg dragging along like a child that didn't want to be put to bed. The doctor stood above her and shook his head grimly, Addie bracing herself to hear the news.

"Well, I suspect you know you got shot," he began.

"That's all I know."

He told her the rest, how they'd patched her up in Rock Springs, but with things so chancy there they brought her to Green River, which was twelve miles west by rail, and were waiting until she came to before taking her on to Evanston. He wasn't even a practicing doctor in Green River, just got caught in the mess of it all, and to her benefit he knew a considerable amount about gunshot wounds. Her bullet, he said with about as much cheer as he was bound to muster, had struck a rib. He got a good hunk of it, but the rest she'd have to carry around. The rib would heal, but she was going to be sore for some time. All and all she'd be fine if infection didn't set in. The doctor paused, completing his diagnosis, and then asked Addie about the pain.

"Right now it's the thirst that's getting to me." She was relieved he hadn't said anything about the baby, and right then it wasn't something she was anxious to bring up. She wasn't willing to believe that Muuk tried to get rid of her and this child he so badly wanted at first. It was her brother, after all, who'd suggested they marry, and Tommy wouldn't have introduced her to a man so full of hate.

Was she even equipped to be a mother? She'd loved her own up to the snowy morning she discovered her gone, up to that morning and well beyond. Her mother had left precious little evidence in Addie's memory about how to be what most folks would call a good mother. Mainly in word and action, she taught Addie that for women the world was hard and unsympathetic, a punctuated lesson without so much as a "See you in the hereafter."

Now Addie made a drinking sign with her hand. The doctor raised a finger and nodded, as if getting her some water was next on his list. As he poured, Addie struggled to pull herself upright, an extended groan underscoring her progress. "There's the pain," she said. The doctor handed her a cup, and she drank the water in two gulps. "You ain't seen nothing like what I saw last night," she said, thinking their medical conversation was over.

Scratching the bridge of his nose, the doctor pulled a three-legged stool next to the bed. "Miss Addie," he said softly. "That's what they told me you go by. You were right here last night full of fever." She didn't see how that was possible, though she wasn't a stranger to such illness. "It's been four days," he continued. "You lost a lot of blood, but I fairly got you patched up." Despite his optimistic assessment, his expression was grim.

"Four days," Addie repeated. She'd once seen her brother struck down with fever for almost three weeks. When he'd fallen, the dogwood blossoms were plump but still unopened, and he lay in the cabin drenched in sweat while the woods were flowering and flashing out in green. He missed the burst of spring. She was young, but it was the first moment in her life where she gave a thought to time. There was no waiting for one boy to gain strength enough to step out of doors to take it all in. This world plunges forward, she learned, not on human time, but on its own terms. It was enough to make a person not want to ever close their eyes.

"Seems like the trouble might be calming down a bit. The sheriff's got a posse rounding folks up. That's one thing. Maybe they'll get who done this to you." She doubted it. She'd met the sheriff once, Joe Young. He was efficient enough, she guessed, but who'd testify against anyone he arrested? Rats don't tell on other rats that get into the corn bin. "Got any idea who shot you? We can get the sheriff here for sure."

She had ideas, though none that she could say without having to explain. "I was a friend to the Chinese," she said, and left it at that, knowing the remark spoke for itself. "And to be truthful, I'm not sure who to trust now. Not the sheriff, or the Railroad, or my own husband."

The doctor raised his white eyebrows.

"But I'll tell you," Addie continued. "Send for a woman named Maye Grood. She's a friend and I'll point her in the right direction."

"I'll look after it." The old doctor took her arm and turned it palm up, placing three fingers of one hand in the center of her wrist. It was a curious thing to do, she thought. But then again, she'd never actually been to a doctor. "What are you doing," she asked, as he grew more quiet and intent.

"Checking your heart. Be still." His hand was cold, and trembled.

Addie would have chuckled if the doctor didn't have such a stern earnestness about him. But she wondered just what kind of doctor he was. She'd butchered a lot of animals in her life, and not one of them had their hearts in their limbs. When she took ill as a child, it was her forehead and chest her mother used to gauge just how badly the sickness had taken hold. But it was her grandmother's healing power that was legendary, both with men and animals. Her remedies, in their variations, always had two ingredients in common: tallow and prayer. The latter of which was the reason her grandmother said that as long as she lived she'd never let some Godless doctor so much as lay a finger on any one of her family.

Addie didn't know if the man in front of her was Godless or not. She hadn't turned out to be much of a churchgoer herself, so it didn't make much difference. And anyway, judging by his gimp leg, it didn't look to her like any prayer of his had been answered.

The doctor was done checking her heart. He laid her wrist at her side and offered a half smile. "Strong," was all he said. "But it's a terrible thing those men did." Something about his demeanor didn't convince her. "Just terrible."

Addie's mind flashed to the purpose of her run to Rock Springs. "Did anyone find Wing Lee?" she asked, grabbing the doctor's hand, but she could tell he didn't know what she was talking about. "He was—" She paused and tried again. "He used to work for me. Was anyone killed?"

"You've just gone through quite an ordeal, Miss Addie." He

patted the top of her hand, and she repeated her question. He was unvoiced for a moment, looked into her eyes, and then with a sigh he told her everything was fine. The Railroad had come in, he said, along with the government—things were quiet, getting sorted out.

"That wasn't my question."

His expression betrayed the gravity of what he was about to say. "I shouldn't be telling this to a young woman who's been through what you have," he began, "but God's honest truth it sounds awful." There'd been a couple dozen Chinese killed, he told her. Some said maybe more. They'd been chased into the hills for the most part, though the railroad was gathering them up along the tracks and taking them in to Evanston. The rumor was they were going to be brought back to the camp under protection of the military. The doctor paused in his story, as if he weren't able to go on, though Addie got the sense it wasn't what he was saying that troubled him as much as that he was saying it to her. He stood, stepped outside the room, and returned with a newspaper.

"This is from Cheyenne," he said. "The day after. Can you read?"

Addie nodded, though there'd been a time not too long ago when letters on a page weren't much different to her than patterns of light on a river's surface, dizzying and mysterious at the same time. She took the flimsy sheets from the doctor. The masthead was dated September 3, 1885, and below, its typeface in perfect columns as if the world could be made so orderly. There was a story about a drowning of young girls in Oshkosh, Wisconsin, a machinist strike in Newcastle, England, and a report that Sarah Bernhardt had fallen down a flight of stairs in Paris. But it was a front-page headline no more than two inches tall and a mere column wide that Addie had been scanning for:

LOOTING THE CHINESE

Rock Springs White Miners
Drive Them Out

ALL THEIR HOUSES BURNED

Three of the Mongolians Known to
Be Killed and Probably More—
The Troubles Reach a Climax

She ran her finger down the column, past the parts the doctor had already told her. Then she read aloud, because hearing it coming from her own voice made it sound more impossible. "At this hour, eleven p.m., it is known that three Chinamen were killed; but without doubt there are more killed, which will be known to-morrow. All the houses occupied by the Chinamen and belonging to the coal company were set on fire and are now burned to the ground. They numbered between forty and fifty buildings. It is probable that some Chinamen burned up in the houses."

The paper came down to her side. It was all too specific and not specific enough. Wing was no more dead or alive than when she stepped in front of a bullet in Rock Springs just a few nights earlier, except now she was certain she was the only one hoping he was still breathing. It hadn't been that long ago, those first tentative days when they weren't sure how to trust each other. It was a business arrangement to begin with, something more later. He preferred bowing to handshakes, and she liked to talk even when she was certain he didn't understand her. At first he preferred not to speak at all, perhaps because she couldn't help but giggle at some of his mispronunciations of words she tried to teach him.

Addie thought of her long-dead grandmother, thinking maybe, for a moment like this, prayer is what she should have been practicing all along. She wasn't sure she could work one up strong enough to be heard against those going in the opposite direction. "When can I get back to Rock Springs?" Addie asked the doctor. Her thoughts were clear. Even if Muuk hadn't shot her, he was capable of going after Wing. She needed to get him out of town. If Wing wasn't one of the ones killed, and Muuk found out, he was in danger for sure.

The doctor stood near the window, leaning against the sill, his crippled leg sagging beneath him at an odd angle. "That don't make good sense right now. You had a lot of bleeding." He looked her squarely in the eyes. "I already asked the sheriff to hunt up your husband to come fetch you, but I suspect he's got his hands full about now."

"Muuk's the one," Addie began, but she stopped herself because she didn't know it to be true, refused to believe he'd actually shot her. "He's my husband." The phrase was bitter in her mouth, almost valueless.

The doctor nodded, walking toward her with a pitcher of water, refilling her cup. "I'll have someone ask around for him by name, and the Grood woman you mentioned. And this Wing—he's a Chinaman, I guess."

"He's a friend," Addie said. She drank to the bottom of her cup. It tasted slightly metallic, like holding nails on her tongue, which made her think of Wing. She had been standing outside the four walls of her newly constructed cabin. The structure was roofless, and she didn't know where she'd get the lumber to finish it. Her husband hoped she wouldn't. When she'd circled the building a third time, she found Wing standing near the entrance that still had no door hung. He looked exceptionally neat, even for him, his queue freshly braided, face beaming. He held a small wood box, and next to him were two long, sun-bleached planks. "Ye go hai bei nei," he said slowly, which she understood only because he was so deliberate about it, and he extended the box toward her.

It wasn't heavy in her palm, and it rattled when she turned it over. She wondered if she was supposed to make something out of the faded Chinese writing and what looked to her like tiny red bats bordering the edges. When she slid the top back, Addie caught her breath as if the truth of the world was right there in front of her. It was close, a couple dozen dark nails. She took the rough little spikes in her fingers just for the sensation of it. In general, she'd found that Dire ran low on kindness, but in that moment her heart felt like all accounts were made even.

"Thank you, Wing," she said. "Thank you." There was more she wanted to say, but she was afraid to let it out, so she said it again, looking directly in his eyes. And though the words were the same, what she meant was she understood that friendship is not an all-or-nothing proposition, except for the commitment itself, and that made her even more determined to be the friend to him that he had been to her.

She wanted to hug Wing right there, Dire be damned. But she didn't. Not for herself; she'd proved she was tough as the worst of them. Wing, though, was another matter. There was no telling what might happen to him if they saw him touch a white woman. It was one thing to work for her, and quite another to be seen embracing, so she offered her hand. Wing responded with a bow, and even though they stood apart, did not touch, in that moment the distance between them closed—for good, she thought.

The doctor gave Addie a strange look, and she knew why. Whites and Chinamen weren't friends, and certainly not a Chinaman and a white woman. "You think this coolie friend of yours was one of them got killed?" When Addie didn't answer, the doctor raised his finger. She could barely breathe, clung tightly to the cup in her hand. The riots hadn't been the finish, but a starting place. Wing was probably in more danger now than before. She asked for a pencil, paper, and something to seal it in. When the doctor returned, she wrote down three questions as best she could.

Need to know—
was it Muuk shot me
were is Wing
can you bring him here

The letters were crooked, but the requests simple enough she was certain Maye would understand. She paused for only a moment, realizing she didn't know if her friend could even read. She'd known her a year, and the fact had never come up, but she'd have to try. She hated to admit it to herself, but right now she was too weak to deal with the consequences of the sheriff asking Muuk any questions. What would he do if he suspected Addie had sent the law after him? No, until she could stand on her own two feet, raise a gun between Muuk and Wing, it wasn't wise to let on to anyone but Maye what she suspected. Wing's life depended on her silence, she was sure. The more these thoughts swirled in her head, the angrier she got, and she tried to rise, but the pain pulled her back into the mattress.

Whether she had a right to or not, she'd always had the idea that she could do anything she put her mind to. But now, when it really counted, she'd been too late, and too reckless, and she was helpless to find out anything more until she could get back to Rock Springs. Until then, Maye would come with answers, as would Muuk if he didn't have anything to hide. None of it protected Wing. She looked at the empty cup in her lap. That's about the sum of it, she thought.

As a teenager, Addie took a seat on the train in Cheyenne just over a year before the night of gunshot and flame in Rock Springs that was her future. It was all she could do to keep herself awake after a long night of trying to hold her eyes open against whatever harm the town might throw at her. Her brother had arranged for a friend of his to get her fixed up with a train ticket. Almost a year had passed since Tommy asked her to Wyoming Territory, and for her entire journey from Kentucky—in wagons, boats, on her own two feet—everyone had been a stranger, and the farther west she went, the more unfamiliar people got, down to sometimes not even speaking English. And even the ones who did speak English sounded odd, or called things different than back home in Orgull. Earlier that day she'd seen a black man on a horse, both of them dusty from a long ride. This man had taken a coin out of his own satchel and paid a white man to feed and water his horse while he went to find a bath and a drink, and the white man looked pleased for the money. "Is that the way it's done out here?" Addie had asked the woman standing next to her at the station.

Looking Addie up and down, the woman made her feel like something the dog dug up. "What is, dear?"

"Whites serving niggers?"

The woman brought a gloved hand to her mouth, a thin, round cloud floating in the sky above her shoulder like a white parasol. Addie thought the woman was entirely too clean, looking in constant readiness to attend church. "Where on God's green earth are you from?"

Addie wondered the same thing about the woman, who removed nearly every r from her speech. God's green uth? It took Addie a second. "Kentucky," she said, finally. "You?"

"My husband and I are from New Hampshire. As for your other question, we certainly don't use that word."

They'd used a lot of words already, Addie thought, so she wasn't sure which one the woman had taken offense to, and she asked as much.

"We say colored, dear."

Now Addie was really confused. "As opposed to what?"

The woman looked to either side, then leaned toward Addie, though not so close, Addie noticed, that they might actually touch. "Nigger," the woman whispered, immediately standing upright again, as if someone had tied her to a hoe handle. "They're human beings, as our dear departed president and no less than our Lord taught us."

Startled, Addie blurted out her next question and removed her hat. "The president died?"

"My goodness." The woman was exasperated. "President Lincoln, dear."

The woman hadn't delivered any real news to Addie. When she was a girl, her grandmother had taken her to a funeral where they were the only white folks. Everyone was crying over Big Martha's death, even Addie, because if Big Martha knew you or even if she didn't, she called you brother or sister, and treated you that way too. But as far as the word *nigger* went, it seemed harmless enough to Addie, though she wasn't stuck on it. If *colored* was what they were saying wherever New Hampshire was in these parts, well maybe that was the way to go. "Colored," she said, trying the word on for size. It didn't seem to fit, felt unnatural, like calling a gooseberry an apple. Still, the woman's look of approval made her feel like she'd accomplished something. Addie made up her mind to use the word even when it didn't feel so comfortable, and maybe she'd use any other new word that came along, rubbed her the wrong way, but made her feel right for saying it.

That was probably going to have to be the way of things for a while. The farther away from Orgull she got, the less she was certain of. She was just a few months shy of her nineteenth birthday, but this journey to see her brother Tommy for the first time in eight years was making her feel younger by the mile. In St. Louis a woman sold her a cup of tea made from corn husk; said it would calm her stomach and clean out her liver. In Kansas City, she worked two months for a couple who found humor in Addie's every curiosity, like the green ceramic buffalo used strictly for serving cream soups; they called it a "turine" and made her say it out loud. The more money a person has, she learned, the more likely they are to make food in one thing and serve it out of another. But it was wasted effort as far as Addie was concerned. Soup tasted best right out of the pot.

A gust of wind pushed through, bringing with it a share of dust, and Addie held her hat to her head. When it passed and Addie removed the hat, poking at its shape, the woman gave a start. "Why, you have the prettiest red hair," she said.

"I don't use that word, red," Addie said.

"Then what do you call it?"

"My goodness," Addie said with a wink, raising a palm to her chest. "Colored."

It was mid-afternoon when Addie finally got on the train going to Rock Springs. The bright, cloudless sky was comforting as an embrace. Addie gripped her cloth sack and leaned against the window. Cheyenne was a surprisingly orderly city, built on a grid that lipped right up to the train tracks, but the precision made her nervous, made her feel hemmed in. It was certainly a change from what she'd seen coming into Cheyenne. Wyoming Territory, the expanse of it all, gave her a grand new feeling, as if all her life she'd been living in a crate and someone came along, ripped off the top, and let all four sides drop away. It seemed as if a person, even a woman, could stand and walk off in any direction they chose. Where else could she think such a thing? The land didn't give you much to work with, it was true, but on the other hand it looked so swept clean that not much was bound to get in your way. And the thing about heading out for fresh places, she decided, was not that she was getting dumber, but that there was a new thing to learn every five feet. It was enough to wear a person out.

Rock Springs was just hours off, and she felt safe enough to take a nap, though she peered down the length of the car at the other passengers just to be sure. Maybe weeks earlier some of them might have given her reason for pause, but now the dusty lot was unexceptional: a father, mother, and son wearily leaning on each other; a paunchy

man with a raccoon tail for a beard, his companion a baggy-eyed colored man wearing a brass-buttoned vest and clutching a fiddle case;
and at the far end, a gray-haired woman and her even grayer husband biting into what Addie thought at first was an apple but took
to be a Brandywine when juice dripped off her chin. What must
Addie look like to these passengers, she wondered, a green-eyed pile
of dirt? Not someone to rob, that was for sure. She closed her eyes
to the clomp of boots and plopped-down bags of other riders, which
became, as she fell asleep, the sound of chopping wood.

Then there was the vision of her mother, her dress soaked with
perspiration as she swung an ax down and through a piece of maple
standing on end, splitting it near perfect as she always did. With
each strike, Addie's mother looked at the divided wood and the
growing pile and then all around her. No daughter or son nearby
to carry it away. "I'm right here," Addie wanted to call out, but her
dream would not let her. So her mother continued, wiping her face
between each perfect blow, never pausing to take aim. She didn't
need to. Her mother's hands held an ax so often they had a mind
of their own. They were hands made for God's earth, her grandmother used to say. But if that was true, Addie had always thought,
He certainly made the rest of the body suffer for it. Addie had felt
the thick calluses of her mother's palms pass as soft as they could
over her cheek, the tenderness a contradiction of sensation, like
coming upon a barbed-wire coil set around April larkspur.

With a jolt of the train Addie popped awake. It had been precious too little time asleep, though as she looked out the window
she saw they'd made it outside Cheyenne. Here again was the land
she preferred, the distant horizon meeting clear sky, calling to mind
the shoreline of an impossibly blue lake. It was a wonder people
chose to cram themselves together in Cheyenne rather than do
what her brother had, get a big piece of land and spread your arms

as wide as you chose. "You must have been very tired," a woman sitting next to her said.

It was the first time Addie noticed she had a companion. "Every inch of me," she said, focusing on the sturdy, scrubbed-clean woman, who had tightly drawn gray hair that kept streaks of its former brown. Her dress was the powdery green of poplar buds. But tidy as she was, her yellowish, rough-looking hands gave away the fact she'd known hard work.

"I figured I better sit here when I saw that you was all alone. A girl your age? It ain't safe." The woman looked around the boxcar in disapproval. "Sure ain't the Palmer House."

Addie had no idea what that meant, but she got the gist. And just exactly what age did she think Addie was? "Thank you. But I do all right." She looked herself over, wondering how that was going to stay true if they made women wear dresses out here. Boots, pants, boys' shirts that buttoned up the middle, and a leather vest did her fine, she thought. The train was going at a good, noisy clip, which made the pair lean into each other to hear what the other was saying.

"You from down near Kentucky by any chance?" the woman asked.

Addie perked up, curious now. "Down near."

"Thought I could hear it. Get pretty good at things like that when you live in the Territory. Everyone speaking this way and that. Most days you don't meet two people from even close to the same place. Unless you're in the mine camps I suppose, then you got all them coolies and Finns and such, thick as thieves."

"Coolies and Finns?" Addie searched her mind. Already there were a few more words she didn't know. She assumed this woman must be talking about people, but what they sounded like to her were different kinds of fish.

"Oh, young lady." The woman sighed, shaking her head as if Addie was at grave risk. She smoothed down the front of her dress. "Where exactly are you going?"

"My brother is meeting me up in Rock Springs, then to his homestead." Addie paused. Rock Springs was her destination, then her brother's place. But where she was headed felt just then like a question without an answer.

The woman huffed and again looked up and down the length of the boxcar. "Homesteading? Outside Rock Springs? And you come alone?"

Addie nodded.

"Then I best fill you in on a few things." The woman held out a palm and jabbed her finger into it. "Whatever land your brother sits on, see to it you got drinkable water. Don't know of many home-steading folks in those parts ain't met with heartache. 'Course, there's a few, and maybe your brother'll be one of them." She took a deep breath as if what she was about to say would take a lungful. "And when you get to Rock Springs, you stay away from the coo-lies. The Finns is okay if they aren't drinking, but the coolies are the most savage lot you'll ever meet. If they get the chance they'll snatch a baby out of a mother's arms and eat it right in front of her. And at night they go underground into their burrows, doing all manner of deviltry."

What was it, Addie wondered, about the women in these parts that turned them all into the preacher's wife? And if this woman was purposely trying to frighten Addie, it was working. She wasn't sure if she wanted to hear more. Outside, the landscape suddenly wasn't comforting at all. The sunlight had a weight to it, seemed to press down on every living thing, left the world flat and dry, the brush more gray than green, the clumps separated and solitary like a wandering army in disarray. And then ahead, Addie caught sight of a dozen or so strange-looking animals, not dogs or deer or cows, not goats either, but still, four-legged. They had long black snouts, tan backsides, white bellies, and one of them had a pair of evil-looking black horns shaped like the pinchers of an earwig. "Are those coolies?" Addie asked, pointing as the train passed the animals. She'd seen them once or twice on her travels but never this close.

The woman looked out the window and then at Addie. Her face held an expression that fell somewhere between worry and sympathy. "You are a green one," she chuckled. "Those are pronghorn. Wouldn't hurt a fly," she said, her chuckle evolving into an outright laugh.

Addie didn't appreciate being called green, nor the fact that this woman she didn't know from Adam was laughing at her. "Then how will I know a coolie if I see one?"

The woman composed herself, nesting her hands in her lap. "That's the bit of good news. You can't miss 'em. They got eyes like cats and tails that grow out the back of their heads and down the length of their bodies. Front teeth like rats and skin so yellow and oily if you ever got hold of one, he'd slip right through your fingers."

As the woman spoke, Addie tried to conjure the monster being described. She'd never seen anything like it, and she wondered, if they were so terrible, why they weren't gotten rid of. She asked the woman as much.

"They import them from California to work in the coal mines," she said. "Those devils are so used to living underground they don't mind the dark one bit. I bet if they didn't have to eat they'd do it for free."

Addie was beginning to sum it up. "How long does it take to train one?"

"I'm sure I have no idea." The woman was becoming impatient.

"Well," Addie continued, "you ever come face-to-face with one yourself?"

"I certainly keep my distance." She assumed a prim posture. "And if you know what's good for you, you will too."

Addie assured the woman she had no intention of getting anywhere near a coolie, and that she was grateful for the information. Then they sat for a few minutes without a word between them while Addie thought about the warning. Maybe if she could get a rope somewhere she could catch one and train it. She'd once seen a man with a dog that wore a pink skirt and balanced on a large blue ball. Maybe people would pay to see a coolie do the same thing. Maybe a coolie was no worse than a cat if you trained it right.

The woman looked at Addie with obvious pity. "I didn't mean to worry you."

"Oh, I ain't worried. I was just wondering how I might catch one and keep it for a pet."

"Young lady," she said sternly, pressing so close to Addie's ear she felt the warmness of her breath. "I'm pretty sure no John is going to want to be your pet."

"John?" Addie was confused. "I'm talking about a coolie."

The woman sat up and rolled her eyes, exasperated but catching on. "John Chinaman, dear," she said loudly. "John Chinaman. That *is* a coolie."

"You mean all this time you been talking about men?"

The woman harrumphed. "I wouldn't go that far."

The approach into the station seemed to Addie to be exceptionally slow. By then her stern seat companion had moved to another part of the car. The woman had filled Addie's mind with a fear of coolies, a fear of miners, indeed, and a general fear of the Territory. And now the train had become a slug on the tracks, prolonging whatever it was she was about to encounter. It was as if the rails were covered in glue, allowing every stand of brush, every rock, to become a dubious welcome party. To her right was the closest thing to a mountain she'd seen since just before Laramie. The land was more boxed in here, but only in relationship to the uninterrupted expanses that preceded it. Rock Springs itself was mostly an unsteady collection of wood buildings that looked to Addie like they'd skimped on nails and paint in the building of them.

Finally the train came to a halt, and when she stepped off, she found she was just one of a handful stopping here. It didn't surprise her that most of the others were headed farther west. There was no sign of her brother on the platform, or at least that's what she thought until a man called out her name. Tommy had changed a lot in eight years. His hair hung to his shoulders and a beard had cropped up in uneven clumps. She couldn't see his mouth for the mustache hanging over it. Everything about him had gotten more extreme, she thought, shoulders broadened, the pace of his step, and the length of his stride. Back home walking through the woods taught a person to tighten up and pull in, but the Territory's openness seemed to allow a person's limbs to swing about as they pleased. The surprising set of changes in her brother made Addie wonder if this is what the place did to people and if she had any say in it all.

"Addie," he said, hugging her tighter than ever before. He smelled like sweet oats, she thought as he stepped back and looked her up and down, nodding in approval.

"Guess I've grown a bit," she said, uncomfortable with his silent appraisal.

"Bet you noticed a few changes in me too." He took off his hat as if to give her a clearer picture of him. He'd obviously wet and parted his long hair, which was sun-bleached at the ends and dark on the crown where light rarely hit. His skin was dark too, which made his green eyes, twins to her own, shine solid as wet stones.

"You remind me of Pa," which was true, but as she said it she knew it wasn't what he'd want to hear.

"That ain't exactly a compliment," he said. "Unless maybe you're comparing his face to my . . ." He fell shy at the word he intended, and instead patted his rear.

Addie laughed and the pair hugged again; this time it wasn't the firmness of the embrace Addie noticed, or the length, which was considerable, but the sincerity of it. She'd never felt anything near it, not from her mother, and certainly not from her father. In fact, she couldn't think of a time in her entire life when anyone other than her brother had held her in their arms this way. If they had, it was when she was too young to remember.

"Where's your bag?" Tommy asked.

Addie cleared her eyes with her sleeve. "A sack is all I got." She held it up, and it sagged beneath her grip like a long-dead fish.

"Was you robbed?"

"I was not. And remember that *you* left home with nothing but a jar of whisky." Her brother smiled at the memory. The ease between them was like old times, and Addie felt her suspicion of the place begin to melt. Then she offered a quiet start at the sight of a man not far behind her brother. It was a coolie, she figured, John Chinaman, just as the woman on the train described. He was small, with narrow eyes that gleamed black, and he had a braid that hung from the back of his head nearly to the ground. Maybe it wasn't exactly a tail, like the woman on the train said, but it was close.

Tommy turned to see what had startled Addie. "Oh," he said. "That's right." He stepped closer to her. "Don't have no dealings with them if you can help it. They'll shake on a bargain with one hand and pick your pocket with the other. One talks to you, just walk away, and don't be like old Lot's wife."

She told her brother about what the woman on the train said, and he didn't dispute any of it except the last part. "Don't make no mistake, Addie. They're men all right, which makes it all the worse because they live like animals and they'll do any job for half of what a self-respecting white man will do. And I tell you something else. There's something brewing around here. I can feel it, and I sure wouldn't want to be ol' John Chinaman about now."

"You talking about a fight between the whites and Chinamen?"

"Not talking about anything really. Just got a feeling if things don't change, there's going to be bullets flying."

As Tommy led her away, Addie looked back one last time. Really, the man didn't look so dangerous, she thought. But then he turned as his eyes met hers, and again a start went through her. It wasn't that his gaze was hard or penetrating, but that it was persistent and indifferent. Though Addie knew she was still moving in the direction of her brother, she couldn't actually feel her steps— Lot's wife on casters.

The walk to where they were staying wasn't long. Tommy explained that it was too late to ride out to his homestead, which was a half day's travel, but that he'd secured a roof over their heads for the night, a bite to eat, and some drinkable water. She took in as much of Rock Springs en route as she could, which wasn't hard to do. Though there were a number of buildings constructed at least partially of stone, Rock Springs seemed a town made mainly of dirt and scrap lumber as far as she could tell, the former seeming the greater of the two materials in some buildings. Then there was the structure that looked like a ship-size long-legged insect dragging itself out of the hillside—the coal mine, she guessed. She'd thought that Orgull was slapdash, but by comparison, her hometown measured up pretty well. Even at this time of day an unspecific but persistent rattle from the mine works jabbed itself in all directions, but none of that noise came from the sound of people talking to each other. This wasn't a ghost town. There were inhabitants, nearly all grown men, each going about their private business. Not one acknowledged Tommy and Addie as they passed, though a few did at least take notice.

Addie tapped her brother on the shoulder, and he stopped. "What's wrong with all these folks?"

"What do you mean?"

"I haven't heard word one from any of them. Not 'Good afternoon' or nothing. And you ain't so much as given a nod to anyone yourself."

Tommy removed his hat and scratched his head, laughing. "We're strangers. And anyway, you got to know how to say hello in five languages to get along here, that's why." They came upon a set of roofs sitting at ground level, which looked to Addie like a bunch of shacks that had sunk straight down into the ground. Each roof had its own nubby stove pipe and was halfway covered with dirt. "Here we are," Tommy said. "A fella I know went to Evanston and said we could hole up here till I took you out to the homestead."

Addie looked around. There were a few other buildings nearby standing aboveground, shabby and makeshift, but more appealing than what she thought her brother was suggesting. "Down there?" She pointed at the sunken shacks.

"It ain't 'down there' when you're down there." The pair walked the short slope and around to the front, where Addie got a better idea of the setup. The shacks were built right into the banks of a creek which announced itself like a skunk the closer they got to piles of floating garbage. She'd grown up on the Ohio River, seen all manner of things dumped in it, but what these folks didn't seem to get was that there had to be a current to carry the stuff off. She guessed they didn't have any sense. After all, a person wouldn't fly a kite on a windless day.

"For God's sake, Tommy," Addie said, waving off the odor, but her brother was already opening the door to where they would stay the night, a windowless rectangle that wasn't much more than a boarded-up cave.

Inside, the only light came from the doorway and a thin shaft from a hole in the roof. A makeshift stove sat in the corner, the same size and squat presence of a sleeping owl. The floor was hard-packed dirt, as was the bed, which was a carved-out shelf in the rear, though at least it offered the comfort of a dusty wool blanket spread along its length. "It sure ain't the Palmer House," Addie said from the entrance, her shadow trapped before her in the block of light on the floor. Tommy returned a confused look, and she laughed. "I don't know what it means either."

Pulling a pair of three-legged stools into the center of the room, Tommy brushed off the seat of one and sat on the other. When Addie took her place, he handed her a tin cup filled with water. These gestures somehow felt grand, as if all a person could ever want or need was a stool and a cup to drink from. The water was sweet, though not cool. They remained side by side for a silent minute, silent except for the fliff of an intermittent wind shifting sand and dirt over the roof, and somewhere in the distance the clumsy sound of random hammering. From her vantage, Addie saw out the door and down into the bottom of the filthy creek. She looked at the remaining water in her cup and back at the creek. "Did this come out of that?"

"Hell, no." Tommy patted her on the back in mock comfort. "They drag their water in from Green River. That there is called Bitter Creek, and if you ever took a taste of it, you'd know why."

"If that passes for a creek around here, I'd hate for someone to show me a ditch."

"Believe me, little sister, you'd rather drink from a ditch."

Addie looked directly at her brother, this new, bearded form of him. Where had the boy gone? If he were on the street, he'd be just the kind of man she would avoid, though even as she thought this, she knew she was prone to avoiding most men anyway. There'd been one, once, by the name of Denny, who didn't think twice about breaking her heart. He'd taken off from Orgull just like her brother. "So you're making a go of it out here?"

"Sure am." Tommy's reply was quick but unsteady. He stood and faced a set of narrow shelves, bringing down a dark, dented can topped by a mound of cloth. "Supper tonight is biscuit and venison."

"How many acres you got planted?"

Tommy paused, sitting down and placing the can between his feet. "Ain't like Kentucky, Addie. Turns out the ground ain't worth a bucket of spit, and where it is, there ain't no water." He told Addie about how when he first set foot on his place, and before he put up some shelter, he could stand in the center and the land was so flat he could see into every corner of his eighty acres. But that was about as good as it got. He'd written Addie to join him before he realized that even if he could clear away all that brush by and by, there was the problem of the rocky soil, and even if he could turn it over enough and pull the largest stones, what was left was so alkali nothing worth eating would ever sprout, no matter how much water you put on it. "Placed all my bets on a homesteading notice got read to me in Missouri," he said apologetically.

Addie tried to picture this land her brother had been so excited about in his letter, the reason she was here, in fact. "So what's it good for?"

"Aggravation," Tommy chuckled, but there was pain in it. "If I just stick for five years, it's mine clear and free."

"You remind me more of Pa than I thought." Their father wasn't much of a thinker, but he did live life with one philosophy, that no matter how difficult a thing was, if you stayed at it long enough, it was bound to work out. It wasn't lost on Addie that the thing he stuck with longest was drinking, and that hadn't worked out for him at all.

"I ought to give you a pinch for that, but I know what you mean." He reached under the cloth in the can and pulled out two corn biscuits and a few dark, thin squares of meat. "Elk," he said, handing her a share.

The biscuits were hard and the elk gamy, but with a fair amount of water Addie managed. Her brother ate his as if it were butter and pie, and she was afraid to know if this was his special-occasion food. "So," Addie said, as she battled a piece of biscuit down her throat, "can you make a go of the land or not? I mean, when you wrote me you had some big plans, but doesn't sound like those will come to pass."

"I thought about sheep or goats maybe."

"Goats!"

"I know'd you'd say something against it. Don't worry, I already did the figuring, and I ain't really the livestock type. But I can't believe that in all of creation those eighty acres can't be done nothing with."

"Sounds like you got Pa's luck." There were other ways to say it, she knew, but they all amounted to an insult to the Maine family judgment. And hadn't she herself just picked up and come out here on a mere notion?

"Like I said, I just got to stick five years and the land's mine. Something's bound to come up." He chewed on the last piece of venison. "So I was thinking, Addie. It's a good thing you come after all."

"I didn't know you was thinking otherwise."

Tommy faced her directly. He put a hand on each of her shoulders, and she could tell he was smiling under his mustache. "I'm sure I could get a job at the mine up top Dire Draw, and I was thinking you could stay on the property till I figure something out. It's just a couple hours away from Dire."

She was adding it up. It was a half day to his homestead from Rock Springs, so Dire was somewhere in between. "I don't know what I come out here for, Tommy, but I can tell you I never had in mind I'd be keeping your house and waiting for you to come home to get fed."

"It won't be like that. It can't, because it's too far. I'll have to stay in Dire, and you'll be tending things by yourself."

"By myself out in the middle of nowhere?"

He laughed. "It's a little farther than nowhere."

"Sounds like you need a wife more than a sister."

"Almost had one," he said, sitting down again. "Emiline was her name, real pretty and sweet. But she said yes to another fella who had better prospects."

She heard his heart in his voice, and, pushing her stool next to him, Addie sat with her arm around his back. "Sorry to hear it," Addie said. "But someone will come along."

"It's for the best, I reckon." Tommy stared at the ground. "I got this idea there's one person in the world can make you happier than anyone else."

"Just one, Tommy?"

He looked at her and smiled. "It's long odds, I know. But it's something to hope for. Till then," he said, tousling her hair, "it's you, me, and eighty acres. And besides, you're the one we got to get married."

There was a response, to be sure, but she decided to hold it. A woman steps into a snare the day she's born, Addie had learned. Her mother warned her about it before loosing herself, which was the difficult thing for Addie, understanding her mother had fled an unhappy life and at the same time wondering if she herself had played a part in the unhappiness. If Addie had done something differently, might her mother have stayed? Could it have outweighed the kind of husband her father became?

She looked around the hovel in which she and Tommy were sitting. Worthless as her father was when the drink took him, even he, at first, managed to keep the family in food and clothes, and the cabin mostly intact. Addie thought of the shabby town they'd walked through to get here. There was its creek with undrinkable water, and the coolies she'd been warned against. And if Dire was anything like Rock Springs, she was better off alone wherever Tommy had his homestead. She looked at her brother and then at the sad little sack that contained everything she owned and what money she had left. And when she found herself nodding, it was as if her body had made up its mind before her brain. "Guess I'll need an apron."

"No," Tommy said, winking. "You'll need guns."

It was an uncomfortable night of sleep, Addie taking the carved shelf with the wool blanket, her brother on the dirt floor with a coat propped under his head for a pillow. He'd fallen fast asleep, but she lay awake in total darkness. Now and then there were voices outside, men speaking words she didn't recognize except for the slurring quality. She'd lived with her father long enough to understand that drunkenness was an international language.

But it wasn't the strange voices that were on Addie's mind; it was that suddenly she was a homesteader with Tommy, which felt like stepping backward. It wasn't an apron she was hoping for, but something else she couldn't name. There wasn't a word for it, the idea that she wanted to make her own way, choose the folks who might help her along, rather than be told exactly what she was confined to hoping for. It was an impractical thought, she decided. It was men who owned, who needed support. Their father had tried to carve out a living on a parcel of land in Kentucky, and that came to nothing, worse than nothing. Her mother abandoned them, Tommy left too, and after a few years of helping her father haul wood into Orgull, Addie practically had to drag him into town as well, away from the place he didn't want to leave and didn't have the discipline to keep up with. By the end, the cabin was more leaky and drafty than it had ever been. The elm that partially hung over the roof split in two, coming down on the roof, to which her father merely replied, "That was your ma's favorite tree."

BRIAN LEUNG

After the elm, the drinking got worse, if that was possible. On his better days her father roused himself in the morning and headed into the woods with his ax and saw, and the mule too if he planned to get any real work done. She could hear him out there sometimes, the thwack of steel against green wood, the thrush and thump of a falling tree. But even on these better days, more and more often the woods eventually got quiet except for the birds and chattering of bitter squirrels. Evening would commence, and Addie knew what she had to do, track her father down before nightfall. The scene was always the same, him sitting on the ground, back against a felled tree. The mule watched her approach with indifference, and it shamed her to think that her father was the duller animal of the pair.

At least, she thought, her brother had not turned to drink. But there was a different problem. From what he'd said about this homestead, even a sober man didn't have much to work with, no trees to speak of, bad soil. Maybe they could keep a few chickens if there weren't wildcats and foxes to snatch them away. If it came to that, she was a good shot, though if there was shooting to be done, a gun was required. Addie pictured this flat dry land with a few chickens, realizing there was one thing she couldn't imagine. What kind of place he'd put up. Was it any better, or at least bigger, than the hovel they were staying in right then? Room enough for two people to sleep in beds at least? The way Tommy spoke, maybe that didn't matter. She'd be alone most of the time. Maybe it was the life her mother had chosen thrown in Addie's lap without asking. She felt for her drawstring purse in the small sack lying by her side. It was thin as a gutted trout, but inside was enough money to get back to Kentucky. It was also enough to stay for a while.

EPISODE THREE

Wing heard the water train approaching, looked up to spot it, then caught sight of the pair far down Dire Draw, two men, one older than the other, or perhaps one was a very sturdy woman. They walked parallel to the tracks, their horse packing canvas sacks. In the wave of heat, it looked like two railroad ties and a barrel sprouted legs and were headed in Dire's direction. If these people were looking for jobs, Wing doubted they'd find any. The Union Pacific didn't have much use for more white miners, and the kind of work a woman might find would be steady but unthinkable.

He stood in a two-walled shed with a pot of simmering broth at the edge of what the white miners referred to as Little San Fran. It wasn't at all the type of place he'd imagined when he left his village. He was going to make his fortune in California like so many others, and like so many others, he discovered too many had come before him. From the whites he heard "Get out!"; from his own countrymen, "Go East!" That is why he arrived in Dire as a camp cook, a skill he was taking to more and more, but for which his young life had prepared him little.

The pair with the horse did not seem in a hurry, looked as if they were talking easily as the younger one occasionally patted the other on the back. Steam from the broth scooped under his chin and up the side of his face. The men he fed would complain that his soup was too thin, tasteless, but he knew if he tried to do more to it, they would criticize it anyway. It was time to move on to other preparations. Certainly he'd be expected to use the salted duck eggs and dried blackfish that arrived the day before. Wing took a last look at the duo making slow progress up the draw. From this distance he was reminded of how small a person became out here. Even two people and a horse became minuscule in this limitless brownish gray landscape. When his parents wrote for news following his departure from San Francisco, he described this very view, the slope of Dire Draw that fanned out into the valley, the black embroidery of train tracks that snaked under a blue so wide and unyielding that in his letter he repeated the character for sky three times in a row. In fact, the sky was not tangible here, gave no sense of ceiling. What he did not describe in his letter was Dire itself, so much of which looked as if a tall wooden building had toppled over and scattered its rooms intact, but leaning this way and that. Little San Fran was only slightly better, more squared off to be sure, less strewn, its buildings the thin red color of blood-sweat. It was UP housing, standard issue. But soot and smoke and dust are indiscriminate migrants, and they found their way into even the most fastidiously kept dwellings. Sometimes even Wing resigned himself to the idea that these were spices in the food he served. At the far end was No. 1, the mine with its sloped tipple that crunched and groaned like an upset stomach until the train arrived to carry away its burden. Once a day the train chugged up Dire Draw and pulled its cars beneath the hovering structure, which laid its black eggs like a prone chicken.

Wing felt a smack to the back of his head. He didn't have to turn to know who it was; Ah Joe, camp boss of the Chinese. "You're daydreaming again, Wing Lee," the man said, first in English, then in Cantonese. Only he didn't yell. He never yelled. Instead he hissed his displeasures. Ah Joe was the fastidious Chinese man who lived in San Francisco for fifteen years before teaming up with Ah Say in Rock Springs and contracting with the UP to organize Chinese labor in the coal camps that were surely going to open up all over the Territory. He'd started on the railroads, and now took on Dire and whatever else came his way as a final fiefdom. He cut his peppery gray hair in the Western style, and no matter the heat, wore a suit with high collared shirts. He spoke of no family in California or China, though sometimes behind his back the men joked that he was married to the railroad, joked about his whore wife named Yoo Pi.

Wing turned, knowing he had to be careful. This man was his lifeline to the company, even back to China. He thought Ah Joe's Cantonese had gotten sloppy, running from his mouth slow as drool. "Don't worry. I'm just getting ready for the eggs and fish. Then cabbage and dried shrimp."

"Too slow. The last cook was much better."

"I understand," Wing said, measuring his tone, but not wanting to back down. "Perhaps the last cook would like to finish here." He gestured toward the cabbage and shrimp on his makeshift cutting block. That was one thing to be said for Ah Joe. At least he made sure they were supplied with familiar foods. The Chinese would rather starve than eat the garbage food of the white miners.

Ah Joe narrowed his eyes and began to reply. Instead, he looked over Wing's shoulder and squinted. It was obvious he couldn't see very far into the distance. "Whites," Wing said.

"More?" He took a suspicious look. "Not from Rock Springs." He slapped Wing on the back of the head again. "Maybe you sell them 'lookee,' stupid girl."

It was a crude joke. Wing had the word clarified in San Francisco, an explanation that required a description of female genitalia, about which he had been entirely unfamiliar. There were some white men willing to pay to see a naked Chinese woman for the rumor that unlike white women, she ran horizontal rather than vertical. When Wing didn't laugh at the insult, Ah Joe waved his hands in front of him as if to wash his hands of the approaching whites. He brought his gaze back to the cutting board, grunting as he turned and walked away. "Finish, stupid girl," he called behind him.

Of course Wing would finish, as he always did, and that was how he was going to make it back to China, bowl by bowl if that's what it took. He grabbed a head of cabbage and drove through it with a cleaver, the sound of the blade hitting wood shooting into the afternoon air. Ah Joe stopped but did not turn around. His body shook slightly, as if he was laughing, and he continued on.

Nobody feared Wing. He knew that. He could hold a cleaver in each hand and nitroglycerin around his neck and the men would still laugh. He was smaller than most of them, and even those whose height he matched had matured their bodies through the hard labor of working in the mines. He had his own strength, to be sure, but it didn't show on his frame. Once, in San Francisco, a small earthquake had toppled two wall-size cabinets stocked full with teas and spices. He had never felt the ground shake before, and didn't know what to make of it. The hanging ducks at the front of the shop swayed in unison like a line of drunken dancers as everything that wasn't secured rattled onto the floor. One cabinet toppled immediately. The second merely tottered at first, and then leaned just enough that it came crashing forward like a square-shouldered giant, slain. The shaking diminished the way a spun coin flutters its way to stillness, left dust floating in the shop almost as dense and kinetic as smoke from a hundred just-extinguished candles. Outside people ran back and forth, yelling to and at each other. But Wing stayed put. Even with the cabinets empty, their contents strewn on the shop floor, it seemed an impossible weight for one man to right, but Wing crawled under the first one, which rested at a 45-degree slant, braced his hands against the front, and strained to walk it up and back against the wall. The other cabinet had fallen at an angle closer to the floor, leaving Wing just enough room to crouch beneath, his back flush against its front. From there, he pressed upward, his legs shaking. Midway he thought perhaps the attempt had been a mistake, but the choice was to finish the job or be crushed. He renewed the thrust from his legs in one heave and the cabinet moved and tilted back, slamming against the wall. Wing slunk to the floor, exhausted.

In Dire, though, he was simply a cook. His strength was redirected not in the preparation of meals but in the appearance of being mere, of being deferential. There was no advantage in showing power, of proving he belonged in the mine rather than over a cookfire. He wanted to return to China, and there were only two ways to do it, dead or alive. He'd already known two men in Dire alone who were crushed by cave-ins, and in Rock Springs there were others; and there would be more. He'd heard, too, the stories of men before him who worked on the railroads, brave Chinese men who laid track in snow tunnels, who were set in baskets made of reeds and lowered down cliffsides, where they chiseled into the rock and set explosives. Sometimes ropes gave and the men dropped to their deaths. Other times they were blown to bits before they could be pulled up. They were easily replaced. That was the price of strength.

The whites Wing noticed earlier drew closer. It was a man, a woman, and a horse. Neither of them took notice of him, which was not unusual. The UP kept the Chinese as segregated as possible. They were an invisible people in these parts unless they were needed for work or were being accused of stealing it. The horse was different than anything he'd ever seen, its torso familiar, but its head more like a mule's. The man's face was red and shining, his shirt blotched with a large spade of sweat, but his female companion wasn't laboring under the journey at all. She was dusty-looking, the color of a sage grouse, and her wet cheeks glowed in the sunlight, but she was altogether upright, unlike the man and even the strange-looking horse, whose head bobbled close to the ground, looked to need rest. This man and woman had what he could not, and he found himself envious. It was a scene he'd been told he would never be part of. Besides returning to China, if he had one desire, it was to have a wife, to be seen with her at his side. When he allowed himself to dream, Wing imagined waking in the morning next to a wife, rising and walking to the window. Outside would be *his* land, not his father's. Instead of rice fields, his home would be surrounded by orange or tangerine groves. Wing could almost smell the perfume of spring blossoms, as if it was a kind of anointment.

He dreamed of these things often, but in the end, reality interceded. The youngest of eight brothers and a favored child, Wing suffered the consequences of their disgraces. One brother, the sixth in line, beat his wife so severely and so often that her village relented to her pleas for return, though her parents themselves refused to take her back. Wing's second brother lost his wife to a Guangzhou businessman, and the seventh brother's wife offered up only stillborn boys. "There will be no wife for you, Wing," his father told him when he was thirteen. "We cannot take the indignity." Youth obscured the full understanding of what Wing would discover in just a few years. His parents weren't merely predicting that he would not have a wife, they were preventing it. The only time he expressed affection for a girl in the village, she was sent away to be married to someone else.

Not long after his parents' warning, he came upon the broadside, written both in Chinese and English, "Americans want the Chinaman to come and will give big pay, and large houses, and food and clothing, all very fine. You can send your family money any time, and we will provide safe delivery. It is a good country absent of mandarins or soldiers. You are made equal with treaties and the American Government. Your great many friends are there now and await your companionship. You are guaranteed lucky and under protection of China God, and the agents of this house. Come to the sign of this house in Canton and we will show you. Money in America is too many for small pockets. Such as are smart enough to grow rich can obtain wealth and honor by application to this office." The broadside had filled him with hope, but now, here in the United States, his options seemed fewer than nothing.

Here in front of him, though the woman's own head was concealed by a well-worn hat, Wing saw that she had that kind of peculiar American hair, not brown or blond but the reddish color of thoroughly ripe lychee skin. Where the sun struck it, there was a shine like the quiet embers of an extinct fire. When she was farther down in the draw he'd mistaken her for a man, but that is what it was, a mistake. The distance played a trick; up close, she was strong, fierce, but not unfeminine. He didn't know exactly what to make of her. Beautiful?

Dire was no place for women, Wing thought; what part of Wyoming Territory was? But if there was a woman who might make it here, this woman looked like she could.

I t took a little over five hours to reach their destination on foot, and Addie wasn't sure it was worth it. Dire made Rock Springs look like a postcard resort, and just like Rock Springs it was split in two halves, only it wasn't an alkali creek but a gully at the top of the draw that separated the main part of camp from the Chinese part. She had not grown up in comfortable circumstances herself, but there was something different about the conditions these men lived in, and she was beginning to put her finger on it. Their family's forest cabin near Orgull had been just one room for all of them. In strong winds it creaked and groaned enough for worry. But there was something about living among trees that made a person feel safe, the comforting green verticality of it all. Here in the Territory, there were taller hills and mountains than around Orgull, but the complete lack of trees was enough to make a person wonder. If an oak or elm couldn't set down a taproot here, what made these men think they could?

On their approach to Dire with her brother's hinny in tow, Addie and Tommy came up the side of the draw with the easier footpath toward what her brother told her was Little San Fran. Most of the buildings were identical, blocky-looking structures, stained grayish red or left plain. There was smoke from a single fire, a Chinaman cooking beneath a kind of shed, as well as from the general growl of the mine operation. Addie did her best not to look at the cook as she drew abreast of him. They weren't heading too close, but the warnings she'd heard about these strange-looking men were enough to keep her on guard. So she averted her gaze, pulled her hat low over her eyes, and stood upright as she walked.

The Chinese half wasn't mansions and gardens by any means, but it was orderly enough to make the half across the gully look like a random scattering of upturned pine coffins. Many of the shacks where the white miners stayed were like the one she and Tommy stayed in at Rock Springs, dug into the earth with a slapdash roof thrown over the top. Others sat aboveground, each of them more stacked than constructed, she thought, oddly fit stones and scrap lumber piled together to form single off-kilter rooms aspiring to be rectangular. It looked to her as if a man could practically touch two walls at the same time by merely stretching out his arms.

Ahead of them, a train chugged through the draw. She'd guessed it was headed into Dire to collect a load of coal, but Tommy corrected her. All the water in Dire, and Rock Springs for that matter, had to be hauled from Green River. Thirty-five cents got you a barrel. They'd tried to sink a couple wells in Dire, but it was too full of sulfur and iron to be of use. The smell of it was known to turn a man green. "Believe me, Addie," Tommy said. "You'll be on your deathbed before you drink any water but what comes on that train." It was a job in itself, he told her, just to get water into your barrel. Some miners ran up to the train with pails and caught the water where it leaked before it could be pumped out into the water wagons. In winter, the barrels were dragged inside to keep them from freezing. The details made her thirsty and exhausted all at once.

Tommy led Racer through the bottom of the garbage-strewn gully and up the other side, but Addie took the footbridge, which looked to be a first cousin to the shacks. She paused in the middle. Dire hadn't built itself up the way Rock Springs had, and was not as immediate to the actual mine. Though the full-throttled rattling of the tipple near the mine entrance made it clear there was life there, Addie was surprised that there were so few people actually visible. It was obvious that the business of this camp was mining and mining alone. Alone. The word came to her, and she understood instantly it would be something she would likely repeat for as long as she was in Wyoming.

She looked back slowly toward Little San Fran, where the Chinaman continued working over the large, steaming pot. He was turned to one side, half concealed by the three-sided shack. This man was small, but not so small as the man at the train station who had scared her so. The cook wore a faded blue, brimless cap with a braided length of hair coiled around his head. His clothes, too, were blue, only he'd cut off the sleeves, his skin a shining light brown, not dark as her own where the sun got to it. The arm that she could see wasn't particularly muscular in comparison to some of the men in Orgull, but she recognized the power of the sinews as he moved, something like a second-year colt. He dropped a crude ladle into the pot and brought it to his nose, nodding to himself with what looked to her like indifferent satisfaction. If she could see his face, she could tell.

"What are you gawking at?" Tommy and Racer stood at the end of the footbridge.

Addie shrugged. "Not sure."

On the other side of a brushy knoll, Dire revealed its core, three well-constructed wood buildings, well-constructed by comparison to what surrounded them. The largest of the three buildings was adorned with a professionally painted sign in thick black lettering, "Beckwith Quinn & Company." These buildings faced the dark-timbered tipple, and here activity abounded. There were at least a dozen men buzzing around the tipple—*crawling* was a better word, Addie thought, for they seemed more like ants working their hill than men. Only they weren't nearly as clean or quiet as ants; these men were sooty from head to toe, which made sense since the earth here was blackened with coal bits—slack, Tommy called it. They walked over the dark ground toward the smaller of the three buildings, which had the words "Superintendent" and "Orner" painted in green above the door.

"We must look like white beans in an iron skillet about now," Addie said, and it came to mind what the place smelled like, overcooked beans.

But Tommy wasn't paying attention. He had a hand above his eyes, shielding out the sun. "Where is he?"

"Who?"

Again, Tommy wasn't listening. He scanned the grounds as they continued to walk. Addie wasn't sure who her brother was looking for, but she thought she'd be surprised if he found him. These men looked the same to her, same smudgy dark faces except for around the eyes. Reverse raccoons, she thought. Except the Chinese, who were cleaner, at least in the face, a condition she chalked up to laziness. Men who work get dirty.

"The superintendent ain't out here," Tommy said as they arrived at his building. He handed Addie Racer's lead. "You stay put. I'm going inside for a minute to see about a job." He winked. "Maybe a Chinaman died. Let's hope anyway."

Addie laughed. "You drag me all the way out here to Wyoming, and *now* you tell me to stay put?" Tommy shot her a smile just before he blasted through the office door with a boisterous "Halloo!" sounding as if he were an unrepentant prodigal son returned. His greeting was met by an equally loud "If it ain't Hell's own!" and then the door closed. Addie slowly turned to the tipple, which looked from the front like the face of an old man, square-jawed and grimacing. She saw now that the men were making an effort not to notice her, making quick glances and then looking away. Except the Chinamen. They went about their business as if she didn't exist. She'd seen evidence of a few women in Rock Springs, but not here in Dire. She'd have to keep her guard up.

Addie pulled Racer closer, positioning the animal between the men and herself as she sat on a bench next to the building where Tommy was trying to haggle a job. Racer was only the second hinny she'd seen in her life. Not much call for mixing horses and donkeys, she guessed. The animal's midsection filled her view, a brindle map, the tawniness of which reminded her of the landscape through which her brother had led her. It felt like the first time since she'd arrived that she was able to catch a breath and take stock of herself. One of her pant legs would need a patch soon, she noticed, but her boots looked as though they'd hold out for a while. She used her hat to swat away dust from her shirt where it showed from under her vest. The yellow in the sleeves was fading, but the material itself was intact. That was one thing to be said for Wyoming. There wasn't a lot of vegetation snatching at your clothes. Back in Orgull it felt like all the woods wanted to do was strip a person naked.

"Fine mare you got here. Odd looking, though." The man's voice came from behind Racer at the rear. Only the four booted legs showed it was two men. When the pair walked around to face Addie, they were about as she expected, blackened from head to toe, but they'd removed their hats, leaving a pale band across their foreheads like descended halos. "Good day," the first said. It was the same voice, oddly proper, and not like any she'd heard before. He was older, graying, with a patchy beard. The other man had thick black hair and a beard that started below his collar and swallowed his face. "Goot day," this darker man said.

The two stood looking at Addie without speaking, as if she were a statue in a museum, or maybe a gold nugget resting on the bed of a clear stream. Finally Addie broke the silence. "Do you all need something?"

The man with the graying beard laughed. "Around here one needs a great many things, but it's no use trying to get them." The other man merely looked back and forth between his companion and Addie as if trying to understand. "But mainly we were just curious, Miss," the bearded man continued. "We saw Tom and you and just wondered if maybe he had found himself a wife." At this, he conspicuously looked at Addie's hand.

Now it was her turn to laugh. "I'm his sister." Part of her amusement came out of the fact that getting married was something she had no interest in. She'd seen the disaster of her own parents, heard stories about her grandfather from her mother. No, marriage was just a man's opportunity to make a woman's life miserable, and no matter what efforts her brother might make in that regard, she wasn't having any of it.

The fact that Addie was unmarried seemed to please the man, who turned to the other and spoke in a language that wasn't English. When she was four, a Frenchman came through Orgull, and when he spoke his language, it was the oddest thing she'd ever heard. "He come down from the moon," Tommy said. "That's moon talk you're hearing." And he let her believe it for a week.

"Ah, ah," the dark bearded man said, smiling, a look of satisfaction coming over his face.

"Yes," Addie said. "His sister." She was suddenly aware of the sun pressing down on her. "If you don't mind," she said, leaning back into the building's slimming shade. Racer, too, shifted her position, so that now the mine operation was once again in Addie's full view.

"I am Emrys Clough," the gray-bearded man said. "And this is Lenhard." With that, he gave himself permission to come into the shade next to Addie, and she thought he smelled more like a horse than Racer. "If you don't mind my saying so, I'm not certain Dire is a place a man ought to bring his sister. All sorts of things might happen. Make sure he keeps good watch over you."

Addie pressed her back against the building and bundled her arms across her chest, holding tight to Racer's reins. She wished Tommy would step out of the building right then and take her to his homestead. "If you don't mind *my* saying so," she said, looking Emrys square in the eyes, "I can fend for myself."

Again, the dark-bearded man, Lenhard, stared at his companion, clearly not understanding the conversation. Then he shrugged his shoulders, made a quick nod to Addie, and walked back toward the tipple.

"He's a good sort, Tyrolean," Emrys said. "Barely speaks a spot of English, but we've come through some tough times together and I can count on him." He looked down at the top of his hat and brushed at it, as if any dust he removed could be an improvement. "I didn't mean to scare you, Miss." His tone was changed now, soft. "I just meant Dire has a reputation."

She didn't take real offense, she assured him. There were men who worked on the riverboats back home like this, she thought. Got so used to only being around other men, they forgot how to speak to a woman, and by that she meant she preferred they talk to her just like they would a man. She wasn't interested in marriage or worrying over. Coming into a new place as she was, Addie figured a person needed to know just one thing; who was honest and who wasn't. She'd gotten word on the Chinamen, which in Dire was half the job done.

The door of the superintendent's office opened, and Addie turned. A quarter of a man's face stared back at her with a flinty gray eye. His skin was reddish and loaded with a thick brown mustache that thinned across his lower cheek like a rat's tail. Without a word, the face retreated and the door closed. Addie noticed something on the side of the building she hadn't before, four years painted in black and crossed through except for 1884, which wasn't fully lived out yet.

"That would be Clive Orner, the superintendent," Emrys said. "We just call him Orner. He's suspicious of women."

"My brother's trying to get work."

Emrys's expression let Addie know that Tommy's prospects were slim. "These days, Miss, it seems like Ah Joe is the only one handing out jobs. And Orner's in on it."

She wasn't in the mood for pessimism so soon. "So you were saying Dire has a reputation." Better to go back to that subject.

Emrys pinched the brim of his hat and put it back on his head. He did not look at Addie but instead stared off toward the top of the draw where she and Tommy entered Dire. "Stop me if your brother told you this," Emrys said, "but did you ever hear how Dire got its name?" Addie shook her head and was about to say she wasn't much interested in a story, but the man's tone changed, as if this was a story anyone who'd come up Dire Draw needed to hear.

Emrys swept his hand across the landscape and began his story. There'd been twin brothers, the Eckonens, who first worked the coal outcropping that would later become Dire's mine No. 1. But that was well before there was a name for the place. It was just the brothers and three mules, and some said if a person came upon the five of them, you couldn't tell them apart. Nobody ever knew the men's first names, so they came to be known as Brother One and Brother Two. At this point in the story Emrys broke into laughter, as if there were a part he was only telling to himself. He continued.

The Eckonens worked the outcropping for two years, packing all their supplies in and taking the coal down through the draw the same way. Just to get by, they had to work the coal seven days a week no matter the weather. Come the second winter, on a cold February day, the brothers started down the draw with a full load of coal on all three mules. There was a light snow that didn't look like it was much to worry about. Traveling through the draw wasn't easy, though. Over time they'd about worn a workable narrow path, but hard rain rutted it deeply, or left it muddy, or both. And where that wasn't true, it was so stony even the mules were tender and slow about where they'd plant a hoof.

Halfway down the draw the snow picked up. In minutes the brothers found themselves in near whiteout conditions, the flakes gathered in bunches fat as a man's hand and coming fierce. It was as if God were right above them dumping the contents of his feather bed. Neither of them could see twenty feet ahead, but by then it was just as far to go back as it was to go forward, so they pressed on.

When the wind came up, the snow ran horizontal, cutting across their eyes, so they had to walk alongside the mules rather than in front of them, and that only made the going slower. Brother One had hold of the lead mule when it stepped in a hole and toppled over sideways and down on top of him. The mule righted itself, but Brother One couldn't; his femur was snapped in two. Tough as these two were, it wasn't automatic what needed to be done. Brother Two thought maybe they could make some sort of lean-to that Brother One might take cover under while the other took the coal into town. But Brother One pointed out the shortcomings of the plan, namely the lack of materials and the idea that there wasn't much out there for a lean-to to lean against.

It wasn't brotherly affection that resolved matters. Brother Two realized that with his twin made lame, their mining days were all but done, so he might as well get Brother One into town. Cussing the whole enterprise, Brother Two released the coal bags from one of their three mules and managed to heap his injured brother on the animal's back.

About mid-afternoon when the weather let up in Rock Springs, one Samuel Banks poked his head out of his shack. The landscape was thickened with snow, the rise and fall of the covered brush like the current of a frozen river. And walking across this was a single mule carrying a man slung over its back. Half frozen and delirious when they got Brother One inside, he fairly got through his story but couldn't say what had become of Brother Two. Three men rode out and found one of the other mules alive, but couldn't find the third and Brother Two. The draw itself, loaded with snow, was too treacherous to navigate, though later when the snow thawed a few men went out but came back with nary an idea of what happened to Brother Two. Some said maybe he took the chance to run off and away from what he owed around. Brother One was sent to Evanston to mend, and the last that was heard from him was that he took a train to California. He never went back up the draw to find his brother or retrieve what few things they owned at the mine.

Addie interrupted Emrys's story. "I thought you said this was about how Dire Draw got its name."

"That's true, Miss." He offered a short bow as if she were an audience member requesting a refund. "Every story has its point, and I'm coming to the one I promised. So like I said, Brother One got his leg mended and a couple toes cut off and went to California, and Brother Two was swallowed up by winter. Now there was the matter of the coal up there practically spitting out of the hillside. So the UP makes its claim the way it does around here, and when they proceeded to start laying tracks up through the draw, what do you expect they came upon but Brother Two and the third mule!"

Addie shook her head in surprise. A living Eckonen brother wasn't something she expected. "Was he hiding all that time?"

Emrys laughed. "You might say. Just by chance they found him wedged underneath his mule, both of them picked clean to the bone so that you could see right through the mule and stare Brother Two's skull right in the—" He paused as if he was unsure. "Well, it isn't quite right to say you could stare that skull in the face, but there you are, Miss."

"That's an awful story," Addie said.

"It is indeed. And here's the last of it. One of the men laying the tracks started down to see if he could fish Brother Two out. But the man running the crew gave him a choice of getting fired or getting back to work. Even then, the coolies were swallowing up all the work, so the man made his choice. No one remembers his name, but that man wiped the sweat off his brow and looked up the draw at all the work ahead of them. 'Dire times,' he said, walking back to the crew. 'I expect we'll leave a few more bones in this draw before we're done.' "

"Dire," Addie said quietly, as if the name of the draw was a secret coaxed out of her.

Emrys shuffled his feet but said nothing, allowing Addie to add things up for herself.

"So they just left Brother Two out there?"

"Well, Miss, every now and then there's talk of locating him so he can have a proper burial, but it never comes to anything. And to be honest, I don't know if anyone's left who could even mark the spot where he fell."

"Maybe I'll ride the train one day and peer over the side to see if I can find him."

"Miss"—Emrys chuckled—"it'll be over Clive Orner's dead body when a woman rides a UP train into Dire."

Addie looked down the draw and at the tracks that ran alongside of it, the land fanning out at the bottom, where the tracks looked harmless as the end of sewing thread. Between where she sat and the bottom of the draw were the bleached bones of a man and a mule. What kind of place was this, she wondered, that could make a person pause to decide if his brother's life was worth more than a load of coal? Somewhere out there was Tommy's homestead, and she knew it wasn't going to be an easy life. She'd arrived in Rock Springs less than forty-eight hours earlier, had been in Dire itself less than two, and she didn't like the new considerations already pressing on her. What could possibly happen that would cause her and Tommy, even for a second, to contemplate the value of each other's life? She was used to looking out for herself, but she had the growing sense that life here was like a hundred dogs snatching at one thin bone.

They'd left Dire Draw and gotten within five miles of the homestead, but the weather was so good Tommy wanted Addie to have one night under the stars before life became work, so they agreed to set camp for the night. Along the way they'd gathered what passed as firewood, and Addie repeated the story about how the draw got its name, and her brother confirmed it to a degree. He'd heard slightly different versions in which Brother One hadn't broken his leg but was shot, or that they'd actually found Brother Two astride the bones of his mule. In any case, every story seemed to agree that at the end there was a live Eckonen and a dead one. "And I tell you one funny thing you didn't mention," Tommy said as they continued through the brush. "If you ever hear a man say I got into a Dire Draw last night, if he ain't a stranger, it means he was playing cards and it came down to him and another man fighting over the pot."

Addie didn't much mind the differences in the Eckonen stories. What bothered her was thinking about how none of them accounted for Brother One's feelings about losing his sibling. She didn't like how a person's life could get twisted around in such a way that what they *did* was changed to make them more interesting, but what they *thought* was tossed away like twice-used bacon grease.

They hadn't found enough wood to build a flame much higher than a foot, but out there, he told her, you learned to survive on what you needed, not what you preferred. She wanted to tell him she knew it was true, but there were places where maybe that was changing. She'd spent time in Louisville, a city too full of crowded bustle for her tastes, but shortly before she left Kentucky she'd gone to the Southern Exposition, where Mr. Edison rigged up more lights in the Exposition Hall, they said, than was even found in New York. It was the strangest thing, standing in that building that was bigger than anything she'd ever seen, thirteen acres under one roof, and by all rights should have been dark as a cave except for the wonder of that invention that made it daylight whenever and wherever you wanted it. She'd seen all kinds of other wonders there too, practical things folks might use to make their lives easier, and she wanted to tell Tommy about them, but decided against it. Why make him feel like he had less than what was possible?

Tommy hadn't had much luck at the mine. Orner didn't appreciate him bringing a woman into Dire. They were bad luck, he'd been reminded, and one was worse than ten because men are less likely to fight over a woman if they thought they had options. And then there was the fact that while he didn't much like them, the Chinese came cheap and the UP sent Orner as many as he needed.

Orner had told Tommy to take Addie out to his place, and maybe, maybe he could get him some work at the mine. The truth was, Orner admitted, the UP didn't have much use for a miner if he wasn't Chinese. But what Tommy had going for him was that he'd once pulled Orner out of a drunken gambling fight just before guns were pulled and a man got shot. And even though the UP was doing everything they could to replace the white miners with Chinamen, Tommy figured Orner knew he owed a favor.

"The truth is," Tommy said, adding wood to the fire, "there just isn't much mine work for men like me. They say ten years ago wasn't hardly a coolie to be seen. Now the mines is full of 'em."

Addie sensed desperation in her brother's tone, not the giving-up kind, but the kind that clings heavy to a person like a rain-soaked coat. In his sober moments, it was the way her father had spoken. He'd been born into the world with only the advantage of a strong back and a strong will, but the combination shackled him to the use of both, and too often the world treated him as if it wasn't enough. She had come to understand that was part of the reason her father turned to drink. Tommy was too young to start down that road. "Let them have it," Addie said as brightly as she could, without seeming altogether false.

"Have what?"

"The work in the mines. When we was in Dire I seen how it does a man, and it reminded me of what Grandma told us. Remember? About how Grandpa died from all the soot in his chest."

"Coal dust," Tommy corrected. His eyes flashed as their camp-fire took hold.

"It's not work fit for humans, Tommy. So leave the Chinamen to it. Let them choke on the jobs they steal from men like you."

"Listen to you. Been here hardly two days, and you sound like some of them in the Knights of Labor."

She didn't know what her brother meant, but he was smiling and sounding better already, which was her aim. And though she wasn't sure what he might do if he couldn't make a go of the homestead or find work in the mines, she was serious. From what she could tell so far, life was hard enough in the Territory, and the Chinese made it worse. One thing was for sure, she wasn't going to have anything to do with them. "Don't need to set my hand on the stove," she said to her brother, "to know there's fire inside."

"I'm glad you come out, Addie," Tommy said. "I weren't at first, but I am now. You're good company."

The words struck her. No one that she could remember had ever said such a thing to her. She'd been told she was a hard worker, a good shot even, but never just plain good company. "I'm glad I come too," was all she said, reaching her hands toward the fire out of habit. Except for the light, they really didn't need it.

"If a man's gonna starve, he ought to at least have his family around to starve with him."

Addie laughed and grabbed her side. "I got a ways to go."

For a while, they did not speak. There would be no more talk about work, or the lack of it, at least for the evening. They watched the fire, poked at it with sticks now and then. Beyond what little crackle that came from the flames, the land was remarkably silent. No night birds or fizzing insects. Just the two of them. Even without the sound of robins and cicadas it was almost like old times, Addie thought, her and Tommy against the world. It wasn't certain how they'd get by, but they would, she knew. The man sitting across the way looked a little beaten down, it was true, but she was certain the optimistic boy who'd been her brother was inside there too. She wondered what her mother would think if she saw how they had made out. Would she be proud of Tommy for striking out on his own? Proud of Addie for getting out of Orgull just as she had done? Was that something a mother was supposed to take pride in, teaching her children to run?

"I don't know how you stuck with Pa all that time," Tommy

said, never taking his eyes off the fire, pulling his hair back behind his ears. She'd never seen it so long.

"It wasn't all bad. He was ornery for sure, but after he got off the whisky, he held steady."

Tom's eyes widened at the news. "You're saying Pa quit drinking."

Addie bounced her head back and forth, looking for the words to split the difference. "I'm saying, in the end he had more good days than he had bad." She told him how it had come to a head, how their father hadn't worked for nearly two weeks, how that hardly mattered because people in town stopped counting on him to deliver firewood on time. It was three days after her fourteenth birthday, a milestone that caused her to look around and take stock of her circumstances. They had two goats, five chickens, some cornmeal, a bit of coffee, bacon fat, and hardly a stick of wood put up for winter, and her father was passed out in the cabin. He'd gone through the last of his whisky, and she knew he didn't have so much as a dime to get more.

Addie was deep into the story and more eager to tell it. "So I got Pa's shotgun," she continued. "And I pulled up a stool right next to his bed and waited for him to wake up."

Tommy leaned forward, the firelight full in his eyes, as if it were coming from inside him. "Come on now. Don't tell me you shot Pa?"

Addie waved him off to keep him from getting ahead of the story. "I done something worse. When he woke, I had the shotgun sitting across my lap. I handed him a glass of water and waited till I knew he'd got his head situated. 'Any morning,' I told him, 'I could walk over here and give you a face full of shot.' He looked kind of startled and got awake pretty quick. 'And if I did that, Pa, if I shot you, maybe killed you,' I told him, 'no one would take a bit of notice because you're already pretty much dead to the world anyway with all the drinking you do.' " Addie paused, remembering the morning clearer than she cared to.

"What did the old man say?"

"He didn't, because right then is when I did what I'd never done in front of him. I cried. And then he cried too, and stood up and put his hands on my shoulders. It wasn't a hug, but that was what he meant by it."

Tommy looked near tears himself. "So he gave up liquor after that."

"He tried, is the point. Things weren't perfect, but they got better." That was all you could ask of a person, she thought, though in their father's case she knew he'd started trying too late. His hands went jittery, and he was irritable most of the time, and those days when he did drink, he filled the whole next day full of apologies, talked of going to church, staying respectable. He wouldn't follow through, she knew, but his bouquets of regret and a few days of sobriety were more than she expected to get when she sat down next to his bed with the shotgun. He was gone now, and she guessed she missed him.

Addie took in the vast plain of sage, almost lavender in the twilight. It wasn't solid like the stretches of grass she'd come across on her journey to Wyoming Territory, not like a cornfield even. Here, each bush seemed to stake out its own little plot, some of them tall as a man, others squat as a baker's wife. "Looks like an army of people standing out there."

Tommy nodded. "I can't tell you how many times I thought that same thing. Like they're all just standing out there waiting. Ghosts." His eyes looked upward into the corner of his mind as his lips thinned into a soft smile.

Addie leaned in closer when she saw her brother scratching his bearded chin. It was his story look.

"You know how Grandma used to tell us this or that person had gone to heaven? And how we should mind ourselves so we could get there too?" Addie didn't know where he was going with these questions, but she nodded all the same. "I've been doing some thinking on that. Addie, I have to tell you I'm not so sure about heaven and hell or even God." He looked at her straight in the eyes, which she took in itself as a question, as if to ask without saying it out loud if she'd ever wondered on the same thing. "Seems to me," he continued, "there's just too much hardship for ordinary folks down here on earth. But then I come and looked out on all this like you just did, and I got to thinking about what happens to us after we die." He winked. "Not that I'm in a hurry to find out for sure. But if there ain't a heaven or hell, it's still a nice idea to imagine a place where we all meet up after it's all over. Where we get to see everyone we loved and fought with and don't none of it matter anymore because we're not scratching an' clawing and elbowing each other for a scrap to eat."

Addie rested her chin in her hands and looked past her brother, imagining for a moment that all those individual shadows were people who'd gone on before her. Already it wasn't like one of his ghost stories from their childhood, not like "The Woman of the Woods" or "The Headless Ferryman" that even their father requested from time to time. Being by himself these couple years had changed Tommy enough that he wasn't thinking like a boy anymore.

"So that's it?" Addie asked in the silence of them watching the diminished light over the valley of root-bound sentinels. "You figure we just go stand around with folks?"

Tommy laughed. "Oh, no, Addie. The way I imagine it, when your time comes and you go to that place, there's everyone you ever knew, and everyone they ever knew, and they're all there to welcome you and pat you on the back, and right behind you is someone else because there's people leaving this life every minute."

That last part was true, though the reality of it hadn't visited her as much as some. While she heard of this or that woman dying in childbirth, or people drowning in the river, there were few dead she'd seen up close. Her grandmother came to mind, laid out on a bench in a pale blue cotton dress, all of her gray and sunken like something was pulling at her skin from her insides.

"And anyway," Tommy continued. "I like to think that maybe it works something like this. There'll come a time when the very last of us brings up the rear, and there ain't no more to follow. And I guess that's when we all head off together at the same time to wherever we're supposed to go."

"Isn't *that* heaven you're talking about?"

"No, because no one gets locked out. That's the best part. It's all or none."

Addie smiled. "You figure Ma will be there?"

"First in line to hug you."

"That's some big story, Tom." Addie wasn't one to get overly emotional, but her eyes welled, not for the idea of it, certainly. Death hadn't been a stranger to her life. She'd known old and young alike who'd been taken from this world, but something about watching Tommy, barely visible even with the small fire and Wyoming's star-ceilinged brand of darkness, something made her feel as if just then he was a ghost himself. Of course, the land didn't make a distinction. "Big story," Addie repeated, drawing the words out slow.

"All right then," Tommy said, standing and placing his hands on his waist. "That's what we'll call it." His voice was almost cheerful, and had none of the gloom Addie had mixed into his story. He gestured toward the plain, at all the souls waiting on him and

Addie, and those to come after. "The Big Story, that's what we're looking at. Where we're headed."

Addie stood and walked to her brother's side. It was as if he had planted a flag on a newly discovered shore. The fire was to their back now, flickering shadows darting away from them as if they were, on their own, reaching to the future. The Big Story, Addie thought. She felt her brother's solid arm rest across her back and over her shoulder, which shook off her thoughts about death. He was talking about a reunion, she reckoned, and a person spends their life getting ready for it so they got something to say when everyone shows up. She liked the idea, and there wasn't a better place to imagine it than from right where she and Tommy stood watching the wide open plain of quiet sage. "So they're all out there waiting for us," Addie said, "just waiting."

"They better be patient," Tommy said. "We're the only family we got on this side."

The fire was out, and Tommy was sleeping. Addie hadn't thought about it before, but he was right, they were all the family they had. Maybe someday their mother would turn up, but it was doubtful. If she had to leave to find a better life, Addie wished her mother had stayed long enough to teach her how a person, a woman, makes a better life right where she stands. It had to be possible. Maybe that was why fate had called her to Wyoming. Maybe the men here were so broken-backed a woman wouldn't have to run, might actually make her own contentment. Maybe she'd stand in front of her mother someday and say, "This is how it's done."

She wanted to speculate about these things out loud, but with her brother asleep, all Addie had for company were her thoughts and the white stars above scattered like seed. The sky was a quiet thing, but not still. Shooting stars streaked and faded like minnows in dark water. She closed her eyes and imagined moonlight dappling the surface of a lake. She was swimming in the sky, thinking about her brother's Big Story, her grandmother, and her mother and father and standing side by side. She knew how her father died, even Brother Two, but it wasn't right, she thought, that a daughter could know more about how a stranger came to his end than what had become of her own mother.

Her father she'd found in the woods, in the late afternoon. It was fall, and he'd been good about staying off the jug to get wood laid in for winter, for them and those in town they supplied. More often than not Addie was with him in the morning pulling her half of the log saw, helping her father fell a few trees. But that day Addie went into town to deliver a load of wood while her father worked on fallen timber dry enough for firewood that season. She knew something was off when she returned to the cabin and couldn't hear anything but the pip of cardinals and the battering of a woodpecker. Either her father had moved deeper into the woods than usual, or he was drunk.

Addie looked at the wall of fiery orange leaves that was the woods that time of year. She had half a mind to let her father just stay there, passed out, stay until he was covered in leaves and ticks. It was what she thought when she stepped out the door and closed it behind her. It was what she thought when she pulled her hat tight around her head and left the clearing for the woods. It was what she thought when she slid over the trunk of the blown-over oak they'd long ago took the branches from, and when she stepped wrong-footed into the creek and soaked her boot. She even thought it when she came to the place where he was supposed to be working, found his silent ax plunged into a maple stump, his saw mid-stroke in the tree itself, and him passed out face-first on the ground, as if he were a denim leaf. She couldn't see the side of his face for his hat, so she nudged him with her foot. "Pa, wake up." He didn't stir. It'd been a long time since she'd seen him this bad. Where was the jug? She didn't see one. She knelt and took him by the shoulders, and that's when she knew. There was no resistance. When she rolled him over she found his face slack, almost young, and his chest empty of breath.

It wasn't a memory she would wish on anyone, Addie thought, but she had the satisfaction of knowing she hadn't left him out there when she thought he'd gotten drunk, and on that count, he hadn't.

It was years before that she'd been introduced to the finality of death. She recalled a night when she was young, sitting on her narrow bed and gently positioning the flour-sack pillow her grand-mother made for her, the one with stitched-on blue flannel geese and hair ribbon bows that tickled her ears at night. She wasn't partial to frilly things, but that pillow was precious to her.

"Do you think if I put the pillow right here," she asked her mother, "that Grandma will come down from heaven and lie next to me?"

Her mother stopped what she was doing at the woodstove and looked at Addie with an expression that, years later, Addie under-stood meant that it wasn't possible but that she wished that it was. In the moment, Addie only heard her mother's reply. "I think that's real nice. I bet she comes the minute you go off to sleep." It was a rare thing to hear her speak so tenderly.

"And you think maybe if I pretend to go to sleep and open my eyes real fast, I'll see her?"

Wiping her hands on the side of her dress, Addie's mother looked worried. She sat at their small table and opened her hands to her daughter, and Addie took her up on the silent offer. It wasn't an embrace, but she felt her mother's firm grip on both shoulders. There was comfort in it. "Adele, baby," her mother said, "it don't work like that." She placed her hand gently over Addie's eyes. "I want you to keep them eyes of yours closed for a minute and think of Grandma's face. Can you see it?" She could, saw every line in her cheeks and the kind way about her blue eyes, the bundled mess of hair that seemed a gray version of Addie's own. "Okay," her mother continued. "Now I want you to think of Grandma hugging you tight the way she did." She felt her mother's hands soft at her shoulders, and in her mind's eye saw her grandmother holding her. "All right, Adele, baby." Addie opened her eyes.

"I saw her just like you told me to, Ma," Addie said.

"That's real good, baby, because that's how you're going to see Grandma from now on."

Addie was caught off guard at this news. "I don't follow," she said. "I know you told me God took Grandma to heaven and that she's with the angels, but are you saying I'm never going to see her again like I see you sitting right here?"

As she recalled the scene, Addie was lying down, listening to Tommy's quiet snore; she couldn't sleep herself. She was thinking of her mother, whom she likely would not lay eyes on again in this life. She remembered the surprised look on her mother's face when Addie herself had been startled to learn that she would never see her grandmother again. Her poor mother, Addie thought, grieving herself and having to explain the disappearing act that is death. "Doesn't God know we need Grandma more than he does?" she had asked.

Her mother was near tears. "Well, Adele, baby. He does." She paused and brought a palm to her face, then looked up and smiled sweetly. "You know how Grandma liked to paint if she had a chance?" Addie nodded. It wasn't something she could afford too often, said it was a waste of the time God gave her, but if she had the brush and paints and a wide enough piece of wood, her grandmother was a happy woman. "Well, God needed someone to help him paint rainbows, and he couldn't think of anyone better to do it than your Grandma."

Finally something was making sense. It didn't make Addie any happier just then, but it was a fact she could hold on to. After that, the first time she saw a rainbow, her grandmother's face came to mind the same as if she were standing right in front of her, and she figured that was God's way of sharing.

Her father had left this world naturally, and she could find comfort in that. But what was her mother's fate? If she was still alive, at that very moment, where was her mother putting her head down to sleep? A daughter should know.

By mid-morning, Addie and Tommy reached his homestead, a plot of land that didn't seem to have any natural borders, nor any particular feature within its fenceless perimeter that might recommend it for ownership. It was brush and more brush growing out of conspicuously gravelly earth blotted everywhere with patches of white that looked like thin puddles of spilled flour. Addie kicked at one to see how deep the white went.

"Alkali." Her brother's voice was clipped but not unhappy. "I ain't going to lie to you. That's the drawback." He laughed and pointed. "And there's the other one."

At first, Addie wasn't sure what it was she was supposed to

focus on. Then, a few hundred yards off was what looked to be the bloated gut of a dead animal, or maybe the underside of a small boat. Neither seemed plausible. "What is it?"

"Home." It took them a few minutes to reach the structure, which consisted of a wheel-less wagon, turned over on top of four walls of piled stones, the whole of it not more than five feet high. "Built it myself," Tommy said.

The pride in her brother's voice wouldn't allow Addie to say what she really thought, which was that it didn't look like the sort of place one would want to even roost a chicken. Instead, she focused on the things her brother had done right. The entrance showed that he'd dug out space inside, and then to keep rain from seeping in, he'd sloped dirt around the walls so that it ran off and away. She thought the effect was something like a toadstool not quite pushed out of the ground. Had she really come all this way to live under a mushroom? "It's something, Tommy," Addie managed. "How did you get that wagon out here?"

"Swapped it for labor at the Grood ranch."

She did a 360-degree survey. Not another house in sight, nor a smoke column that suggested one. No trees, of course, which in Orgull had been their mother's milk. Here the land didn't offer so much as a callused teat. "I suppose if we get attacked by Indians," Addie said, trying to make the best of things, "we'll see them coming from way off."

"That ain't going to happen. They pretty well run them off a long time ago. Now and then you'll see a few come through, but they're licked."

She'd meant it as a joke, and she gave Tommy a look to underscore the point, taking off her hat and wiping the sweat off her brow with her forearm. Maybe it was the way the sun hit her skin, or the movement of muscle beneath, but the image of the Chinaman cook back in Dire came to her mind. He was also someone far from home. She'd seen China on a map, a land she could no more imagine than the ocean that separated it from the United States. But he'd come to this shore and then some. Maybe it wasn't right, he and his kind taking jobs from men like Tommy, but a person had to appreciate what this Chinaman cook was doing. He left everything behind and was making a go of it here in the Territory. If he can do it, she thought. Then again, the way she heard it, the difference was, if he failed there were a dozen more to take his place, which was why Chinamen seemed to do so well, she guessed. Here, it would be her and Tommy, and if either of them missed the mark, there was no one to pick up the slack.

So there it was surrounding her, all of Tommy's cards on the table, the unworkable land, thin job prospects, and worse, there wasn't even a third thing. "A man'l 'spect you to follow him like a dog," her grandmother told her once, "so a woman's gotta act like a cat." At the time she was too young to hear it, but now she was beginning to understand. Maybe the situation wasn't quite what her grandmother meant, but all the same, now that Tommy had convinced her to pull up stakes, it wouldn't hurt to keep that advice in mind. At that moment, none of it made her feel under immediate threat, but the Chinaman cook notwithstanding, Addie thought it was an open question as to whether folks came to Wyoming Territory to live or to die.

EPISODE SIX

The man who walked up Dire Draw with the fire-haired woman had gotten a job in the camp. Wing saw him fumble into the mine with the Finn who'd lost his partner in a mine accident not long before. They looked unlikely to bring much coal out. The new man sagged and stumbled with his gear, and the Finn seemed unconcerned, only smiled and laughed at his novice charge as they arrived at the entrance.

Wing quietly searched the white side of Dire to see if he could catch a glimpse of the woman who had been with the new miner, but she was nowhere to be found among the crumble of shacks. What had happened to her? When he first saw her, she'd looked as out of place as he felt, as if Wyoming was a shore and they had been on the same boat. But what if he did see her, meet her? He couldn't speak to her in English. And why would she listen to him? The arrangement, the order of things, was clear from that first day he set foot on the dock in San Francisco. Whites spoke. The Chinese listened. If a reply was to be made, there were a few Chinese who did this . . . for a price. The Six Companies in San Francisco, Ah Say and Ah Koon in Rock Springs, and here in Dire, Ah Joe was the voice of Chinese miners.

It was a ridiculous thought, anyway, to think he would ever stand so close to the woman that he might share even a Chinese word, a simple "Nei ho." And beyond that, what was there to say about his unhappy life anyway, or even about that early time when he caught pleasure by the shirtsleeve? The woman couldn't possibly be interested in how he'd generally passed the days for nine years, or how at first he measured the San Francisco days by their gradations of gray, or how at night there, if he could put together enough money, he attended the Royal Chinese Theater on Jackson Street, sometimes the Lung Look with its wonderful parquet floors. If he told of these things, surely she might think of him as a lazy dreamer. If he told her that for a few months he had been an actor on one of these stages, surely she would find him frivolous, soft. How could she possibly understand his excitement at seeing fifteen hundred people squeezed into the theater, half of them sitting on the backs of seats with no upholstery? There were the private boxes he would never be able to afford and a partition for women, vendors milling about the crowd selling candy and fruits. And the productions, no scenery to speak of, everything a suggestion. A handkerchief might be a cherished dove, an escaping soul, or a bouquet, all in one night. The stage was a simple raised platform with two doors for entrances and exits and an orchestra in the middle, not a traditional Chinese orchestra, but close. There were cymbals, a guitar, a gong, and the scraper of the catgut.

It was by chance that Wing had been introduced to Sing Ten,

who was preparing a new play—a lampoon, he said. He looked Wing over head to foot. "You don't have any experience, boy. But you look the part." The man wore an exasperated expression and allowed his graying queue to lie over his shoulder and hang down his left side, which made Wing uncomfortable. "Can you sing, boy?"

Wing nodded. It was true. In China, he was the youngest of eight sons, and his parents considered the number a symbol of an auspicious voice. Although he was not number one, would never manage the family accounts, he was doted on by both his parents, encouraged in music, singing, and storytelling. Often at the evening meal his father tapped the side of his bowl with his chopsticks and simply looked at Wing, meaning he wanted to hear one of his son's stories.

"Let's hear it then," Sing Ten said, crossing his arms. They were standing outside the Lung Look Theater. The evening had chilled, and there were just a few men walking the streets.

Wing began a song his mother taught him as a child about a white heron that turns into a woman at night.

He sang. "No, no," Sing Ten said, stomping his foot. "Like an American woman."

Sing Ten had found Wing's impromptu audition acceptable. "You're trainable," was what he said, and in six weeks Wing was painted up and cinched into a corset to play a San Francisco socialite married to a fat, drunkard banker. The woman finds herself taken with a Chinese dockworker. From there, the inebriated husband is made to look the fool at every turn as the socialite and her suitor scheme to take his money and leave Gold Mountain for China.

For a first role, it was not too difficult, and Wing managed to carry his part off to fair success. He was onstage a great deal, but it was mainly the men who sang, leaving him to make broad coquettish gestures, or to sing brief but cunning lies to her husband. In the beginning Wing enjoyed the experience, learned to anticipate the laughter and cat calls. But when the newness wore off, when for the millionth time he had sung, "Just one more sip of beer my love?" while the lover pickpocketed the husband, he grew bored, started to resent the audience for the drivel they applauded. And then he resented himself, both for being in the play and for having once been part of the audience cheering the very same kind of thing. He found himself imagining his parents in the front row, both offering disapproving looks.

"Can't we do something more serious?" he asked Sing Ten one night while counting receipts. After all, Wing had seen more traditional Chinese stories on their very stage.

"We put on what sells tickets."

"Remember that song I first sang you?" Wing asked. Sing Ten's attention never left the money stacked in front of him, leaving Wing to speak into his blue cap. "What if we made that into a play?"

Sing Ten continued to focus on the receipts but offered a grumbly chuckle. "You have a few lines, and suddenly you want to write a play and run the house?"

Wing placed his hands on Sing Ten's desk and leaned forward to make eye contact. "I was only thinking—"

"Ayyah! Don't be impertinent." Sing Ten raised a hand and brushed the air for Wing to leave.

Later, Wing took a certain satisfaction in hearing that his replacement had been booed off the stage, and the production closed just a week later. That evening with Sing Ten, Wing decided he would not return. He would write his own play, something that mattered. Maybe it would be about the heron that turns into a woman at night, or maybe a story with two people who aren't schemers, but true lovers.

Laughing at himself, Wing shook his head. He was standing in Little San Fran, looking at the white side of Dire, imagining the story he would not tell the fire-haired woman not because she wouldn't understand his language, but because ultimately it was a story of failure. He was a cook in a mining camp in an American territory not even deemed worthy of being one of their states. He was not a writer of plays. The necessities of life had thwarted inspiration, though he felt that perhaps he carried a dormant seed waiting for a spring he could not predict.

EPISODE SEVEN

Tommy didn't need to worry. Addie guessed she'd make a try at living, but she hoped that would mean more than just getting by, and that she'd have some say in the matter. She was alone, standing in the bright open plain under blue sky, unsure if she should feel large or small. One thing was for sure, it was as if all the rabbits got word of Addie and her brother's shotgun. In nearly three hours she hadn't seen even the wisp of a tail taking off into the brush. She wondered if this meant something in those parts, if it was some kind of omen. Or maybe it just meant there wouldn't be rabbit for dinner, she thought. She'd been at this new life a month and had become accustomed to one or two gutted rabbits dangling from her waist, which slowed her progress some, but it was also like keeping score. Addie was used to being ahead, and with nothing at her waist today, she was frustrated the rabbits were winning.

She was about three-quarters of a mile from Racer, who at that distance, yellow-gray in the sunlight, looked not unlike a week-old biscuit. Lots of things tended to look like food, she noticed, when you're hungry all the time. Behind the hinny, in the sunbaked distance, was a brown splotch trailing dust. Most likely wild horses, and if it was, she needed to get back to Racer before the hinny got any ideas. Addie ran through the brush, dodging what she could, plowing through the less formidable. By the time she reached Racer it was clear that the herd of wild horses was a double-hitched wagon with one driver. Addie mounted Racer and waited. Wild horses she needed to get out of the way of, but a person, well, it would be impolite to ride off, she thought, when it was obvious the wagon would go by using the double row of wheel ruts below Racer's hooves. She pulled the hinny off the trail so the wagon could pass.

With a hundred yards between them, Addie saw that it wasn't the kind of driver she expected. Holding the reins was a woman, bonnet on her head, rifle in her lap. Another woman out here, she thought. It was like being the last two peas on a plate. The wagon slowed up as it approached, and now the woman took her rifle up to her side, pointing it skyward, which Addie didn't take offense to. How was the woman to know a person on a horse out in the middle of nowhere wasn't laying in wait to hold her up. But quick as the rifle went up, it went back in the woman's lap, and some brand of astonishment flashed across her face. Now she was stopped even with Addie, the kicked-up dust storming past them as if it had its own business to attend to. There they were, the two women, each of them silent, staring pea to pea.

"Howdy," the woman said. She had a bullfrog voice and was missing her right lower front teeth. Her dress matched her bonnet, light blue, and covered her entirely, neck to ankle. Addie guessed her to be forty, and the dress, threadbare at the elbows, looked not too far off from that. She pulled a blue handkerchief from beneath her sleeve and wiped her face. Addie did the same with her forearm but stopped midway when she felt the grit pulling across her skin.

"Ma'am," Addie said. They were silent again. On Addie's part it was due to the strangeness of it, like two does coming face-to-face, useless to each other on the surface of the thing, but a relief nonetheless. Addie noticed the wagon tray was full, but with what she was unsure. It was covered with a canvas tarp. "Headed into town?"

"The husband took ill again." She shook her head. "Seems like he's either broke down or gallivanting off, and I got to hold things together." Pointing behind her with a thumb, she spoke of her current objective. "Got to get our whatnots to Rock Springs. This is our ranch." She gestured with both hands, and Addie felt a little guilty. Without fences, the land was all just open space to her, and here she was hunting on this woman's property.

"I'm sorry," Addie said. "I was hunting rabbits."

"I'm sorry you're hunting rabbits too." The woman laughed, slapping the buckboard. "I'm Maye Grood, and if you're apologizing for being on our land, don't think nothing of it. The Groods don't eat vermin, and the fewer of them making hay in our garden the better. Difficult as it is to raise anything up fit to eat." Maye stopped herself, Addie noticed. "Not that it's unheard of to eat rabbit, you understand."

She had a generous, honest smile, even if it wasn't complete, and the whole of Maye put Addie at ease, reminding her of a doll left outside too long, but still pretty. "Staying at my brother's homestead not far off. Addie Maine."

"Tom Maine your brother?"

Addie nodded, surprised to hear the quickness with which her brother's name had popped from Maye's mouth.

"He's a good man. Helped us build the summer kitchen. That wagon he's got for a roof come from us." One of her horses got impatient, shook in its harness, and Maye tug-tugged the rein to quiet it.

Addie wasn't sure what to say, if she was supposed to be impressed by the roof over her head, or if Maye was simply offering a point of fact. She didn't have to think about it long.

"If you ask me," Maye continued, looking into the distance, rather than directly at Addie, "I'm not for sure your brother's exactly the homesteading type."

"He ain't," Addie said without hesitation. "But we didn't have much when we were young, so I think maybe the land feels good beneath his feet even if he has to buckle his back to keep it."

Maye nodded. "Sometimes I think it's women better suited to this godforsaken place." She told Addie about her own circumstances coming to Wyoming. She was seventeen when her family set out from Missouri. There had been some dry years for everyone, and farm to farm along the way the story was the same: corn to cattle had withered, and people were pulling up stakes for places where the rain was a little more reliable. She'd never been out of the state before, so every day seemed to bring a strange new thing. "I remember we was out on a low grass prairie and we come upon a flock of sheep and I had no idea what they was. I'd seen cows and goats, but never a sheep, so they was wild animals to me. Ma and Pa had a good laugh." Addie recalled her own confusion when she saw a pronghorn from the train, and was comforted by the fact she wasn't the only one.

Maye told Addie how her family reached Cheyenne and set up camp just outside of town. It was then she realized that Wyoming Territory was their destination, but didn't know exactly what it was they were going to do now that they were there. Her father hadn't mentioned homesteading or ranch life even once. They traveled for days past Laramie, pitching their tent every night. Maye woke up

one morning, ready to gather her things for that day's trek to wherever they were headed, but her father just smiled and told her not
to bother. They were home. Maye smiled at the end of her story. "I
can't say I'd recommend this life to a girl the age I was then, but I
come into my own all right." She pointed to Addie. "And you look
like you'll do fine." With that, she reached under the canvas and
fished her hand into what Addie made out to be a sawdust-filled
barrel. "It ain't much," she said, handing Addie two brown eggs,
"but welcome to the Territory."

Addie accepted the gifts in both palms like they were precious
objects. And they were. She couldn't remember the last time she'd
held an egg, much less two at the same time. They may as well have
been gold nuggets the way she stared at them, appreciated their
weight. After a series of Addie's effusive thank-yous, and Maye's
horses clomping their agitation at the delay, Maye announced she
needed to get to Rock Springs, but that Addie was welcome to visit
the ranch anytime. "It's good to take a day now and then to just be
with other womenfolk," she said, though Addie wasn't sure quite
what that meant. Maye patted her rifle. "And remember, love 'em
as we're wont to do, but in Wyoming, more often than not a gun is
more use than a man."

The morning after meeting Maye, Addie was bringing Tommy
a few days' worth of cooked rabbit and one of the eggs, which
she boiled so as not to risk breaking it. To get the pair back to
their shack after receiving them from Maye, Addie took a cue from
Maye's sawdust barrel. She filled her hat halfway with brush, placed
the eggs inside, and tossed in more brush until they were covered.

Now, even though she was bringing Tommy his share, it was

her own breakfast that was on her mind. She'd fried her egg, which is what she thought about all the way into Dire. As eggs go, hers hadn't had any qualities that recommended it above others, except that as it plittered in the skillet it wasn't the thought of an egg or the memory of an egg, but a real egg shining in the hot fat, and all of it for Addie. Plenty wasn't something she thought about often, but it occurred to her just then that there were times when a single egg could indeed be plenty, and this was one of those times.

She thought about that and the woman who'd supplied the eggs, Maye. She had a husband; didn't seem dragged down by the fact. And she was headed somewhere, not running, but moving on like she had a choice and knew what she wanted. That was the secret, Addie guessed, knowing what you wanted and then going after it. But how does a person figure that out? she wondered. What did she want? In all her young life she'd never asked herself a clearer question, was never so stumped for an answer. So there was a starting place.

As she rode up Dire Draw alongside the railroad tracks, Addie kept an eye out for the bones of an Eckonen brother and his mule, imagined finding the alternate version of the story that placed Brother Two fully astride the mule's spine. Here and there she pulled up the hinny to take a second look at what turned out to be sun-bleached wood or skull-shaped rocks.

Dire Draw itself, despite its name, maybe wasn't such a bad place for a person to lay down their bones, she thought. After all, the draw didn't do anything except just be, and the animals here seemed to get along just fine. It was human beings that were sometimes just too tender and raw for such a place. But the draw itself was harmless, quiet as a church on Monday, and all the more solemn for it. But still, it didn't sit right with Addie that they'd let

Brother Two's bones just lie there. Could laying down track really be so important that a man's last dignity could be ignored?

The answer to Addie's question was clear when the tipple at Dire came into view. It wasn't laying track that was important so much as what it was aiming toward. Maybe it was the sweet odor of the daytime meal, but as she passed Little San Fran, Addie found herself looking for the Chinaman cook, though he was nowhere to be seen. She imagined he must be responsible for the meal she smelled, which was not poultry she was certain, and not beef. Pork maybe, though she'd heard the Chinese shipped in all manner of things to eat that a right-minded person wouldn't feed a dog. Still, if what the Chinamen were eating that day wasn't something she'd let even close to her mouth, she had to admit she couldn't tell from the pleasant way it rode the air.

Somewhere among the few grimy faces emerging from the mine was her brother. Most of the men, she knew, would eat inside the mine. She watched as the Chinamen headed one way while the other miners went opposite without a word or wave between them. A hand did go up, however, and it was aimed at Addie: Tommy, her smudge of a brother, approaching her with another man just behind him.

Addie slid off the hinny and brought the satchel of rabbit and one boiled egg down with her. Tommy was all smiles, though through the grime she saw that he was tired. His companion was taller, broader in the shoulders, had hair nearly as long as her brother's, and appeared to her to be all grimness. His eyes were bright blue, almost like they were lit from behind, but there was no kindness in them, but no maliciousness either. This man never looked side to side, as if the only thing that mattered was what was in front of him, and at that moment what was in front of him was Addie.

"Sis," Tommy began, "I want you to meet Atso Muukkonen."

Addie nodded, remained focused on the quality of his eyes. She was sure he didn't blink.

"I call him Muuk," Tommy continued. "And he don't seem to mind much. You know Finns."

She didn't, but it wasn't a point worth pursuing.

Muuk took off his cap and scratched at his hair, creating a haphazard part. It was as if a lever had switched in his brain, and he suddenly realized he was in the presence of a woman. It was the kind of nicety she didn't care for much, but that's what men were taught to do. He lowered his gaze. "Miss Adele," he said. He had a deep voice with a kind of internal tremor like the low notes of a harmonica.

"Addie, if you prefer," she said.

Tommy patted Muuk on the back. "He's probably been practicing that for a week. Don't speak much English."

"I speak when I need," Muuk said. His accent had a strange musical quality that struck Addie as a kind of sadness.

The three of them ate supper together in the slim shade outside Muuk's bachelor hut, he quietly dipping dried beef in canned tomatoes, Tommy gnawing at a rabbit thigh as he told Addie about his new partner in the mine. Muuk was Finnish born, from a place called Kisko. His father brought him to the copper mine there when he was fourteen, but when work gave out they came to the United States and tried their hand at dairy cattle. It wasn't but a few years after they arrived that the entire family was beset by hard times. When Tommy got to this part, he scratched at his beard and turned to Muuk as if to ask permission to continue.

Muuk swallowed and nodded. "I do not complain at this."

When she was forty-two, Muuk's mother delivered a stillborn

boy, Tommy continued, and lived a month of grief before dying herself. Within a year, his father and sister died of consumption.

"Venla," Muuk said. "My sister."

It was the first glimpse of tenderness Addie saw in him, and the recognition must have shown in her face, because Muuk cleared his throat and finished the story.

"I missed home, Finland. I have a friend there I like very much. Panu Lankinen. I have no money to go back, and it cannot be with my friend, so I come to Rock Springs." He paused and shook his head, then stared into the ground. "But the UP bringing the Chinamen, and now here."

" 'Bout eighty of them to our thirty here in Dire," Tommy added. "Getting to be a Chinaman's world, sure." He smiled, shaking off the thought, and patted Muuk on the shoulder. "That's more words than I've ever heard you say at one time." He winked at Addie. "Must be the company."

Muuk looked up, first at Tommy, and then at Addie, where he held his gaze for what felt to her like a curiously long time. This was a man, she could tell, who wore in his expression every one of life's scars, the weight of living itself.

"That's where I come in I guess. Muuk's last partner got his hand crushed." Tommy held out his hand and spoke the partner's name. "His name was Eetu?"

Muuk nodded and laughed. "Idiootti."

Tommy was laughing as well. It was an odd response, Addie thought, odd because they were laughing at the memory of a man's injury. She wondered if it was Dire that turned men hard like this, or if it was the kind of place hard men sought. If the latter was true, she misunderstood her brother, and the idea of that bothered her.

A gust of wind seemed timed to remind the trio that the men

had to return to work. Muuk tossed the empty tomato can aside and held his hand out to Addie, palm up. It was callused, black in the creases and wide as a Christmas pancake. When she didn't respond, he said, "Your hand?" Addie duplicated his gesture, offering her own palm. She'd never thought she'd had what most people might call girlish hands. They were dry and showed they knew rope and wood and reins, but by comparison to Muuk's, her fingers took on an unexpected delicacy that surprised her. "Hyvä," Muuk said. "Good."

"Looking for a new partner?" Tommy said. "Or just sweet on my sister?"

Addie drew her hand back.

Now the three were silent, Muuk looking both Addie and Tommy in the eyes, going back and forth as if to check if he'd made some offense. A section of newspaper fluttered between them, breaking the silence, and Tommy stomped on it like he was killing a bug. "Watch this," he said to Muuk, picking up the scrap and handing it to Addie.

It was mainly advertisements. "What am I supposed to do with this?" Addie said.

Without saying a word, Tommy pointed to one of the ads that was all text, and she understood what he wanted. "I cure fits!" she read. "When I say I cure I do not mean merely to stop them for a time and then have them return again. I mean . . ." She'd come to a word she didn't know, but she gave it a go. "I mean ra . . . dical cure. I have made diseases of fits . . . epil . . . epsy of falling sickness a lifelong study. I warrant my remedy to cure the worst cases. Because others have failed is no reason for not now receiving a cure. Send at once for a trea . . . tise and free bottle of my infallible remedy. Give express and post office. It costs you nothing for a trial and I will cure you. Address Dr. H.G. Root 133

Pearl Street, New York." She hadn't read out loud in a while, and was relieved to be done with it.

"What do ya think about that," Tommy said, slapping Muuk on the back. "My very own sister can read."

Muuk smiled. "Hyvä!"

Addie felt her cheeks go red at the attention, and in an attempt not to acknowledge either man, she focused on their near identical lunch buckets. Tommy bragged on her some more, told how she could throw a knife and had won a sack of potatoes in a shooting contest back in Orgull.

"And I'll tell you what else," Tommy said. "That there Dr. Root has got the right idea, going into business for himself. Only way a man can make a real go of it in this life."

"That, and maybe homesteading," Addie said with a grin. She was still staring at the lunch buckets, but with a different purpose now. Nearly every miner carried one just like them. "Muuk," she began, "do you have a chunk of beef and canned tomatoes every day?"

Muuk looked embarrassed and confused by the question, so she put it to Tommy.

"I ain't thought about it," Tommy said. "I guess so. Sometimes it's elk or corn, and he don't have a can all the time."

"And the Chinamen? What do they eat?"

"Babies and dogs."

"Be serious." An idea was growing in her head, and she needed some information from her brother. "When I rode by Little San Fran today, whatever they were cooking smelled pretty good. What do you suppose that was?" It was coming back to her, the funeral her grandmother had taken her to years ago, Big Martha's, the black woman who seemed to have no limit to the space in her heart for everyone she met. After her funeral, Addie and her grandmother stayed to eat. Mostly it was things she knew, ham hock and beans, collards, chicken. And then there were the crisp little meats her grandmother warned her against. "Don't take none of that," she'd whispered. "Them are gizzards, and we don't eat gizzards." Addie nodded without saying the warning had come too late. Before her grandmother sat down next to her, Addie began with the gizzards, not knowing what they were, and she liked them, the saltiness, and too the way they managed to be crisp and chewy at the same time.

"Addie," Tommy said, "I'm happy to say I ain't got no idea. I never wanted nothing to do with their kind. I just let them alone. Though I'd like to knock their heads together." He turned to Muuk. "You hear what I heard? Some of them is paying Orner for the best rooms in the mine?"

Standing, Addie smiled at her brother. "Stop fretting about the Chinamen. You can hold your own no matter what." Muuk stood as well. "At least there's one gentleman in the crowd," she said, though she recognized his politeness just to be nice. She looked at the pair of them. It took two men per room in the mine, so maybe partnering up wasn't such a bad idea in the wide open. With that thought she nodded and turned toward Racer, thinking about two items Tommy left with her at the homestead, a LeFever shotgun and a 45-70 rifle. She was going to trot over to Little San Fran and find the source of whatever it was that they were eating over there. More than that, she hoped to find the Chinaman cook responsible for it. She needed him.

"Wait," her brother called out as she left. "What are you doing?"

"No time." She didn't bother to turn around. "I got business."

EPISODE EIGHT

It had been a gamble to ride all the way to the homestead and then back again to Dire the next morning, but Addie managed to make it to the narrow bridge by the appointed time. Just the day before she'd been sitting across from her brother and Muuk as they ate their midday meal. No men ever looked so hungry to her as miners, she thought, which was why she let the pair digest their poor little meal while she went off to Little San Fran. She'd caused quite a commotion riding through the Chinese quarters. She guessed it was uncommon enough for a white man to come through, and from their reactions, just about unimaginable for a woman to be among them. The area was orderly, that was one thing. Same dirt to walk on, but the housing was sturdier, had a little red paint to it. It was clear who the UP was looking out for and who they weren't, men like her brother and Muuk.

An odd-looking Chinaman stopped her in front of his little joss house with its single pewter incense holder sitting just in front of the doorway. "You must be the young lady everyone is speaking of," he said. "Addie Maine, I believe." This man was too finely dressed for Dire, Addie thought. He wore a gray wool suit with a red silk vest and matching bow tie, the two set off by a surprisingly bright white shirt.

It was Ah Joe, the Chinaman boss Emrys Clough had mentioned who managed most of the Chinese affairs. "That's me," Addie said. For a moment she thought to get off her horse, but with a number of Chinamen milling about, she thought it safer to stay in the saddle. She explained her proposition to Ah Joe, and they agreed to meet at the bridge the next morning.

She waited in the dry and windless morning. Beneath the bridge the gully was loaded with discarded cans mounded like mushrooms. Ah Joe was wearing the same outfit as the day before and was approaching with a smaller, younger man who she hoped was the Chinaman cook she'd asked about. They were stoic in expression, so much so Addie wondered if she was in for some disappointing news. She'd had the idea that she could earn some money by bringing game into Dire. But she needed someone in the camp to peddle it for her, maybe even take orders. She thought if she got a coolie to work for her, she might get some business out of Little San Fran because they would trust one of their own.

When Ah Joe neared the bridge, his face exploded into a smile and his arms pulled up into an open gesture of friendliness. The young Chinaman smiled as well, but less broadly and all the more sincere for it, and his clothing was much more subdued, the same indigo cotton shirt and loose trousers as most of the Chinese wore, only he'd cut off his sleeves. It was this latter detail that made Addie sure that this was the same Chinaman she'd seen cooking over a large pot the day Tommy first brought her to Dire.

When they arrived in front of Addie, Ah Joe extended his hand and offered two sharp quarter bows. "Miss Addie," he said thickly. "I am Ah Joe, as you remember. Happy to serve you."

Addie looked at Ah Joe's light brown hand. She had never touched a Celestial, and it never occurred to her that she'd have to now. It remained between them like an unfinished bridge. I've held the nethers of goat, Addie told herself, may as well do this. She met the gesture firmly and found Ah Joe's hand warm and soft, and she knew immediately that he didn't do much with it except strike bargains. She looked at the young man, whose eyes were directed downward. Up close he was slight, his clothes concealing that fact poorly. Still, she saw in his arms a kind of musculature that's more efficient than showy, the difference between taking game with a spring trap or with one shot from a gun.

"You may call this man Wing Lee," Ah Joe said, with a tight sweep of his other hand.

"Not Ah Wing?" She'd thought all Chinese names began with Ah.

Ah Joe chuckled. "Of course, if you like." Then he said something in Chinese, and Wing looked directly at Addie. Only it wasn't an uncomfortable thing. He was young; young as her? Or was it just that his face wasn't smeared with coal dust like so many of the others? Or maybe it was that the whites of his eyes were so supremely bright. His eyes. Their shape reminded her of two little fish facing each other. She understood now that was why she couldn't look away from him that first day. She couldn't see his eyes then, and she wanted to. This moment was an opportunity to get her fill. His deep and easy gaze caught her, like a silent refutation of all the things her brother and everyone else had said about the Chinese. In this moment she felt like maybe they were the same, two people just trying not to get swallowed up in this strange place, and the thought made her uncomfortable because this feeling had struck her heart once before, just as quickly, and it turned out badly.

"Hello, Wing, I'm Addie," she managed. She thought to offer her hand as Ah Joe had done, but Wing merely nodded and smiled without showing teeth.

Ah Joe clapped his palms together. "Addie, not Adele? Very well. Wing Lee is a good boy. Very fast to learn whatever you need." From there, Addie listened to Ah Joe for several minutes as he ran down Wing's availability, what he thought was fair pay, and what the limits of his duties ought to be, all of this peppered with praise for Wing's industriousness and his variety of skills. She knew this same tone from the barkers at the fair, and the situation wasn't too different, she thought, from paying a few coins to see whatever it was behind the tent flaps, be it the bearded woman or the man that lifted dumbbells with his mustache. Only this time it seemed like the reverse, that all the strangeness was out in the open, and maybe she was about to plunge through the tent flaps and find everything familiar.

"That's all fine by me," Addie said after Ah Joe came to a stopping place. She wouldn't be asking Wing to do 90 percent of what Ah Joe praised him for anyway. He had experience with butchering, which was good, and cooking. But she didn't need to know about useless details like Wing's superior musical skills. She doubted a Chinese song would ever be the key to her next meal or keep a roof over her head. "What do you think, Wing?" Addie asked. The new hire acknowledged her with a nod but did not speak. She tried again. "That all sound fair?" Nothing.

Ah Joe cleared his throat and spoke in Chinese, Wing nodding at each pause. Then Wing turned to Addie and smiled, this time showing a row of distinctly straight teeth. "Yes," he said, almost in a whisper.

Addie caught on and cocked her head. "He don't speak English. Am I right?"

"Very little." Ah Joe did not elaborate, or apologize. He merely waited.

Oh, that was a fine thing, Addie thought. She looked into the sky, where a hawk was circling. Ah Joe had gone through all that, and *now* he was telling her she wouldn't be able to communicate with this Wing? Maybe her brother was right, the Chinamen couldn't be trusted. It was bad enough that she had to hire one in the first place, Addie thought, but one that didn't speak English? How could she manage that? She shook her head in doubt, lips pursed, rattling off a series of questions about Wing's history as Ah Joe had told it, questions she thought she ought to be certain of before they sealed the deal. After all, she was taking Ah Joe's word for everything. And she threw in a final question just to be thorough. She'd heard Little San Fran had rooms dug out beneath the buildings where the men smoked opium, gambled, and went out of their heads. What did Wing have to say for himself on that count?

Ah Joe looked incredulous. Instead of translating he stopped and put his fists on his waist. "Miss Addie. Wing has not asked *you* such questions. He has not asked for proof that you can pay him, has not questioned why you are a woman willing to live alone. It is not usual for whites to associate with Chinese, but Wing has not shown suspicion. He has not asked you about these things, but he would be right to."

She was caught short. It was true, if she was honest with herself. It hadn't occurred to Addie that this Chinaman cook would want or need to know anything about her, or that there might be reasons he would decline her offer. In truth, she'd been cheated in her life often enough, and it had always been at the hands of folks that looked and sounded a lot like her.

"See this boy's eyes," Ah Joe continued. "He is the sincere hard worker."

She did look, not just at Wing's eyes, but at his remarkably placid expression, as if it were impossible for him to be troubled by anything. Or maybe Ah Joe wasn't fully translating. She chose to believe the former.

"Wing must go back to work. I can have Ah Cheong write down the answers to your questions if it is necessary. He writes very fine and clear English."

"I'll tell you what," Addie said. "You have that man do that. But tell Wing here I'm going to sit down and do him the same courtesy." Ah Joe looked uncertain about what she was offering. "I am going to write down for him how it is a woman like me ended up in Dire, and I'm going to tell him just how I can afford to pay him." She pointed at Wing, whose face held an expression of kindness. "Go on," she said to Ah Joe. "Tell him."

But Ah Joe was stuck on another point. "You will write this yourself?" He showed the fingers of one hand as if he were holding a pen and wrote on an invisible piece of paper between them. "*You* write?"

"I can," she said firmly.

Ah Joe turned to Wing and spoke in Chinese for what seemed to Addie like a long time, as if they were talking about more than what she and Ah Joe had just said. Was it possible the Chinese didn't like the idea of a woman who could read and write? She tried to picture a Chinese woman, but nothing materialized. Where she was from, men were pretty hard on their women, but they needed them too. It was women that kept them fed and as mannered as possible. If a man lost his wife, more often than not any civilizing he'd got over the years left him by and by until he was more like a cur dog than a man. Yes, Addie had concluded, men need women, but the reverse wasn't necessarily true.

Their protracted conversation seemed curious. The deal is off, she thought. It's like everyone said, you can't trust a coolie. And then Wing raised his right hand, palm upward, bringing it near his chest. "Wing," he said softly. "Wing." Then he gestured forward in Addie's direction. "Ah Dee," he whispered tentatively. And then again, more certainly, "Ah Dee."

"Miss Addie," Ah Joe corrected.

Addie looked at Wing's open hand, at his slender fingers, not brown, really, but maybe the early russet of a ripe peach. "It's all right," she said. "I like it. Ah Dee."

EPISODE NINE

He had never met a woman like Addie, had never met anyone at all like her. She was even willing to play with her name. He could pronounce it like Ah Joe, but she was willing to hear it another way. The American women in San Francisco he mostly saw from a distance, and they fell into two categories, those outfitted in enough fabric and lace to make three dresses, and those who wore dirt as comfortably as a hat. But Addie was neither kind. She was rough to be sure, dusty, but not with yesterday's dust. And her hair was a mystery to him, that reddish color she alone seemed to own. In his homeland her independence would have been an unattractive liability. A husband there would be expected to tame a woman like her, to make her subordinate. But then what would be left?

He wanted to calm whatever doubts Addie might have about him. He would be honest about the relevant parts of his life, dem-

onstrate that he was trustworthy and industrious. Ah Joe had arranged for Ah Cheong to translate a letter for Wing because it was
Ah Cheong who produced all the official documents between the
Chinese at Dire and the UP. But when Wing tried to dictate his
letter, he found that Ah Cheong only kept remembering his own
story, offered suggestions and details that Wing had no interest in.
Particularly, he seemed to have an obsession with rats in San Francisco. To hear him tell it, the entire city was overrun with them.
After nearly an hour of this, Wing sat down and wrote the letter
in Chinese. When he was done, he returned to Ah Cheong and
thrust the paper into his hands, telling him it contained not more
or less than what he wanted to say.

The next day Ah Cheong handed Wing the document. He
claimed the only correction he'd made was the spelling of Addie's
name, which Wing had offered as he pronounced it. Ah Joe had
insisted on his own spelling. The letter's penmanship was immaculate, evenly lined and without so much as a smudge on the thin
paper. Wing made a show of his frustration that he could not read
the words themselves. How much more certain it was, he elabo-
rated, that Ah Cheong's skill would make him prosperous in this
country while poor Wing was destined merely to be a cook, and
now, the employee of a woman.

Later, when he was alone in the cellar dug beneath his barracks, Wing removed the folded letter and did the thing no one
knew he could. He read in English.

Ah Cheong's letter was officious. He had turned Wing's journey
into a properly ordered list, but it sounded mechanical, all gears
and levers, little that sounded human. He would have to do it himself. Addie wouldn't know his hand from Ah Cheong's, certainly,
and he could show her it was a man she was hiring, not a machine.

Miss Addie:

You have been very kind. I am sorry you have so many words I do not know. This letter is a reply to the many questions you put to me through Ah Joe. I regret that I do not have time to answer all of them at this moment, but I believe there are many I can answer by telling you how it is that I have come to this place.

I arrived in San Francisco in June 1875. I was fourteen. This was in the early evening and many of us were allowed to come from below and stand on the deck. Though we were told we were near landing, the fog made me feel as if we had sailed into the sky instead of California. The ship proceeded slowly as we approached the mouth of the bay, which is fairly narrow, so it felt more like entering the claw of a crab than a golden gate. It was a very long voyage, and I was anxious to set foot on land. It was strange because the smell of the salt air seemed to condense and press upon us more than on the open ocean. Then our sails opened full and our ship was making fast time again. My ears were filled with small thunders from the wind. As we passed an island the largest fish I have ever seen jumped out of the water as if to take a look at us. It was big as me and silvery white. Far off, winking yellow light showed the city rising before us. It was like a mountain of tiger eyes watching from a shadow place. This was when my excitement started to turn to fear. Finally, forms appeared on the water, ship masts of all kinds, like fish bones, and then the flickering of lamps defining the shore. San Francisco. I must say here honestly. I cried, not because of happiness, but because now there was proof to my soul I had left China and my family. I cannot express my fear enough. As terrible as the voyage was, as soon as I saw the docks I realized how far away I was. You asked about my family. This is when I thought about them most and I only hoped that I might make my fortune and return to them quickly because they have troubles. When I got off the ship I did not know what to expect. There were very many people on the dock yelling in Chinese. It was like a tree full of chirping birds. But then I heard a man's voice yelling, "Take this wagon! Take this wagon!" It was my dialect, so I followed the voice to its owner, Hong Koow. He took me to a wagon where several other men from the ship were already waiting, each of them clutching their few belongings just as I was. Everyone would be taken in by the Six Companies.

As our wagon proceeded up the hill there were some boys in very poor clothings who threw stones and potatoes at us, and yelled angrily though I do not know what they said, but their faces were angry, their teeth yellow like dogs. But I understood why we were put in a wagon rather than walking. It wasn't a far trip to our destination but it seems to me now that it felt very long and strange. I had never seen such a collection of people. I know they were men, Miss Addie, but they may as well have been monsters. So many with furry faces and wide hats that flopped over their eyes, big noses, dark skin and very white skin. We passed them all as we went up on the hill deeper into the darkness of the city. I know they call that place Gold Mountain but on that first night it felt like being buried alive in coal.

You have asked, too, about my experience. I do not think I have butchered animals such as you have here. But I believe mostly all are the same. Birds have two legs, animals have four wherever you go. In San Francisco Hong Koow housed me for three days. On the first full day I mostly slept and tried to learn to walk on land again. I must say whenever I stood, or even when I sat up, I could still feel the ocean moving beneath me. But on the second day I ate an early meal of rice and some very fine port. My host agreed to take me outside after. The sky was

much brighter than when I arrived two days before. There were
so many Chinese on the streets, so many if I didn't know better
I could have believed I was still in China. Everyone seemed so
busy. My host introduced me to many people, and coming by
work was very easy and helpful to pay my crossing debt. Indeed,
in the first few months I had three jobs, which I will not tell of
here. Most importantly to you is my work cutting meat. Hong
Koow introduced me to Look Toy, my new boss. This man was
short and well-fed and looked like a toad. He told me to return
the next day if I wanted to work. It was very lucky. I told my host
that I wanted to go back to the harbor since I did not get to see
it fully. But he said that it was not a good idea since there were
men who did not like the Chinese and they might harm me if it
was just one or two Chinese alone. So he took me to the top of
a building where we stood on the roof and I could see much of
the bay. It is something you must see if you can. On clear days it
sparkles like bits of green and white porcelain. It is full of so many
ships and boats of all kinds. There are even some of the kind
found in China. Sometime I can draw one for you if you like but
for now imagine a long flat boat with a large orange fish fin for a
sail.

On my third day I went on my own to see Look Toy. Mostly
his shop was for meats dried and fresh. Pork, some goat, duck,
and chicken. Dried fish and shrimp and some local fresh fish. He
had a sign which means WE RECEIVE THE GOLDEN HOGS. It was a
very messy place with poor business, but Look Toy said that this
was his partner's doing. He had been a lazy man and bad luck
in business. Just two weeks earlier he disappeared, but Look Toy
supposed maybe his partner was dead because several men had
come to the shop and insisted that he repay the debt. So this is
why Look Toy said he hired me because it would take two people

to make enough money for the debt. At first my pay was very low but I received meals and a room above the shop and a dollar a week was to be paid to Hong Koow for securing my position. At first this was an agreeable arrangement. Look Toy seemed very serious about improving business. We cleaned the shop in every corner and sold meats at very low prices to get customers to return. Since Look Toy's partner had cut all the meat I was put in charge of butchering. I was not very good but I guess his partner was worse, so he was pleased with my work. There I learned to cut up a whole pig so many ways the only thing we threw away was the grunt. Everyone was happy and Look Toy said soon I would get a raise and money I could keep for myself. But this was not to be. As I now know is not unique to San Francisco. Look Toy began spending less and less time at the shop until I only saw him in the early evening when he would take the day's receipts out of the wooden box and leave. After several weeks of Look Toy forgetting to pay me and Hong Koow, I was wise enough to keep a little out of the box, a few coins at a time until it equaled a week's pay. Then sometimes Look Toy would not acquire the poultry, some days we would have no pork and people began to yell at me as if it was my fault. One late night three men who I did not know woke me by pounding on the shop door. At first I thought it was Look Toy drunk again, as had been happening more frequently. But these men were in search of Look Toy. They did not introduce themselves. The one who spoke had a fat bumpy nose and wore a flat cloth hat that sagged on his head like an unstuffed pillow. He was short and wide-cheeked and used several dialects until he discovered mine, which I hated because on hearing this I found myself looking directly at his front teeth that were brown from tobacco. I tell you this so you know the type of men. Highbinders if you have heard of such. Behind him *were two taller men who stood shoulder to shoulder, almost as if they were joined as one. Their outmost points were tall and their faces low and gloomy like vultures. Look Toy owed them money, they said, and insisted I show them our cash box, which I did, but they were unsatisfied with the amount. They told me if they could not find him that they would expect me to pay his debts. When they left I ran immediately to Hong Koow's. He was awake, and very understanding of my troubles. He asked how much I had saved to send home to China. When I told him that sum he said I should bring it to him and he would use at least some of it to secure my safety. Sadly he had to use all the money meant for my family. And eventually I had to leave the city. So, Miss Addie, that is why I am here, in this Wyoming Territory. I believe I have told you everything I can.*

With Humble Respect,
Your servant, Wing Lee

When he was done there were just two things that bothered him, the way the letter began and ended. He had been right to use the correct form of her name. It was Addie, but Wing intentionally mispronounced it when they met, and now he was sorry he was stuck with saying it that way. He was trapped in his own lie now. And too, he wished he had thought to end the letter by simply writing what Addie called him, "Wing," but what was he to do? The full name was formal and this was a business arrangement.

EPISODE TEN

Tommy brought her Wing's letter. It was Sunday, and he'd ridden in on a borrowed, deaf mule. The surprise for him was he didn't have to tether it. Addie had managed a small corral for Racer, complete with a shed big enough for him and a second horse. She'd gotten the lumber from the Grood ranch. Maye Grood offered it and wouldn't take a cent. "We might could sell it," Maye had said, "but the Lord tells me you ought to have it. By and by it'll come back to us. Maybe you could teach our boy Aulis to ride."

"Done," was the only word Addie needed.

"They're good folks," Tommy said. He and Addie were sitting together on a bench she'd fashioned from a wood plank and piled stones. She read Wing's letter aloud, looking up now and then to gauge her brother's interest. He'd cut his hair and had a shave, or what passed for one in Dire, and his clothes looked washed. It was as close to the Orgull version of him as she'd seen since she arrived in Wyoming.

Wing's letter was written with tight, orderly letters on both sides of a paper thin enough that the printing showed through. She'd thought the Chinamen had things easy, but Wing's letter suggested that wasn't so.

"I don't see how anything good can come of you mixing with those Chinamen," Tommy said when she finished. "That letter proves it. They can't even trust each other." He was rubbing his hand, bandaged with strips of cloth, torn from what, Addie couldn't tell.

She rolled her eyes. "I ain't mixing. It's business." She looked around the homestead, hoping Tommy's eyes would follow. The cabin seemed just a larger version of the bench on which they sat. "This is *your* dream, Tommy. And I'm happy to help. But the only crop we got out here is game. And if that means hiring a Chinaman to earn us some to get by, then so be it."

Her brother stood, staring directly at the wagon-topped cabin he'd assembled. "Ain't much of a dream, I guess."

"It'll be fine one way or another."

"But I ain't much of a *man* if my own sister has to gallivant around shooting rabbits and sage chickens so I can hold on to a pile of rocks with a smokestack." He turned, and his tone stiffened. "I think you ought to get married."

Addie laughed. "Sure thing. Next time I'm in Dire I'll pick up some flour, coffee, and a husband."

"I'm serious, Addie. I got someone in mind."

She looked at her brother closely. His own expression was firm. "Who?"

"Muuk."

She couldn't believe what she was hearing. The strange Finn she'd met not a week earlier? Him?

"Hear me out. He's solid, lets me bunk with him. Always got his eye on me, watching out. Took to me faster'n any man I met, been a real friend in the mine. Seems kind of sweet on you, too. Told me so out of the blue when we was sitting on the gob pile. And besides, it'd be some security if anything happened to me in the mine."

She loved her brother, but she was beginning to believe he couldn't think even one step ahead of himself. He'd wanted her on the homestead so he could keep the land. If she got married, then what? In any case, the whole notion was out of the question. She was just starting to get an idea that maybe there were bigger things ahead for her, and marrying a stranger wasn't one of them. "Not only am I not marrying Muuk," she said, "I don't plan to ever get married. And nothing's going to happen to you in the mine." She thought of her own parents. Why had they gotten married? They didn't seem to like each other all that much, except if they were both drinking, which meant they never remembered the times they got along. Once, her mother had held her dirty left hand in front of Addie's face and pointed at the copper adornment that served as her wedding ring. "If a man ever asks you to marry," she told her daughter, "just remember it ain't a ring he's putting on your finger. It's a harness."

"At least consider it?" Tommy said.

"I don't see *you* hitching your horse to no wagon."

"It's different for a man." Tommy squared his shoulders. "We can take a hard life and come out the other end. We can sleep in dirt, take a bath in dirt, and think nothing of it. We're badgers. A man can stand up to another man and it's a fair fight. And he can protect his woman."

Addie laughed. "So you want me to marry a dirty, fighting badger? I have to say, Tommy, you don't recommend your sex too well." It was an exasperating conversation, and she made sure her tone showed it. "And if all men are like you say, well then, who protects me from the man protecting me?"

"You ain't getting it. Look at me," Tommy said. He stood and turned with his arms raised until he faced Addie again. "I'm clean as a duck. Proof a man can chip off the grime and make himself presentable." She could tell he was certain he was right. "The point is, if you'd been my brother instead of my sister I wouldn't have gone to all the trouble. That's what a woman does for a man, makes him spruce up, calms the waters a bit."

Addie wasn't sure about that proposition. It didn't seem that her mother had much impact on their father. But then again, Addie herself made inroads with him. She looked at her own clothes, not dirty, but worn enough she warranted some new ones. And that's where she discovered the problem with her brother's thinking. A woman gets married and suddenly she doesn't only have to worry about herself, she has to worry about her husband too, and if they have kids, that's her job as well. A husband, she figured, is kind of like the glass on a pocket watch. It's basically useless for telling time except that it protects the works while doing absolutely nothing.

"With no disrespect to Muuk," Addie said, "I'll stay out here with the rabbits." She pushed her palm at Tommy for emphasis, shutting him up. "Tell you what," she said. "See that knothole on the door? If I hit it with my boot knife, you'll promise never to talk such foolishness again." The knot was fist size, and they stood about twenty feet off.

"If you do, I'll warn every man in Dire they better not cross Addie Maine."

In Orgull she'd practiced with a larger knife, so the bet wasn't a sure thing, but she stood in line with the door anyway. Blade behind her head, handle gripped not too tight, Addie took aim at the knot that seemed to stare back at her like a glazed eye. In a second she'd stuck her target almost true center.

"Ain't you just the dainty thing," Tommy laughed.

She'd won, but they might have continued their argument if not for the unexpected sight of a pair of riders headed their way. They waited, unsure of what to expect. There were so few visitors, usually you could tell a person before he was in front of you, but both she and Tommy were stumped. She thought to get the rifle, but the glint off a bridle called her off the idea. It was unlikely they'd have trouble with someone using shiny tack. In minutes the riders were at the homestead, but didn't dismount. Both of them wore suspiciously clean range clothes, and the taller of the two had a blondish gray mustache that fell broadly from his upper lip like a woman's hoopskirt. He pulled eyeglasses from beneath his vest and pinched them to the bridge of his nose. "Warren," he said, tipping his hat. "Francis Warren. And this is John McCourt." His companion tipped his hat as well, revealing a distinctly pale baldness.

Tommy stepped forward in a take-charge manner that made Addie want to laugh. "Thomas Maine," he said. "This here's my sister Adele, and you're galloping across my homestead."

"Indeed," Warren said. "No offense. We're just riding range, checking on property."

"What can I do you for?" Tommy seemed to puff up, and the two men on horseback took note of each other, clearly not impressed.

Looking over the top of his eyeglasses, Warren repeated himself. "Just looking at property." Then for good measure, added, "I'm treasurer for Wyoming." Something about the statement brought both him and his companion to laughter.

"Rough life out here," McCourt said, patting the neck of his horse. "Never understood the appeal of ranching."

"Yet you're checking on property."

Warren ran a hand under his mustache. "*I'm* checking on property. McCourt here is just making sure I don't get lost." He looked at his companion and offered a cue Addie couldn't decipher. They tipped their hats once more. "Ma'am," Warren said, turning his horse. And with that they rode back in the direction from which they came.

"What do you reckon that was about?" Addie said.

"Don't know. Seeing if I was keeping my homestead agreement, I expect." He did a slow 360-degree turn. "Must be something about this place I don't know." Addie joined him. It wasn't a likely place for coal. For that matter, it seemed an even less likely place for men.

The renewed optimism in Tommy's voice about the homestead was misplaced, Addie thought, but then again, she was glad for the distraction. It meant no more marriage talk, and she planned to get even further away from it now. "You didn't tell me exactly what happened to your hand."

He looked down at the makeshift bandaging, some of it bloodied at the knuckles. "Oh, hell. I was laying there on the floor, picking out the damn kerf, and a piece of the face come down on me."

Kerf? The word reminded her she wasn't sure exactly what her brother did in the mine, and she confessed the fact.

He explained to her there were two men to a room, and that a lot of work was done by those two men getting the room ready before even an ounce of coal could be mined. His job was to cut a gash, a kerf, along the bottom of the coal seam about five feet in. "You're practically burying yourself," he said, "laying there, pulling all that slack out with your pick." He explained that he also made a vertical cut there, while above, Muuk drilled holes into which he tamped black powder, sealed them, then poked in the squib they lit. "Then you get the hell out and wait for the blast."

Addie shook her head. "Certainly explains why you all come out of there looking like tar babies."

"That ain't the half of it. You got to work in what amounts to pitch-black, and your face is so caked with coal dust your partner is practically just a pair of floating eyes. And if the lamp on your cap goes out . . ." He paused and retrieved a piece of iron from his pocket about the size and shape of a rooster spur. "If your cap goes out, you got to fish around for your pick to lift up the wick just to get some light going again."

Addie nodded, knowing her brother too well to interrupt.

"And the smell. All that smoke has to go somewhere, only there ain't nowhere for it to go, so it just fills in like you're a berry in a pie full of sulfur."

Addie didn't like the sound of any of it. "It don't seem safe at all, Tommy."

"Safe?" He rolled his eyes. "There's things falling down around us all the time, and maybe you hear it but don't see it." He leaned into Addie wide-eyed for effect. "Nine men got killed last year alone."

She didn't want to think about her brother working in such conditions, and shook her head to record her disapproval.

"Addie," he said, laughing, "gophers and moles spend their whole lives underground. You think I don't match up?"

She wasn't as sure as he was on the point. "There's a man I want to ask you about," she said, changing the subject, "and it isn't Muuk."

Tommy walked to the door where she'd stuck the knife and

pulled it from the knot, returning to Addie with a casual step. "Who's that?"

"Besides the fact he's a Chinaman," Addie said, "what do you think of this Wing as a man?"

Tommy threw up his arms, the knife blade flashing in the sunlight. "As far as I can tell he cooks and does little odd jobs around, so maybe he's okay. I don't know. But if he's anything like them that's in the mine, he'll cheat you sure. Like I said, they're paying Orner or the pit boss to take the best rooms."

The statement made Addie do something she'd never done with her brother. "Is that true, Tommy?" she asked.

He looked at her, surprised and hurt. "I heard it," was all he said, which was enough for her to know she'd made her point. He turned back to the cabin and tossed her knife, which thudded against the door and dropped to the ground.

"Ain't you a dainty thing?" Addie said, elbowing him in the ribs, coaxing a reluctant smile. Tommy wasn't the right person to ask about Wing, she guessed. She'd have to make up her own mind. Wing didn't seem at all like the kind of man Tommy had described. None of the Chinamen were, when she thought of it. Maybe that was why they were so hated. She certainly hadn't seen any of the things she'd heard about them, that they boiled the flesh off their dead, that they kidnapped white women and sent them off to China. Even Ah Joe, who seemed the type to take advantage of every opportunity, had struck a fair bargain with her. And now here in Wing's letter, if what he said about himself was true, he had been through even more than her to end up in Wyoming. She wasn't convinced he was so trustworthy that she'd forget to watch her dealings with him, but Tommy forced a comparison that caught her off guard. Other than her brother, she realized, she'd rather spend time with a Chinaman cook than Muuk, or any man in Dire for that matter. It wasn't the kind of thing she was about to say out loud, but she did venture one thought. "If Wing weren't a Chinaman," she said, looking up at Tommy, "I might like him."

Tommy rode off on his borrowed mule about midday, which was good timing, Addie thought. She still didn't have a lamp, so she needed the daylight to compose her letter. She was sitting on the ground, using her bench for a writing table. In front of her were a freshly whittled pencil and two pieces of paper she retrieved from inside. The first piece of paper was for a first try, the second to copy it over neat if it was necessary. Wing had paid considerable attention to his letter, and she thought she owed him the courtesy of the same, though it certainly wouldn't be as neat and proper. She hoped he understood that she was at a disadvantage. Reading something was a lot easier than writing it, and he'd had help with his. She was on her own.

She didn't know where to begin, so she just started.

Wing, thank you for your letter. You have had some time of it. I must apologise for our meeting if my questions ofended you. In business as you have shown in your letter you have to be careful. I promise not to treet you like Mr. Koow. I will pay you befor I pay my self. I have had it hard to. My ma left me when I was a girl and I had to chop wood with my pa to make a living. I got to Wyoming Territorie by a boat and wagon and a lot of walking. Then I took a train. I was with a husband and wife out of Independence in their wagon headed to Salt lake city. Lots of folks

*going west but it is ruffer getting north. On the prary once we had
to burn some bufalo chips because we had no wood but I never
once saw a buffalo.*

Addie paused, letting the pencil fall from her fingers. "Hell,"
she said, looking at her writing. "I can't give him this." Her letters
were clumsy, and each line, if you could call them that, rose and
fell across the page like moving water. It looked to her as if a child
had written the note, which made sense. After her mother and
Tommy left she had the idea to go to school more regular. She had
made a deal with her father so she could go in the mornings for
reading and writing, but she had to work after that. She was so far
behind, her teacher told her to focus on reading, which would be
more useful than writing. So she did it, even outside school, read
cans at the mercantile, tossed-away newspapers, tried a tattered
copy of *The Marble Faun*, which confused her to no end because it
didn't seem to have a single deer in it. Yes, she read and got good at
it, but writing, that was another matter altogether.

Nope, Addie thought, her letter just wasn't going to work. She'd
have to ride into Dire and speak to Wing directly, get Ah Joe to
translate. And she had an idea that would be better than words,
would satisfy them more than a whole book full of words. She gave
her letter another look, the pencil lead gleaming in the places
where she'd pressed hardest. It was a hopeless little thing, like a
baby bird pushed from the nest. Which is what she felt like just
then as she set the paper down and looked around. It was true, the
ground beneath her felt warm and safe, but the land was wide and
empty everywhere she looked, and above, not so much as a cloud
for company.

They stood on the outer limits of Dire's Little San Fran, near the open hut where Wing cooked. It was just their fourth meeting. At first it unnerved her, his near silence. Addie spoke to him even though she knew he didn't understand English, and it was odd to her that so few sentences—even when they were Chinese—came from his mouth. Though in one way it worked out better than if she were working with a white man. At least Wing didn't interrupt her or question her judgment, or think what she really ought to be doing was thinking about getting married.

All of Dire was still fairly quiet, as no miners had yet come out for the midday meal. She understood that most of them usually ate in the rooms they worked in the mines, but Tommy had told the camp she was coming. She and Wing were going to try selling spit-roasted rabbit to the white miners. Two days earlier she gave Tommy two of these to divide up as samples, so that the men would have a taste of what she had to offer. Today there were eight rabbits altogether, Addie taking five, leaving Wing to take the other three to Little San Fran with Racer. She was still uncertain if the Chinese would be interested.

"Now remember," she said. "Get the money first, then give them the game." Wing nodded, but the blank look in his eyes didn't register confidence. She held out a coin and tried again, speaking slowly as she closed her fist around it, pulling it fast to her chest, then thrusting out the rabbit.

Wing laughed and nodded, repeating her action, showing he understood. Addie laughed too. She supposed anyone watching their little performance would think the rooster had snapped off her weather vane. But there was something serious about all this too, and she was relieved she didn't have to convey the true worry she had, that perhaps Wing was too gentle, would be cheated by the Chinese miners. Or even that she was overly trusting of him. She couldn't say with 100 percent certainty that he would come back with her money. Even without English he had a charming way, which Addie promised Tommy she'd mark up to deviltry until he proved otherwise. It was cold comfort too that Dire was also out in the middle of nowhere, so she knew he couldn't ride away on Racer—at least she assumed he couldn't.

When a few men exited the mine, Addie took her leave from Wing, understanding that he need only wait for the Chinese miners to return for their meal in Little San Fran. She looked back a couple times, saw him flop the dark rabbit meat on his chopping block, Racer's reins firmly in his grip. He waved with an empty hand, smiled.

The rabbits she carried, two in one hand, three in the other, were awkward to hold but not heavy. She'd be glad to be rid of them, not only for the money but because she'd had her fill of the smoky odor. But it was precisely that smell of freshly cooked rabbit that sold them with hardly a word. She assumed she'd have to quarter them with her knife, but all but one were bought whole, with two or three miners going in together for each. She saved a half for Tommy and Muuk, but they didn't come out of the mine, and when she asked after them, all she was told was they'd been having trouble with their room and they were still working the walls hard.

She watched as Orner approached from his office, ambled across the sparkling black ground as if maybe Addie was his destination, or perhaps she'd just be in his way. And because the tipple had quieted while its operators ate, she could hear each gravelly crunch of Orner's steps. He was one of the UP men that thought he had to wear a suit to make sure his miners knew exactly who was boss, and his fit him perfectly, vest and bowler, shiny black shoes. But it was that mustache trimmed long and thin on either side of his face that made him distinct, like an insect with pulled-back pincers. "Miss Addie," he offered smoothly, tipping his hat. "Hear you're selling game."

She didn't like his voice, which curved out of his throat like a snake. "I am."

"Hear you're working with one of my China boys."

"I am." She wasn't sure what he was getting at.

He ran his finger across one side of his mustache and looked over her head. "Can't say that I recommend it."

Cradling the half of the rabbit she'd saved for her brother, Addie raised an eyebrow. "You're saying not to trust men you hired?"

"I'm saying you don't know these Celestials the way I do. Sure, they work out for me real good. But listen here, little lady, they'll lend you two bits with one hand and steal four from you with the other. No telling what they're bound to do to the lesser sex."

"Want to buy some rabbit?" Addie asked, to show how much she thought of his advice.

"The Chinaman touch it?"

"I gutted them. I roasted them."

He looked at the meat, then at her, tipping his hat good-bye. "All the same, I'll pass."

When he was a few paces away, she called after him. "Hey, Orner!" She waited until he turned around. "The way I heard it, you sell the best rooms in the mine to the Chinese."

Opening his mouth as if to speak, he paused, looked around, then shook his head, smirking as he turned and continued to his office. She knew she shouldn't have said it, for Tommy's sake, but there it was.

Including Orner's little visit, fifteen minutes was all it took and she was done. She headed across Dire back to the collection of dust-red buildings that was Little San Fran, but there was no sign of Wing where she'd left him. The rabbits weren't on the chopping block, and Racer was nowhere in sight. Except for a few Chinese miners sitting outside their barracks, eating from bowls, the area was completely still. She stood at his hut near the chopping block, saw the three dark streaks where the rabbits had lain. She waited. Nothing. She'd been wrong about him after all. Worse, Orner was right. Wing had taken off with Racer, maybe thought he could sell him. And do what? Did these people eat horse meat? She couldn't say she hadn't been warned, and not just by Orner. Tommy had been adamant on the point. It was her own fault. She guessed she'd have to wait till the evening, when her brother came out of the mine.

Addie stepped back toward the white miners' side of Dire, but stopped when she thought she heard Racer's nicker. She walked through Little San Fran, past the reddish barracks and the joss house, where she caught a glimpse of Racer's hindquarters and switching tail. Did Wing really think he could hide in broad daylight? She approached the corner of the building slowly, removing her hat and peering around the edge. There was Wing and another Chinaman standing in the shade, their backs to her. They were exchanging money while Racer drank from a bucket on the ground. Just as Addie thought to step out and halt the transaction, Wing raised his last rabbit, which the man accepted, both of them bowing. Slipping the coin in a leather pouch, Wing patted Racer on the neck, whispering in his ear when the hinny's head came up from the bucket. Then the pair were off around the other side of the building, where she watched them walk to the hut with the chopping block.

She wanted to punch Orner, and her brother for that matter, for sowing all those doubts. Trusting Wing isn't the problem, she thought. It's that I don't trust myself.

EPISODE TWELVE

Eleven days had passed since the riot, and Maye was due that morning in Evanston, where Addie had been moved from Green River. She'd sent Maye a note with three simple questions. Certainly by then she would have spoken to Muuk, found out about Wing. Perhaps she would have thought of a way to bring him to her. The timing was good because the better she felt, the more frustrated Addie was about staying in bed, and if it had been any injury other than a gunshot, she might have had the strength to ignore the doctor and gone back to Rock Springs herself to see if Wing was okay, to see if Muuk would show himself. Certainly not her spirit, but every time she tried to rise, something in her body weighed her into the bed like an anvil on her gut. It wasn't possible to leave.

And where *was* Muuk for all this? What husband is not at his wife's side when she is laid up in bed for such a long time? For all their troubles, they were married, and unless he'd been arrested without her knowing, wasn't it at all a suspicious thing to other folks that he remained in Dire?

On Wing's account, she couldn't afford to wait for answers. She pulled herself up, the pain crisscrossing her abdomen as if it were stroked with sword blades, challenging her ability to breathe. Looking to the door, she imagined how many steps it would take. Maybe it was just a matter of getting outside the building's threshold. They'd picked up the fleeing Chinese along the railroad tracks and brought them to Evanston. Was Wing among them? She'd heard the miners gave Beckwith Quinn & Company three days to get all the Chinese out of town. Then they intended to set on the Mormons for not joining the Knights of Labor.

She paused, sitting at the edge of the bed, frustrated by her weakness, and tried to catch her breath. Frustrated not for herself, but knowing that somewhere beyond this dim room Wing needed her. There were too many dreams about him to count, brief dreams that felt strange and real at the same time. Just that morning her sleeping mind had placed him lying on a solid field of perfectly white snow, he in the familiar blue clothes with the cutoff sleeves, his eyes closed, his queue a long curving sinew like a black root. On his chest, held by both hands, was a nest of three young birds, their necks craned upward, mouths agape, but soundless. Then Wing's eyes opened and he sat up, the nest now in his lap. He looked at the young birds, mimicked their hungry silence as he plunged a hand into the snow and retrieved a handful of worms, which he dutifully fed his featherless charges. Each one gulped its worm, waited eagerly while its siblings were fed. When Wing completed the task, he lay back, replacing the birds on his chest, then slowly fell into the swallowing snow, whiteness overtaking blue until he was gone and only the nest of well-fed birds remained.

She didn't know if she could take much more. She had a fighting chance in her waking life, but dreams did as they pleased, and her current situation made her feel even more helpless. And then there was that odd and impossible feeling that the one person she needed at her side to find Wing was Wing himself. As a team, she'd come to feel they could do anything they put their minds to. Now she could only hope that he understood she knew she had made a mistake, and that he wanted as badly to find her as she him.

She pressed her arms on the edge of the bed, but the pain would not let her stand, so she lay back once again, clenched her teeth against tears, and looked around, hoping no one noticed. The bed in Evanston was smaller than the one in Green River, and there were seven more just like it in the long rectangular room. If it really was Muuk who'd put her in this prison, first she'd get Wing out of harm's way, and then if the law didn't take care of her husband, she'd find a way, face-to-face, consequences be damned, because she knew what was right.

She looked around the room, sighed at the placidity. The beds were occupied with patients of various levels of infirmity, the most lucid of which peppered Addie with requests to hear her version of what they were calling the massacre, her version and what she was reading in the papers, since as it turned out she was the only one of them, slow as she was, who could read.

She told them what she could. Things weren't quieting down, as far as she could tell. The trouble seemed to have moved to Almy, where the white miners there had also told Beckwith Quinn & Company to pay off the Chinese and get them out of town, or they'd be fired upon. For now, Almy was shut down, as was Rock Springs. Governor Warren, who'd just been appointed by the president that year, was trying his best to convince the secretary of war to send U.S. troops to protect property and lives. The governor was the same man who'd ridden out to Tommy's homestead, Francis

Warren, and she didn't trust him. Here it was a week after Rock Springs had leveled Chinatown, and the UP was picking up terrified Chinamen along the railroad tracks, with plans to haul them back to a camp near Rock Springs.

M aye was sitting on a chair next to the bed when Addie woke from one of her many naps. By the light, she could tell it was midday. Maye looked tired, pale, as she had a right to be. She was almost eight months pregnant. "I shouldn't have asked for you," Addie said, pulling herself upright. "Guess I wasn't in my right mind."

"I'm glad you did. Aulis is downstairs, but they said he was too young to come up." Her belly was large, the quality of her dress material reminding Addie of a plump sack of flour. The weight of it gave Maye a look of being bound. In months Addie would look the same, and she feared it—not being pregnant, but how it would weaken her at the very time she needed to be strong. Maye's hands rested on the mound of her dress, one of them containing what Addie recognized as the note she'd given the doctor in Green River.

Addie put her finger to her lips, looked to her right, where the woman next to her slept. Her name was Euphemia Cole, a woman in her fifties, but her toothless condition sunk her a couple decades more, though nothing about her struck Addie as unusual. She'd been run over by a wagon team, and somehow managed to get crushed rather than killed. "She'll be in our business sure if she wakes up," Addie whispered. "Nice, though."

Maye's expression was suddenly less weary, her blue eyes widening with relief. "I was just so worried about you, Miss Addie. How are you?"

"Pretty well patched up, I think. Though my innards have been giving me fits." She pointed to the note in Maye's hand. "Sorry for the chicken scratch."

"Aulis made it out for me." She looked down at the paper. "I hunted up Muuk like you asked."

"And?"

"First, I ain't never met him, and he's about how you described."

"Sorry to hear it."

Maye shrugged, as if she felt sorry for Addie. "Wasn't sure just how to ask a stranger if he shot his wife."

"Of course," Addie said calmly. A person couldn't come right out and ask a thing. She could have sent the question directly to Muuk in that case. She figured Maye might just generally put her ear out. "So how did you go about it?"

" 'Muuk,' I said, and Aulis was sitting there in the wagon as my witness. 'Muuk, did you shoot Miss Addie?' " Addie felt her throat tighten as Maye went on. "And he just stared at me with those icy blue eyes of his. So I asked it again. We were outside the tipple, and then he kind of looked around real slow to see who might be listening."

Addie felt her body tense, realized she was squeezing her blanket as tight as if she was wringing water out of it. She hadn't meant for Maye to come out and say it like that. Muuk would know the accusation had come from Addie. If he'd been angry enough to shoot her before, what was he likely to do now? "Maye . . . " was all Addie managed.

Maye continued her story, put her hand on Addie's leg and told how Muuk walked up flush with the wagon and looked directly into her eyes. "She shoot me," he'd said, and he spat, waving his arm. "All of you." Then he walked off.

"What did he mean by that?"

Addie understood exactly. "Wing," she said quietly, though she wasn't sure what he meant by "all."

"Right." Maye nodded. "The Chinaman. I told you how I felt about that. Still no cause to shoot you." She was shaking her head, which Addie took to be more about her circumstances with Wing than the fact that it was likely she was shot by her own husband.

"If," Addie said. "I don't know for sure it was Muuk."

"Sheriff Young is asking around, but he told me . . ." Maye shook her head as if to indicate the unlikelihood of finding a witness. "No one's even spoke up against them arrested for the riot."

"And Wing?" Addie was hopeful, but she saw immediately in Maye's face there wouldn't be good news.

"I can't say, Miss Addie. Went to Dire to see Muuk like you asked, and it took us more than a few hours to get the wagon into Rock Springs. Barely made the train." The woman in the next bed, Euphemia, began to stir, and with no little effort Maye quietly scooted her chair closer to the head of Addie's bed. "It's a mess there. They got Chinamen living out of boxcars because everything in Chinatown got burned. And they got I don't know how many army there trying to keep things calm."

"But Wing," Addie pleaded. She'd heard and read enough to know things weren't settled in Rock Springs. What she didn't understand was why it was taking so long to account for the men that were attacked. Wasn't there a ledger to check against, a way to mark the deceased and living? "Did you ask for him by name?"

Placing her warm hand on Addie's cheek, Maye's voice grew as sympathetic as it had ever been. "I did, Miss Addie. But they're still sorting things out, and everyone's got a different story. But I'll tell you this. One old fella gave some hope."

Addie'd been staring at the ceiling, but now her eyes darted to Maye's. "About Wing?"

"When I described him, what work he does, the old guy said chances were if he wasn't a miner, he wasn't one killed. Said he was likely run out like most of them Mongolians."

There'd been a time when she didn't know the difference, but now Addie hated those kinds of names. But it wasn't worth trying to correct Maye, especially after all the effort she'd made to get to Evanston. "That's something, I guess," Addie said.

"I'll ask again when Aulis and I go back through."

"Something else I should tell you," Addie said, and then she paused, waiting for a sudden cramp in her abdomen to subside. "I intend to fetch Wing from Rock Springs and get him away from here. The two of us." There, it was said out in the open, the thing she wanted, the choice she would stand on, and it felt right. The most important decision she'd ever made, and the burden of it fell away now that she'd spoken her intentions.

"Miss Addie," Maye said, shocked, "you're carrying a baby. You can't be carrying a Chinaman too."

"I have to do it, Maye. It's my fault he ain't safe."

"If heaven's not got room for a Chinaman, I can't tell where on earth you think you two can live. You three."

She had a point, more than she knew. It seemed to Addie that maybe anywhere they went was like going more to hell than heaven. But maybe they'd go to California, or the Northwest. At least on the coast hell would have water and an ocean breeze.

Maye was sitting fully upright now, groaned softly as she adjusted herself in the wood chair. They spoke for another hour about how things might turn out. Addie could tell that even though Maye was supportive, she was hopeful that Wing was gone, not dead, but just one of the ones that ran off and didn't look back. Mostly they let the topic go, spoke at length about Maye's son, Aulis, and her husband, who seemed to be around the ranch less and less the larger Maye grew. "I'm sorry," Addie said as Maye stood to leave.

"For what?"

"That I forgot I'm not the only one with troubles."

"Miss Addie, I wouldn't wish your troubles on a cur dog."

She leaned over, braced herself on the bed, and kissed Addie on the forehead. "And that last question," she said. "In your note. Guess you see I couldn't bring Muuk with me."

"Figured as much." But Maye misunderstood. When Addie had written, "can you bring him here," it was Wing she was asking for. No one understood, she thought, watching Maye totter out of the room.

Nothing was as it should be anymore. The nurse and doctor referred to her as Mrs. Muukkonen, which was strange to her. Hadn't it been just yesterday that she was a girl deciding to leave Kentucky to join her brother in the Territory? Hadn't it been just the day before that which set all this in motion, the day her mother left?

She was ten years old and had woken in near darkness that morning in Orgull, shivering under the dark wool blanket that covered her entirely, a membrane just thick enough to keep away the draft while still letting in the cold. She could not hear Tommy asleep next to her, could not feel the rise and fall of his breathing. If he was up, he was outside, because the cabin itself was completely silent. Pulling the blanket slowly off her head just enough to see out, Addie adjusted her eyes to the thin morning light. The cold nipped at her forehead. Why hadn't her mother freshened the stove yet?

Across the room she saw the reason. There was the mound of her sleeping father, and just on the other side would be her mother. If they drank after Addie had gone to sleep, they'd be in bed for a while yet. But then, there was something else, Tommy sitting against the wall but leaning forward, his arms wrapped around his knees. Covering his shoulders was their father's black coat. She guessed he was asleep too. Something was wrong. It was too quiet. Addie reached above her head and pushed open the window panel at the side where the deer hide covering the space was loose. Light came through in a brownish glow, darkened by what Addie knew was the U shape of snow clinging to the sill outside.

She sat up straight and wrapped the blanket around her. Standing, she saw that her father was in fact still asleep, but her mother was not next to him. "Tommy," she whispered as she approached her brother. "Tommy." When he didn't stir, she shook him, and he raised his head slowly. He was bleary-eyed, the blondish fuzz of his young beard and long curly hair somehow making his skin look even paler than usual. "Where's Ma?" Addie continued.

Her brother raised a finger to his lips but didn't speak. She saw that his eyes weren't just bleary from sleep, he'd also been crying. Then he pointed to the door. Addie clutched the blanket closer to her, following her brother's direction. The latch was makeshift, braided strips of a flour sack looped over a bent nail. On windy days they sat a chair in front of the door to keep it from flying open.

The light from outside fell into the room like a chunk of ice. It had not been a heavy snow, three or four inches at most, but every stone and leafless branch was covered in white, and leading from the doorway were three sets of footprints running nearly parallel to each other, one returning to the cabin, and two moving away from it until a near intersection where they congealed into a static swirl before the smaller set continued on into the woods beyond the pin oak that defined the edge of their property. Addie didn't need an explanation; her mother was gone. She looked at Tommy, who had put his head back down. "Does Pa know?" Addie asked quietly.

Tommy shook his head.

"What did she say?"

He turned toward his sister. "That she was sorry she couldn't bring us with her."

"That's all?"

"And that she's maybe going up to Louisville. She said she couldn't take living out here in the middle of nothing, living on nothing."

Addie looked again at the bluish landscape and the tracks that marked her mother's escape. It couldn't possibly be that easy, she thought. A mother couldn't just walk out on her family and never look back. She sat next to her brother and took his hand. It was colder than her own. "Think Pa'll go after her?"

Tommy shook his head and gave Addie a worried look. "I expect he'll beat one of us first."

Addie knew he was right. Their father would take to the whisky and then come after one of them, probably Tommy. In good weather they could outrun him, speed through the underbrush, maybe scramble up a tree. Addie's favorite was a tall beech not too far off that had limbs complicated enough that their drunken father couldn't negotiate them. Now, she stood and tiptoed across the room near where her father slept. Almost at the head of the bed she gently lifted the floorboard and removed a corked green jar. Tommy gave a stern look and tried to wave her off, but she persisted, replacing the board and returning to her brother, jar in hand. "He'll think Ma took it with her, sure." She handed it to her brother. "Take it out to the woods before he wakes up." It would buy them a week or so before her father could put enough money together to get another jar's worth.

Tommy accepted the jar and uncorked it. It was white mule as usual, and its aroma inserted itself in the space between the brother and sister as if the air was dense with invisible needles. Taking a swig and grimacing, Tommy handed the open jar to Addie, who followed his lead, pinched her eyes shut with the swallow, then returned the jar to him.

"Maybe we should just light out too, Addie."

"And leave Pa?" Their father wasn't a particularly good man, but it still seemed like a terribly disloyal thing to do. "Who'll take care of him?"

"*Us*, if we stay, that's who. And you know it's true. He'll work us to the bone just to make up for Ma being gone." Tommy clutched the green jar and looked toward the door. Addie understood that if he stepped outside, he wasn't coming back. But that was okay, she thought. She could hold her own. She'd seen her mother handle her father plenty of times, and besides, where would they go in the middle of winter? Her brother could find work, sure, maybe shoveling coal, but who'd hire *her* to do anything? And if Tommy stayed close enough by, she'd maybe see him now and then. No, she was better off here for now. She hugged her brother, and the pair stood without words.

Addie watched as her brother made a fourth set of tracks in the snow. Tommy did not look back. Each of his breaths held briefly in the air as if he was a train outbound. From now on it would just be the two of them, she and her father. Her mother had never been a particularly affectionate woman, but she was often a buffer, standing between Addie and Tommy and their father's anger. Now, even at her young age, Addie knew she would become the woman of the house.

She closed the door.

Her sleeping father's back was to the room. When he woke, he would be groggy from the previous night's drinking. No doubt this time her mother had gotten him drunk on purpose. But it wouldn't

be unusual for her to be out of bed before him. He'd be more concerned about heat in the stove, coffee, and maybe a biscuit with a
sliver of salt pork. Addie sighed and looked above her, imagining
the bright winter sky beyond the dark ceiling. God lived up there,
she was told, so she asked him to bring her mother and Tommy
back someday, then turned her attention to restarting the fire in
the stove in preparation for her father's morning.

I t was in the spring when she got a second letter from Tommy.
Six years had passed since the first one let her know he was
headed west. Neither had been written in his own hand. Now she
sat with the new letter in the shade of a pair of leafed-out dog-
woods that stood just a few hundred yards from the Ohio River,
wide and muddy from spring rain. In her hand she held an envelope
addressed to her at the Orgull Mercantile. It'd been sent from Rock
Springs, Wyoming Territory, and was only the third letter she'd
ever received in her life.

> Dear Addie,
>
> First day hear. To much to tell and I don't want to wear the
> fella out whose putting this down for me. Got me a homestead
> and a hinny. I ride out tomorow and that means I got to make a
> go of it for five years. Come up if you can. It ain't to bad. If you
> come through Cheyene to Rock Springs, ask for Benjamin James.
> Lots of folks their don't speak English, and their ain't too many
> women, so don't be suprised. Come West, Addie.
>
> Tom
>
> P.S. They give women the vote here.

West, Addie thought, so many people were headed out there. The breeze in her face was coming from that direction, and above, the big white clouds too. Even the sunlight, all from the west. It was as if the elements had come to collect her on behalf of Tommy. This time she didn't think of her father, or how he might manage. "I'll do it," she said out loud, and she wished someone had been there to hear her.

Had she known what she was signing on to, maybe she would have stayed in Kentucky, but here she was in Wyoming Territory, shot, married, and desperate for news of Wing. She needed to find him and see her plan through. She'd told it to Maye to make it official, something she couldn't take back. And once she found Wing, got him out of Wyoming, figuring what to do next would have to come later—a kind of figuring, she thought, that might occupy the rest of her life.

Maye was gone, leaving Addie with the women in the beds flanking her, one shrouded in blankets and never awake, it seemed. The other was too awake, Euphemia, the woman run flat by a wagon. Still, her curiosity hadn't been damaged, meaning that when Addie was brought a copy of the *Chieftain*, Euphemia struggled into a better view to watch the curiosity of a woman reading.

Addie took advantage of the light forcing itself through the near-shut curtains. It was September 13, and nothing that she read comforted her. No one had been brought to justice, and it wasn't yet clear how many Chinese had been killed. More than a dozen had been burned alive and at least that many shot, was what she guessed. The Knights of Labor held a special meeting in Evanston to make a series of resolutions.

"What's it saying?" Euphemia asked in response to Addie's cluck of disapproval. At every sound like this, Euphemia was at the ready with this same question.

Addie explained the meeting, and how she had a pretty good idea of how it went. "I seen one of them Knights come into Dire and rile everyone up."

The Evanston meeting produced a series of resolutions that condemned mob violence and the riots in Rock Springs, but also seemed to blame the Chinese for the very same thing. Beneath that was an article reprinting Governor Warren's reply to a petition signed by 380 Evanston citizens in which they demanded that the Chinese laborers be paid off and sent back to China. When Addie arrived at the section where the governor stated that such action was being taken, she laughed.

"Oh? What's it saying, honey?" Euphemia asked again.

"That they're letting the Chinese go home."

"Well, that ain't bad."

Addie sighed. "But it ain't true. That governor and the UP planned to have the Chinese back in Rock Springs the very next day."

"Oh," Euphemia said. She leaned toward Addie and squinted at the newspaper. "What else you see, honey?"

Addie read the small sections beneath the column. "Says here that you can make yourself better with Fig Syrup. Or if you got liver and kidney complaints, you can buy some electric bitters for fifty cents."

"Oh," Euphemia said again.

"How about this?" Addie pointed to an advertisement for a circus coming into town. It featured a sketch of a horse in a strange gallop, all four of its legs in the air. A shirtless man stood on one leg on the horse's back, while a shirtless boy rode on the man's head.

"J. B. Cushing's Great Overland and Ocean to Ocean Circus. The old-fashioned one ring show of our boyhood days." Addie looked at Euphemia, who seemed immediately engrossed, her toothless mouth slightly agape. "We do not gall the people by advertising a crowd of cheap performers appearing at the same time in three separate rings, but give you 30 first class artists. 30 in one ring. Each and every performer a Star! Each and every art a gem! Admission one dollar. Children under 10 years, 50 cents."

"Oh," Euphemia said again, brightly.

"Ever notice you say 'Oh' quite a bit?"

"Hadn't thought about it, honey. But it's serviceable. Might be the finest word there is."

It was the first moment in the short stretch of time they'd been bed neighbors that Euphemia had ventured an expertise in anything. "How's that?"

Offering a wide-open smile, Euphemia showed every bit of her gums. Addie had known a woman in Orgull without teeth who ate everything in mashed form—potatoes, carrots, turnips, beans, all of it a mushy paste on her plate. Occasionally she'd take bread, pieces of which she popped in her mouth and sucked on like hard candy until it was gone. "It's just a plain little word," Euphemia continued. "Anyone can say it. Everyone does." She pointed at Addie. "Go on. Say it!"

"Oh," Addie offered without emphasis.

Euphemia nodded. "See, right there's the beauty of it. The way you said it"—she mimicked Addie's pronunciation—"it's like a little chunk of wood ready to be carved at." Euphemia became more animated. "Ain't you a pretty thing?" she asked the air in front of her in a mock baritone. Both arms were above her head now, and she smoothed her hair as if preparing for company. "Oh," she replied in a girl's giggling embarrassment, fanning off a blush. Then, "Oh! I didn't see you there."

Addie laughed. She got the idea. "Oh. I thought there would be cake." Her body preferred that she be still, reminded her so after that burst of laughter. At that moment she ignored the pain, ignored the too-dark room and the musty wool blankets. She rolled her eyes. "Oh, was he ugly!"

"Yes," Euphemia said, waving Addie off. She was on the front side of a belly laugh, and it was clear she wasn't trying to avoid aggravating her injuries.

"Oh, but you're such a good teacher, Euphemia." Addie winked. "Ohio is a great state."

Euphemia shook her head and caught her breath. "That last one's cheating." The pair settled for a moment before Euphemia continued. "I know there's quite a few we ain't mentioned, but I'll tell you the one I like best." She looked directly into Addie's eyes like a starving woman about to share a last morsel. "It's in them times when everything comes clear, when all of everything you didn't understand just opens up like clouds parting and without even thinking you just say it real soft and a little longer, and nothing comes after. Oh . . ."

"I'm not sure I ever had a chance to say it that way."

"Well, sure, honey, that's this life. But it'll come to you someday, and you'll know just what I mean."

Addie looked at the newspaper sitting on her lap, at the long columns dedicated to the riot at Rock Springs. She could use that moment of clarity now. Everyone was arguing about whose fault the riots were and what to do about the Chinese. Even the governor of the Territory was making pronouncements. But the only thing she was interested in was finding out what happened to Wing.

Addie closed her eyes so she could see him. He stood in front of her in blue, sleeveless as always, and smiling. It was the day he surprised her by showing her how quickly he could field-dress a pronghorn. By then she was spending more time with him than her own husband, but Muuk either didn't notice or didn't care.

The animal was a kind of gift from the land, which most of the time proved to be fairly stingy. Addie and Wing had ridden out to her brother's homestead to bring back whatever lumber they could use for a roof that could keep the weather off her and Muuk. They were barely into the task when a large buck presented himself on a little rise not thirty yards from where they worked. At first Addie ignored him, which was a difficult thing to do. If a person weren't hungry, she'd often thought, you might look at a pronghorn and find something handsome about it, maybe beautiful, but you didn't want to be downwind of one, which they were. Every breeze brought with it something like the sour odor of a spittoon that'd gone too long without being emptied.

Besides the fact they smelled him in the air, the coloring of this buck made him hard to turn away from. He was exceptionally black in the face and thick necked, with stripes leading to his breast like white daggers on a tan field. There was no doubt in Addie's mind he knew he was special, lingering in the same spot, grazing without concern about two humans staring directly at him, something she recognized as the same kind of cockiness a lot of males of her own kind were prone to. But she was done with the business of bringing meat to Dire, decided to let the opportunity pass. The buck lingered, and before too long Wing presented her with her rifle. He was the left hand telling the right hand to do what it wouldn't admit it wanted to do. He knew her that well. With one shot she hit him true, made him run fifty feet or so before he staggered and finally dropped.

Wing managed the pronghorn with ease, as if it were the size of a lamb. They dragged it by its hind legs, but watching him, it was clear to her that Wing didn't require her help. For tools he had only a hatchet and a wood-handled knife nearly as wide as a hand spade, the latter of which he plunged into the white breast of the pronghorn and followed through clear to its bung hole. It was almost delicate, the silence of it, how he avoided the intestines, and then, too, how the ends of his blood-tipped fingers looked, at first, like shining rosebuds.

She'd never seen anyone dress an animal that size so fast and manage to stay so neat. The first time Addie dressed her own deer, her entire front side was soaked with blood, including her face. But Wing somehow confined the blood not beyond the elbows of his sleeveless arms and mere flecks on his shirt. At one point he looked up from his work, pausing. "Addie," he said. "I have been thinking I should thank you."

"For what?"

"Since I left China, I have only thought about myself. No one else. You have reminded me how important it is to help someone else."

"But I paid you."

He looked at the pronghorn, then back at Addie, smiling. "Not again, you will not."

She tried to resist the sentiment, not because she disagreed, but because she felt it pulling her toward him. "There's other folks need help more than me," she said.

Returning to the work on the pronghorn, Wing seemed to ignore her response, spoke instead of a kind of liberation Addie had delivered to him. He had spent nearly a decade thinking only of himself. Every day seemed to him more like living a strategy rather than a life. Then Addie came along, relieved him of this burden. It felt good to give, to assist her. And it was *her*, a white woman who had no cause to be kind to him, *her* that opened his heart to a lesson he'd forgotten long ago, that to give oneself freely in service of another was to recognize a multiplicity of centers in the universe. "Please know," he said to Addie, "I am here for you when you ask, and here when you don't ask."

Whatever discomfort she felt when their conversation began had disappeared. No other living soul had looked her in the eyes this way, made her feel important and vulnerable all at the same time. More than that, until Wing spoke it, she didn't even know it was something her soul wanted to hear, and without thinking she replied. "I need you, Wing," she said.

He smiled again, and moved on. "You can help?" he asked when the pronghorn had been fully emptied. She knew what he meant, that they needed to hang it by its head to let it cool further. While she held it up against Tommy's old shack, Wing used rope to secure it to a jutting piece of wood, and that was when it happened, when the buck slipped and they found their cheeks pressed together as they hoisted it once again. Maybe it was the comparison with the still-warm animal they held, but Addie was struck by the heat of life she felt coming from Wing in that brief moment. She backed away, unsure, exactly, what this sensation was. She looked to see if he'd experienced the same thing. What she saw were single streaks of blood beneath his eyes, as if he were streaked with war paint. The image lent him a kind of fierceness that shook Addie once again.

S he'd been thinking about that day with Wing and the prong- horn long enough that Euphemia was simply staring at her, as if the next thing Addie was going to say would be the most important sentence of her life. Addie slung her legs over the side of the bed. There was no time to waste, no matter how much her body hurt. She was going to Rock Springs to take Wing away before something else happened, like Muuk putting his finger on a trigger.

"Where you headed, honey?" Euphemia asked.

"I can't sit in this bed a moment longer," Addie said.

Euphemia's eyes widened. "Oh."

Three weeks had passed since they met, and their arrangement was going well; their game was selling, and Addie paid just as she said she would. Ah Joe allowed someone else to cook for Little San Fran twice a week while Wing assisted Addie. On this outing they came up over a ridge. The top of White Mountain was an endless expanse of brush, and not a peak as one might think looking up at it from Rock Springs, not a peak unless one counted Pilot Butte, a brown mass that stood in the distance, solitary as a ship on an open ocean against a great blue sky. "That's where we're headed," Addie said, pointing. She told him she'd hunted on this land, but today with Wing at her side was the first time she planned to ride right up to the butte and climb it. If he ever did make it back to China, she said, he should have better stories to tell than what it was like to be a cook in a coal camp.

He heard all this, but still pretended not to understand what she was saying. And while that wasn't true, it was true he didn't understand what they were doing. A few weeks earlier he thought they'd made a simple agreement that he would prepare and sell game she brought in. But now he was on the back of her horse, holding her at the waist, with the purpose of what seemed to be the pleasure of the ride itself. There had been a distinct change in her graciousness, he thought. After their first few times together Addie seemed to go out of her way to make him feel like more than just her employee. It was a level of kindness he'd never experienced from any white person, and this made it all the more difficult, more awkward, that he still hadn't admitted he could speak English. He wanted to, but didn't have the courage to put the anonymity of his abilities in another person's hands. Which meant, if he was honest with himself, he wasn't sure he could trust even Addie with this part of his life.

The shame of his withholding from Addie made it an even more awkward thing to be clinging to her as they rode on Racer's back, to be relying on a woman for balance because it was impossible for him not to notice how strong she was, how much he enjoyed the cord of auburn hair brushing his face. She'd tied it with twine in three places, allowing him to see the back of her ears, their curves beaded with delicate freckles. Then there was the scent of her, which was something like the sweetness of freshly cut wood. Every detail was strange to him, this woman who was not Chinese, down to the fact that she was in charge.

The wind was at their backs, so the ride wasn't bad. Addie pointed out that they lucked on to a wild horse run coursing directly to the butte. Wing wondered at these explanations. If she thought he didn't speak English, why was she always talking to him as if he understood? It was curious too that she never resisted trying to teach him her language, which was the way of so many whites. Even Ah Joe tried to coax English from him. Were his acquiescent bows and confused expressions not convincing, the little yeses and noes he offered too precise?

Racer came to such an abrupt stop that Addie and Wing lurched forward in the saddle. It was one of the advantages of riding a hinny, she told him; they won't walk into danger. "Something's spooked him." And just as Addie said it, they saw what it was. A couple miles ahead of them was a billowy streak of thrown-up dust trailing like the tail of a yellow comet headed their direction. It looked like a band of marauders overtaking a village, only there was no village out here to rob. Wing's grip on Addie's waist tightened. In Little San Fran the UP kept him and the other Chinese protected, mainly from the white miners who hated all of them, he knew. Just two days earlier a fight broke out in the mine when Bank Teters claimed that Bang Gee and Ah Guu stole the room he and his partner worked for days, getting it ready for extracting coal. The men were paid by what they produced, so the stakes were not small. But with the Railroad supporting the Chinese and with Orner on their side, Wing felt safe living side by side with such tensions. Out here on the plain was a different story. Tough as Addie was, she was a woman, he was a Chinese, and there wasn't anyone to protect them but each other. "Who?" he risked.

Addie laughed. "It ain't a who; it's a what. Wild horses." She reined Racer off the run a dozen yards. In a few minutes the herd was nearly on them. Racer jittered, but Addie held him still. Maybe they were curious about the three-headed animal, or maybe they were just passing through. The herd was led by a large brown stallion with a white forelock. The collective sound of their approach was not like thunder, as he'd heard it described, but more like hearing a deep pot of water come to a rolling boil. The stallion and his mares seemed to barely take notice of Addie's little troop as they passed. Up close the horse's coats were of a quality some might find ugly, Wing thought, but perhaps because they turned out to be horses and not men, he appreciated their roughness; they were lean, built to be free. He even liked the cloud of dust that wafted over him and Addie, the smell of horses and earth mixed together; it almost had a heat to it.

"That was worth the trip alone," Addie said, brushing the dust off her arms. She turned to look at him, smiling at the futility.

He wanted to agree, but knew a misplaced yes would give him away. He'd been thinking so much about what to do, even confessed to Ah Cheong about his ability to speak English. "You're not a stupid cook after all," was Ah Cheong's simple reply. Maybe today Wing would just get it over with, tell Addie he spoke her language. She might be so angry with him she'd leave him to walk back to camp. Could she keep his secret? Would she?

Wyoming Territory hadn't promised to be a complicated life, but it was. China was a hard one as well, and he'd known grave hunger there, but he missed the tangerine trees of the Spring Festival, the certainty of a laundered *cheung po*, the sleeves of which he cut off when he arrived in Dire because he couldn't stand to look at the dirt they collected, the reek of the food he cooked. In the worst of times back home there was still the occasional wedding banquet with nine courses, always nine because to speak the word meaning "nine" is also to say "long lasting." There was nothing like it in Dire. Even in San Francisco he had the pleasure of the barber of his choice, where for a few coins he had his face and head shaved, ears scraped, eyes cleaned, back pounded, and queue combed and braided with black silk to accentuate the length. It was an altogether different life here now, which he'd almost gotten used to until he was hired by Addie.

They scaled the side of the butte between massive sections of rock separated like layers of onion. Addie was sure as a goat, clambering ahead of Wing, then pausing to give directions. Half-way up she pointed to a rock with a name and date carved in it, "Cleveland Thomas 1879." "Seems like everywhere men go," Addie said, "they got to be just like a dog walking through the woods, lifting their legs to every tree." Wing wanted to laugh, but knew better. There were some words of hers he allowed himself to recognize, *yes, no,* a few others, but mostly he tried to imagine her speech like individual flowers floating on a deep lake, avoided their meaning as much as he could and simply received her voice as a kind of beautiful random song. It was like the *hua mei* his father kept, the caged little song thrushes. Each morning they were set outside, his father gently rolling up one panel of the cloth coverings. "The sun must greet them slowly, or they will not sing," his father said. And they did sing.

"What are they saying?" he'd once asked. His father leaned an ear toward the cages as if he were an interpreter, nodding and smiling. The birds were giving up their secrets. They seemed not so much his father's pets as another set of children, siblings to Wing but speaking from black-streaked beaks in a language only his father understood. Wing imagined he was one of them, wished he owned the feathered eyes his father was so fond of, the white circles so perfect it was as if they were painted on. When his father stood erect, he stroked the thin mustache that grew long from both sides of his upper lip. Wing repeated his question. His father touched Wing on the tip of his nose. "I can only tell you this. If you listen carefully for your entire life, you can one day answer your own question."

Addie faced Wing from above. She was standing on the lip of the butte, directing his progress. I should tell her I speak English, he thought again. It's a mistake to pretend I do not understand what she says. Not yet, he told himself, unsure not because he didn't trust her, but because he *did* and was unsure why. The truth was, in a way she was like his father's thrushes. He heard her words, understood the practical sense of them, but it was the woman herself he didn't understand. If I listen long enough, he told himself, maybe one day I will.

When he finally made it to Addie's side, she stopped speaking and merely smiled, gesturing at the view. It was as if they were at sea, standing on the mast of a sailing ship. The landscape was vast and flat, interrupted by greenish brown mountains so far in the distance they reminded him of ocean swells. There were no cities, or towns, or even houses, and why would there be? Nothing on the surface suggested this land as a destination.

That was all it was, just land and a bright blue sky that held two small clouds floating side by side, their shadows swimming over the plain below like dolphins. "Bok Hoy Tun," Wing said, pointing. Addie repeated the word and pointed to the clouds as well. But it wasn't her pronunciation that troubled him so much as the realization that she probably thought she was learning the word for "cloud." He shook his head and turned his hands into a pair of swimming dolphins swimming side by side. Addie again looked at the clouds, then back at his undulating hands. "Backoyton," she said, nodding. "Fish?" she offered, placing her hands at her cheeks like gills, pursing her lips. He laughed. It wasn't correct, but he understood it was as close as she could get. Unless he said it in English, no amount of swimming hands or fish faces could lead her to what he meant, "Goddess of the Yangtze."

The top of the butte itself was breezy, a flat and random quilt-work of lichens in various shades of orange and green, with low-lying brush taking advantage of the collected soil in cracks and fissures. As they ventured farther, a startled pair of nesting hawks rose from just beyond the butte's edge, screeching at the invaders. He understood how they felt, living in a place where one must treat every new encounter as a potential threat, and he admired their loyalty to each other, and to their nest, an empty bowl of twigs. These birds were protecting an unknown future.

"Sometimes I wonder, Wing," Addie began, walking toward the edge of the butte opposite from where they had disturbed the hawks. "I wonder if I should ever come out here for Tommy. I get to thinking it just ain't the type of place people ought to live. I know there's coal to be had, but the UP is the only one that benefits. The rest get broken backs." She paused and sat down ten feet from the lip of the butte, patting the space next to her. When he joined her, she continued. "I mean, look at what just happened. Those men the other day were fighting over rocks like it was gold. And even if it was, it's the Railroad's gold. And then I see Tommy's face all cut and bruised and him telling me about how Bang Gee and Ah Guu stole a room, only he didn't exactly see it and never had trouble with them before, but by God he was willing to throw in when the fight was on." Wing understood. The tension had gotten bad enough that it caused the mine to be shut down for the day. Ah Joe sent all his men back to Little San Fran. Orner, too, had made the white miners go back to their shacks.

As Addie continued, Wing remained silent, watched her cracked lips as she spoke. She stopped and looked at him, laughing. "You don't understand a word I'm saying. No matter; just thinking out loud."

Wing ached to say, I do understand, and I know why you're speaking. Because you're as hungry for someone to hear you as I am. He wanted to tell her this because they were sitting together alone, high above a landscape that offered no sign of other human beings. They were out there, he knew, but dwindled by remoteness. Without her he would be half again smaller, and now that he'd met Addie, he couldn't bear such a feeling. And so he did say these things, opened his heart to her in Chinese. Spoke softly, lightly clasping his hands in front of him as a show of sincerity. He told her of the many nights he lay awake in his bunk wondering the same things. He told her that the past weeks with her had been a special gift to him, had given him renewed hope that there was something for him beyond a coal camp called Dire.

As he had done for her, Addie listened to him without looking away. He had the full attention of her green eyes, and it struck him briefly that he was so used to looks of disdain from white faces that she was all the more remarkable in her attentiveness. It gave him permission to continue in his own tongue, and for once Wing didn't feel guilty for speaking to her in Chinese because he was able to use all the words he was certain of, and she was willing to hear them.

"Well," Addie said when he finished, extending her hand, "I know how you feel."

He accepted the gesture and shook on it. The firmness of her grip never ceased to amaze him.

"Never told you this," she went on, as they continued to shake hands, "but that first time we sold rabbit, Orner tried to warn me off working with a Chinese. But I guess I've come to trust you more than anyone except maybe Tommy. If I didn't have you two . . ."

It was all right, he told himself. Now. "I . . ." He paused, did not let go of her hand, noticed that she had not released his. It had been so long since he had trusted someone that he almost didn't recognize the feeling as it washed over him. The risk was to test it. A wisping breeze puffed at Addie's bound hair. "I know how you feel also," he said in English. He let go. It was a connection for her to extend again if she wanted.

Addie's chin rose slightly and her eyes narrowed, but she did not speak. Instead, she nodded her head slowly, stood, and walked to the edge of the butte, where air currents pushed upward, sending her hat flying off her head backward, and landing it near Wing, who trapped it at his side. Addie turned and untied her hair, wind throwing it upward like flame. Her expression was full of decision. "English, Wing?" she said. "This damn place." She paused. "But I suppose it's a relief. There's something been weighing on me." She took a breath and paused, then spoke again about the first day they'd sold game together, how she thought he'd taken off with Racer, then worse, thought she caught Wing selling him. "I'm sorry for not trusting you either," she said. "These have to be the final lies between us."

Her tone contained both admonition and invitation. He'd made the right choice in more ways than one. He'd been given a way out, after all. Just two days before, Ah Joe had made a proposition Wing would have said yes to at any other time of his life. Ah Say in Rock Springs needed a courier. The miners there had money and letters to send to China, and there would be more to collect from those at Almy and in Evanston—Dire too. They would pay Wing's passage to San Francisco and back to China if he would safeguard these items and whatever else was added in San Francisco. He had not made his fortune in America, had left behind his family, and here was an opportunity for return, but his first thoughts were of Addie and his sense that she needed him, the certainty that he needed her.

Before he gave Ah Joe an answer, he went to the joss house, the *miu* built for men who carried China in their hearts while they labored with their backs. There, Wing did something he'd given up on not long after arriving in the United States; he lit a joss stick and prayed. It was a room filled with gilt and red silk. There were shining statues of deities he no longer honored. Tin Hau, wrapped in orange and yellow embroidered robes, was positioned against the wall in the center. She was black faced and stern, indifferent looking. Here she seemed out of place, helpless, this goddess of the sea shipwrecked in a territory without so much as a lake. So he did not pray to her or the ancestors, but instead turned to his own heart, which he knew contained answers. It was the most difficult decision of his life, and the voice he heard was clear and direct. China did not need him. His life there would be the same as when he left, and it would always be there if return was what became necessary. Now, however, there was Addie, who even in such a short time made him feel like a better man.

There really wasn't a choice. When he returned to Ah Joe, he uttered just three words. "I will stay," he said.

Ah Joe raised an eyebrow, tilted his head slightly back, as if he was suspicious of Wing's decision. "You are Chinese today," he said. "You will be Chinese tomorrow. That is your only currency to white men here, and it can be spent in just one way. Remember that you become counterfeit otherwise." He turned to leave, but spoke a final thought. "Worthless to them."

It was a strange warning, but now on the butte with Addie, it seemed unimportant. He met Addie where she stood, and offered her hat. "Hold it for a while," she said, turning to the wind. "This life is so knotty. Ever since I came west, nothing but."

It struck him, the direction from which she'd come to Wyoming, because to him, San Francisco had been east, and Dire even more so. Still, he thought he knew what she meant. "We will know peace, Miss Addie," he said. "It will wash over us as a wave of beautiful calm, and it will remain."

"Sure's something to look forward to."

He nodded. "It is how this world will sound, maybe tomorrow, maybe after nine thousand western skies. But it will come."

They stood side by side, experiencing the flood of air that rushed up the butte like an invisible river. "One language is never enough," he said. "Yutgo yee yuen hy ngau." The pair of clouds they spotted earlier had merged into a white pictograph on a blue field. If he turned his head just slightly, it could almost be read as "heart." He thought to tell Addie, stayed silent. It was also a form of communication, the comfort of not having to fill the air with words. There was time for that later, and it would be true and easy. Even the hawks were quiet. For now it was enough to allow the earth's voice, to hear the wind in their ears. There was nothing in front of and below them, he thought, nothing and everything.

Four days after Addie and Wing stood together on Pilot Butte, Addie was conducting business in Little San Fran with added confidence, now that they had spoken their trust. She was handing Wing rabbits when the noise began. Men scattered from out of the mine, disoriented as termites from an overturned log. It was all clamor and rush, unintelligible calls from coal-blackened bodies. Addie watched, perplexed, until she saw other men running to the mine, and then ashy wisps licking out of its entrance. "Tommy," she said under her breath, and then she too was running toward No. 1, Wing at her heels.

The men were a loud black clot around the mine entrance, Chinese and white crushed shoulder to shoulder. Orner stood at the fuming entrance of the mine, arms raised. Addie overheard "collapse" and "patience." She scanned the dark faces for her brother, called out his name, then a face turned to her, two blue eyes and an expressionless mouth. It was Muuk, and he was shaking his head. Why wasn't Tommy with him?

Addie pushed through the crowd, squeezed between shoulder blades, the men uninterested in her scramble other than the momentary distraction of being jostled. At the front, Addie herself had become a blackened mess. She stood face to face with Orner, the only man in Dire she hadn't liked from the moment she saw his face. But now she needed him. "Orner," she said firmly, "my brother in there?" She couldn't tell if the air smelled of smoke or coal dust, or a combination of both.

Orner looked at Addie with a sour expression. "Not all the men have been accounted for," he said. Then he looked at the miners, right through Addie, she felt, and he began to lay out the plan. They would wait to be sure the mine had stabilized, then they'd send in a search party, seven men as soon as it was safe.

"How long is that going to be?" Addie asked.

Orner examined her again, brows looming sternly over his angry eyes. "Little lady, there are rocks down there the size of houses falling from the ceiling. Timbers broke like God's matchsticks and sharp as frog gigs. We'll get those men out, but we're not losing any men to do it." Now his voice was at a growl. "I suggest you just get back to your meats and whatever else it is you do with the Chinaman. Let the God-fearing take care of their business here."

Addie held her place for a moment, then turned slightly. The men were mainly silent except for the brief whisper of translation by those who understood English. Again she found Muuk's eyes, only now she noticed tears threading across the darkness of his cheeks. She knew how to read this even if it wasn't being said. Her brother was one of those unaccounted for. She raised her eyebrows as a silent request to Muuk for information, and took his unchanged expression as confirmation of her suspicions. He shook his head slowly, as if to ask Addie not to do what she was about to do, as if he felt her fast beating heart and clenching fist.

Orner went down in one punch. Addie rushed past him, feeling the sting in her knuckles. "Let her go," she heard him say. "Let her die," he repeated as she plunged into darkness. At first, the light and the tracks leading down the shaft were enough for Addie to see her way as she called out to her brother. When the balance of light and dark turned in the latter's favor, she looked behind her, up the slant of shaft to the surface, hoping for a fraction of a second that some of the men would follow—nothing. But the look back provided one bit of comfort. Lying on the ground behind a pile of rocks, a miner had dropped his cap, its lamp still lit.

On her head, the lamp offered just enough light for the few feet in front of her. She came upon a mule hitched to a pit car. The animal was strangely quiet, as if it was patiently waiting to complete the work it did every day, which was to pull coal up the tracks and return for another load. Addie touched its neck, and it turned its head toward her, the lamplight glimmering in its otherwise dull eye. It was the deaf mule her brother had borrowed. Then she heard it, the man's call, not Tommy, she knew, but she rushed toward the distant sound, discovering the increasing rubble of a collapse as she went, at first just melon-size rock fallen from above, displaced timber, but when she got near the voice, the true seriousness of the situation was clear. There were two more abandoned caps providing still orbs of light. Orner was right. Every support beam on one side of the room was obliterated by huge slabs of fallen stone.

The man shouting was Chinese. He repeated his call, and Addie found him sitting upright against the wall. He pointed to his broken legs, one of them showing bone. Then came another sound, a moan from the darkness. Her first thought was Tommy. Following the wall of the shaft she found a man laying facedown, making sounds like a shot buck just before it expires. She carefully turned the man over. She didn't think he was Chinese, but the light was so dim and his face so blackened that she couldn't tell. Her lamp dulled, threatened to obliterate what little she could make out. She remembered what her brother had shown her, a squib he'd called it, and she searched the pocket of the injured man until she found what she was looking for. The wick lifted, the light reintroduced the man's face. His mouth drooled, glistened with blood. He coughed and she tasted the saltiness on her lips. Neither of the two men was getting out on his own, she knew, and she wasn't sure they could wait for Orner's men.

"I'm going to get you out of here," Addie said, but the man's expression didn't change. She repeated herself, louder, and then came a voice from behind her.

"Damn it, Addie." It was Tommy, hoarse, but her brother for sure. She called his name. "Get out of here," he shouted from the darkness. There was strangeness to the sound in the mine, the way it deadened the voice.

"Can you get to me, Tom?"

"Stuck. You can't do nothing. Go," he called. Addie touched the cheek of the man in front of her, assuring him she'd return. Then she was groping over fallen rock and calling to her brother. Every reply from Tommy seemed angrier, more urgent. He wanted her to turn back. But she allowed the light from her lamp to crawl in front of her until it fell on the back of her brother's head, shone on his sweat-soaked shoulders. He was lying facedown, and it wasn't until she'd pulled almost on top of him that she saw the extent of his predicament. Slabs of rock extended beyond his waist, though they clearly weren't crushing him.

"It's my legs," he said, puffing into the gravel in front of him.

Addie took his arms at the elbows and pulled gently, but there was no give, and he cried out at the effort. She'd need help.

"You ain't stuck," Addie said, trying to confirm her brother's situation, maybe alleviate the true urgency of his predicament. "You're just lazy."

"It's more comfortable than what I sleep on at Muuk's shack." The pair were silenced by a thump and tumble of rock farther down the collapsed shaft. "I ain't telling you again, Addie. Leave me be and get out of here before they're writing songs about the ghosts of Tom and Addie Maine." He craned his face upward. In the light, his eyes were red as a bloodhound's, but clear in their green core. They were her father's eyes, which caught her off guard.

"I got to get help."

"Sure," her brother said firmly, "but don't you come back."

She knew better than to reply, but as she turned, Tommy grabbed her hand. "You'll be all right, sister," he said, pulling it toward his cheek. "I know you'll be okay." And there was something final in his voice that made her feel uncomfortable. It was what the old women at church used to say when a husband took ill and it was clear he wouldn't make his way back.

"Hang on, brother," she offered, which was what those same old women said even when they knew a person was crossing over. Addie squeezed Tommy's hand, and he let it go without looking at her.

"Wait," he said. "Addie, I got to tell you something." His voice was as sincere and pure as she'd ever heard it. "Remember when you first come, and I told you I had an idea there was one person in the world for each of us that could make us happier than anyone else?"

"I do," Addie said.

"I just want you to know, little sister, for me that person is you." It stung her heart to hear him say it, as if he didn't think he'd have another chance. Addie kissed him on the head and started off. When she was a few feet away, she turned and looked at him again, what she could make out. He lay facedown, arms angled in front of him as if he was about to stroke through water. The lamp on her cap began to flicker, so she turned once again and made her way back, using the inconsistent light.

EPISODE FIFTEEN

The miners were now yelling outside the mine, but none seemed overly anxious to follow Addie down there. In the minutes after she'd gone in, Orner seemed more interested in restoring his authority than following her, or rescuing his men. He'd gotten off the ground, beat out the dirt from his sleeves, and pulled his hat low over his eyes. Then he began barking orders, reminded the men they got paid for coal, not for standing around, and come payday they'd know it.

It meant nothing to Wing. He only thought of Addie. She was perhaps the only real friend he'd made since he came to this country. When Orner asked for rescue volunteers, Wing's was the first hand to go up, but the miners around him chuckled, and Orner didn't give him a moment's consideration. Five Chinese and two white men were recruited, though it wasn't clear when they'd actually enter the mine. It was one of the few times in his life that Wing felt entirely helpless.

One day in his village, when he was six years old, a runt piglet took a liking to Wing, perhaps because Wing compensated for the young pig's lack of size by making sure he wasn't pushed away from its mother when nursing time came along. An older boy in the village nicknamed *Sau Jai*, "Stupid," saw Wing doting over the piglet and began calling him "mother sow" between sounds of suckling. Sau Jai was a pudgy boy, born with one arm noticeably shorter than the other, a deformity that left him with few friends and parents who barely claimed him. Still, it wasn't long before other children joined him in his taunting of Wing.

With Wing not responding to the taunts, interest waned, and Sau Jai upped the stakes. He rushed Wing and snatched the piglet from his arms. With the squealing animal in his grasp he ran toward the pond, the other children running after him. Wing popped to his feet and gave chase. It was summer, the hot humid air making him feel like he was running not into a wall but through one. Still, he was gaining on the chubby boy. In front of him Sau Jai ran toward the pond at full speed, now holding the wriggling piglet above him with both hands as if it were a torch, his shorter arm seeming no liability and proof to Wing that Badness is an adaptable creature.

When he neared the pond's edge, Sau Jai used his momentum to fling the piglet into the water, barely able to stop in time to save himself from falling in. The other children squealed with delight, tossing twigs and small rocks as they watched the piglet flail. Wing was stunned, tears already coming. He knew what he had to do. He must jump in and save the piglet that came to this misfortune merely because it had received kindness from him. Yes, he must jump into the pond, raise the piglet above the water, swim to the other side, then run away from the children, he and the piglet, run through the rice fields, past the hills where his ancestors were buried, to a place where cruelty wasn't rewarded.

This is what I must do, he thought, though his feet stayed planted on the bank because he could not swim. Instead he watched the piglet, which had never seemed smaller than just then, a pink pound of flesh in an expanse of dark water. Pigs could swim, Wing knew, but the confused piglet had swallowed too much water, and it wasn't long before it was Wing alone who stood at the edge of the pond, staring at what looked like a lonely stroke of bright paint on a lifeless canvas.

Addie had been in the mine perhaps twenty minutes, but to Wing it seemed longer. It was an irresponsible thing she'd done, even if it was for her brother. But then again, that was one of the qualities Wing liked best in her, the capacity to put others first without giving up her own dignity. In a place where it seemed like everyone was competing to survive, she showed him you didn't have to cut another person's throat to do it. Still, she wasn't indestructible, and Wing was anxious for others to go into the mine and bring her out. Orner's crew of seven men were gathering equipment for the rescue, though Orner himself stood at the entrance, facing down the crowd with a stern gaze, perhaps as agitated at the interruption of coal coming out of the mine as the fact there were men now trapped in it. But it was two faces emerging from the darkness of the mine behind Orner that made Wing and the other men catch their collective breath. Addie, now completely blackened, wearing a miner's cap, its lamp extinguished, was leading a mule up the tracks. It was hitched to a pit car, though the cargo wasn't the usual coal.

A cheer went up when the crowd saw that Addie had brought up two men, the mule rocking its head away from the attention as the men pressed forward. "You're safe," Wing said excitedly as he came alongside her. Behind her the rescued men groaned as they were lifted from the bucket.

"You spoke English," she warned.

He hadn't meant to, but there it was, his secret out in the open. He looked around. In the commotion it seemed she had been the only one who noticed.

Orner was at Addie's shoulder. He looked neither happy nor appreciative. "That was a damn ignorant thing you done, little lady." Wing noticed the pink glow on Orner's face where he'd been punched.

"My brother's still down there. Stuck."

Orner looked at Wing and narrowed his eyes. "Git," he said, suggesting a direction with a sharp tilt of his head. "You ain't got no business here."

Grabbing Wing by the elbow to keep him in place, Addie continued speaking to Orner. "What are you going to do about Tommy?"

Orner allowed a short, thin growl and ran the fingers of one hand across his mustache. "What's the situation below?" he asked, looking up to the sky as if answers might be found there. After Addie explained what she'd seen, he shook his head. "Don't sound good at all. But if you ain't cursed the mine, we'll get your brother out." He turned abruptly and began shouting to round up the seven men who would go into the mine. "We got two out," he said, "but Tom Maine is still down there."

Wing looked at Addie, who was now getting pats on the back from both Chinese and white alike. He hadn't appreciated the way

Orner used "we" when it was Addie who'd been the brave one. He caught her eye, and she shook her head softly, smiling.

When she double-squeezed Wing's hand, it caught him off guard. Her touch was hot and calloused, and if his eyes were closed he might have guessed the gesture had come from a man. But his eyes weren't closed. It was Addie.

Wing was surprised at this new feeling of affection, something he'd felt just once before, in China, for a girl in his village. Her name was Sun Foy, and even by the time she was eight years old she had made a name for herself in the village by refusing to wear her black hair any other way than pushed over her shoulders and straight down her back. Her exasperated parents relented to this child who wanted nothing in her hair but the breeze. It was not vanity, Wing understood even then. It was self-determination. They'd been friends as children, but later there were feelings that his father called "young asparagus." In the first seasons after planting, the shoots are thin and speculative, tasty, but not bountiful enough for harvest. But then, gradually, as the root ball expands, there comes a season when it's time.

When she reached fifteen years old and he was thirteen, Sun Foy was told she had a suitor in the neighboring village. There was a day when all the older women went to that village to inspect the young man who would be her husband. He stood in front of his family home with crossed arms as the women spoke out loud of his various flaws and virtues. Then they returned to Wing's village, Sun Foy's parents were informed that the young man was a suitable match, and that was that.

Such a marriage arrangement wasn't unusual, but even so, Wing resolved that if he ever began to feel for another girl what he felt for Sun Foy, he would treat it like a weed, cut it down, tear it out by the root, and let it dry in the sun. He had no idea his parents wouldn't give him the choice. So what was this sudden feeling, he wondered, this shock of affection for Addie, who stood before him, tarnished by coal dust, a white woman standing among men as if she were one of them? It didn't feel like "young asparagus," not quite, but it was close enough.

Addie was distracted by Orner's directions and the miners at her ear, every pat on the back or shoulder echoed in a powdery burst of dust, as if each congratulation was a detonation. Wing didn't wait for Addie to notice he was leaving. He backed away until the denseness of men required that he turn entirely. This was not a good thing, he thought, this feeling. Nothing right could come of it. He was Chinese, and she was white. They could not be friends. They could not be anything. As he walked toward Little San Fran, Wing was resolved. This situation was named Difference, and it was a suitor from another village already carrying Addie away.

EPISODE SIXTEEN

A red cow. That's what Addie was thinking about. It was the last item on the list she'd been keeping during her first winter in Wyoming.

Sunday: Had cold
Monday: Pluged hole in Racer's shed
Tuesday: got some dirt in eye. Maye checked on me.
Wednesday: Snowed most all day
Thursday: Snowed most all day
Friday: Snowed most all Day
Saturday: put red cow in shed with Racer

Winter kept Addie at the homestead three days, but with the snow covering the whole of the shack, she was managing to stay warm enough, and there was the rarity of plenty of fresh water, drifts and drifts of it. Plus, she had time to think about a lot of things besides the red cow, mainly that final image of her brother's face, his shining green eyes above the dark fields of his cheeks. She wished she'd been able to offer Tommy just four more words, "I love you. Good-bye." After his death she spent a month in a dull haze from which both Muuk and Wing tried to draw her out, efforts she met by repeating the regret of missing those words. But now it was that red cow she'd run across out on the plain that occupied her thoughts. With Tommy gone from this world, she wasn't sure what she was going to do, so anything that took her mind off the uncertain future was a blessing. And the cow was a hard thing not to think about, since it had announced itself by thumping against her door not two hours earlier and was now crowded with Racer out in the corral shed. What she was going to do with it, she couldn't say.

It was the second time she'd come face-to-face with the cow. Not long before Tommy was lost to the mine, Addie rode out past the Grood ranch, where Maye told her a good lot of pronghorn had been lingering for a few days. Particularly, they seemed of the size Addie might easily field-dress alone. When Addie got not too far from the herd Maye told her about, she saw what looked like a luminescent orange brick right in the middle of it about the size of two cotton crates side by side. A warm wind surprised her from behind, and in seconds the pronghorns had caught her scent and were trotting away. But the brick merely rose on four legs and showed itself to be a cow. Addie rode closer, and while the pronghorns were having none of it, the orange cow stood its ground, backside facing Addie, its head turned in her direction. It raised its ears, which were the size and shape of magnolia leaves.

There wasn't another cow in sight as far as she could tell, and when she got not ten feet from the animal she was pretty certain it wasn't branded. Still, it didn't spook, which meant it had at least been around horses. Maybe she could get a rope around its neck and take it back to the homestead, or to Maye's place, where someone might think to claim it. She slid off Racer, rope in hand, and approached slowly. There was nothing remarkable about its shape. It was anvil-headed with a bourbon-barrel rib cage just like any cow, and though its udder was high and tight, there were four teats to it as one would expect. Its color, though, that was another matter. She'd never seen anything like it. Red wasn't the right word. Maybe orange, but it was deeper than that. Then, too, there was the way the coat shone in the sun, crisp as a flash off fresh copper, almost seared the eyes if she stared too long.

As she raised her hand to touch its hindquarter, the cow slowly turned to face Addie. Its wet, shiny nose was peach colored and came level with Addie's face. She ran her hand slowly down the side of its neck and it pushed against her palm for more. If she didn't know Wyoming better, she'd swear someone had raised it as a pet. It made her smile to think of some old bachelor rancher who, instead of a dog, kept a cow at the foot of his bed.

When she raised the lasso end of her rope, the cow let out a soft bellow that sounded definite, not like *moo* but an extended *noooooo*. It was convincing enough to make Addie reconsider the whole enterprise.

Addie stopped at the Grood ranch on her way back. "Don't know a ranch with a cow like that," Maye said. "Might be that squaw man Thompson's, but I doubt it." Addie knew who she meant. Wiliford Thompson lived out a ways in a tepee with two sons and a Shoshone wife. "Can't believe you just left it alone."

"What else could I do?" She'd caught Maye in the middle of closing down the ranch's summer kitchen, Maye's sleeves rolled up to the elbows, showing pinkish white forearms that ended in hands brown as roots.

"If it been my husband, the hide a that thing'd been nailed against the barn already and I'd have beef in this here pot." Maye handed the pot to Addie, picked up two herself, and headed toward the house.

"That don't sound right."

The statement caused Maye to stop in her tracks and turn. She was smiling and shaking her head. "Didn't say it was right. Said what'd be done." She took Addie's pot and combined it with her own load. "And sometimes what's done turns out to be what's right."

"But—" Addie began before she was cut off.

Maye lowered her head and looked at Addie with one eye. "Got a last piece to say, Miss Addie. If none of that makes sense, the one thing that'll get you by in this life is this: 'What's done is done.' "

Addie hadn't quite understood fully what Maye had meant, but it was coming useful to her now. She cracked the door a sliver to check on the state of things. It wasn't so much white outside as baby blue. The snow had stopped, but the wind blew cold and sharp, like it was sluicing needles. The shed was holding against the storm, though it was supporting a lot of snow. She'd have to figure out what to do with the cow, certainly couldn't afford to feed it.

Addie closed the door and pressed her back to it, then looked around her brother's dimly lit shack. It was a small dream for a man, this homestead, a decent one, and it saddened her that Tommy wouldn't get to see it through. There had been days since his death she was certain that at any moment he was going to knock on the door and walk in with a smile. Instead, the knock she heard that morning had come from a cow, because that's how life was now. She was alone in the world, the last Maine she knew of. No family back in Orgull to return to, no Tommy here. She remembered his Big Story. Maybe she'd see him there one day. But on this earth, what's done is done.

Aside from the wind, the homestead was silent, voiceless. Tommy's would not be heard again, and there was no reason for Addie to speak to the air. At first, it suited her to remain quiet, but maybe now it was time to move forward. It wasn't so much that she had much she wished to say, but what little she did, she thought, might only be understood by Wing. Certainly he would listen. But there was also a hard truth facing her now that Tommy was gone. Life had struck its worst blow, which felt to Addie like a kind of punishment for wanting more than just living day to day. What would Tommy want her to do now? she wondered. The answer came surprisingly fast, as if he'd whispered it in her ear the moment she asked. Next to her was Racer's saddle. When the weather let up enough, she'd put a rope around the cow's neck and take it in to Dire. What's done sometimes turns out to be what's right, Maye had told her. She'd put a test to it. She'd trust the cow to Wing for butchering and have him share it among the men, Chinese and white alike. Then it was time to have a conversation with Muuk.

The 1926 Maibohm convertible plowed forward, a yellow-and-black rhinoceros on wheels. Buckley was driving, Addie in the passenger side. His father, the man she'd known as Orner, spawned a son late in life and met his maker in a fight with his young wife before the boy was two, gone too early to raise a son that might live up to the shorter version of his name most men would have adopted by his age. Addie was more than Buckley bargained for, she knew, but then again, he was living in the wrong part of the country to be wearing what he was wearing, a narrow-brimmed straw hat, new wool suit, and mother-of-pearl cuff links.

The road to Dire Draw was paved, two lanes, though Addie couldn't say it was a smoother ride than the days it was a ribbon of sand and mud rut and she'd come up that way on horseback. She was pleased with the speed, however. The older she got, the faster time went by. Made her feel like a car might be the only

BRIAN LEUNG

thing to help her keep up. The smell of sage hadn't changed at all, that morning's rain bringing it into the air sweet off the high desert plain. It brought to mind her brother, and she said his name quietly. Tommy. The only blessing of his death was at moments like this, all these years later, when she saw his face young and fresh. Age couldn't touch him. This place was his home, never truly hers, but still, it felt good to be back, if only for Tommy's memory. Confronting Muuk after all these years—that was another story.

"A thousand miles seems like an awful long way to travel for lunch," Buckley called over the engine and rushing air.

"Just a few inches on a map," Addie said. "Who wouldn't do that for a friend?" Though as she said it, she understood more and more that it wasn't just Ah Cheong's farewell she had come for. There was something she needed to take back, though what that was she wasn't quite sure. So much had been taken from her, from this place. She recalled lying in that bed in Evanston, hearing the news of how Wing died. How could she go back to Muuk then? Her mother's voice had come to her then, whispered. *Run, run.* She didn't think about it, just put Wing's wood chest under her arm and headed west. It had been a mistake, she knew now. Muuk hadn't been held accountable, and Wing deserved better.

Buckley played his left hand into the wind. "Guess they'll be folks there you haven't seen in forty years."

"It's the ones I'll never see again I'm going for." Buckley's expression showed he failed to understand, but she didn't explain. She'd only admitted it to herself days earlier and planned to look Muuk straight in the eye and ask if he was the one who shot her. If he said yes, she guessed she wasn't too old to make a fist.

"Sure is a whole lotta nothing out here," Buckley said. "May as well be blind and deaf."

She smiled, but was too polite to say it. Poor kid, he didn't know how far off he was from describing himself.

At the bottom of the draw where the road paralleled the tracks, a train pulling three empty coal cars sat still as a caterpillar at rest. Two men stood in front of it, kicking at the railroad ties. One of them she guessed as the engineer. Addie poked Buckley in the shoulder without turning away from the train. "Pull up next to them," she said. "Let's see what's going on."

"Why you want to do that, Miss Addie?" Buckley asked. "We can't do anything for them." He didn't know Addie well.

She looked at him sternly and shrugged. "I'm curious."

Buckley complied, guiding the big fat wheels of the car just off the edge of the road. They were about fifty yards away from the train. The engineer caught sight of them and offered a half wave before going back to stomping on the tracks. Addie grabbed her cane and unlatched the door, which swung itself open from the slant. True to herself, she was wearing a white cotton short-sleeved blouse high to the neck and khaki aviator pants tucked into brown boots. The sun was sharp and direct on her cheeks and nose. She wished she'd thought to unpack her hat.

"You're not going over there?" Buckley asked as Addie took her first steps into the knee-high brush. He had a voice plinky as a child's piano.

"No," she called, stepping forward, "I'm not." Behind her she heard the slam of the driver's door and the crunch of gravel beneath Buckley's useless dress shoes. The car was his mother's, the clothes, from her money.

Addie kept her eyes on the engineer and his partner, neither of whom took notice that she was headed in their direction. With Buckley three steps behind, it was easy to imagine she was out there on her own and young again, in her hand not a cane but a walking stick she'd picked up along the way, though that itself would be the biggest stretch of the imagination, since hardly a thing out here grew tall and thick enough to produce a stick with the strength to lean on. The sage brushed against her pant legs, feeling like hands not so much trying to hold her back as much as urge her forward, like sentries laying down arms.

By the time she reached the tracks, the engineer was standing, hands on hips, eyebrow raised. He was unshaven and red-faced, fifty, Addie guessed, but he might have been older. His partner could have been his gray-haired twin. The engineer removed his cap and scratched the back of his neck, clearly baffled by the presence of the odd pair approaching. "What can I do for you, ma'am?" he asked as Addie came near.

"I'd like you to take me up the draw in your train here." She stood at the base of the raised tracks, shiny black clinkers scattered all about her boots, the man looking down at her by about two feet. She figured standing side by side they'd be the same size.

"Sure," he laughed. "Three rides for a nickel."

"You're not serious," Buckley added, coming up alongside Addie. "As a cave-in."

The man looked down his lumpy nose. That phrase didn't get used much anymore. "You're not a city woman."

"Not much." She climbed up to where the man stood. In her day the tracks stopped about midway up the draw between a heap of squat wood buildings and a lanky tipple that loomed over everything. But now, she saw there wasn't much left of old Dire, and the tracks went farther into the draw and around the bend. "Adele Maine," she said, extending her hand.

The man took a half step back and looked her over. "Miss Addie? I can't believe it. I'm Aulis Grood." He looked at his partner, who offered a faint expression of recognition.

"Little Aulis!" The two laughed and shook hands eagerly.

"Read you was coming. Didn't think it was true. Guess I was expecting a young redhead."

"My hair was never what you'd call strictly red."

Buckley remained at the foot of the tracks staring up at them, mouth open. "You know each other?"

"Used to," Aulis said. "And excuse my manners. This here is Mix Teters."

She shook the man's hand and began to introduce Buckley, but they already knew him. So she turned and told him how she came to know Aulis, and in the telling, she realized how much and how little there was to say. His mother Maye had been a godsend, and she'd taught Aulis to ride a horse. But then, after all, she hadn't stayed in Wyoming long enough to really know him. Then there was the fact she didn't care to recall. The day she left Evanston, she got word that his mother had died in early childbirth. It was as if Wyoming had in mind to wipe out every last person she cared for, the curse of her young life. "I was so sorry to hear about your mother," Addie said.

Aulis nodded. "It was a hard life after she passed, but these things we can discuss in heaven."

It was the phrase that once helped pull Addie out of a difficult time, and she was glad to hear it again.

Aulis gestured toward the Maibohm, which, dusty as it was, gleamed an unnatural yellow. "How'd you come by that, Buckley?"

The car's large black wheel wells looked suddenly to Addie like claws at rest, a big fat crab, she thought. "Mother shipped it from Chicago," Buckley said.

Addie interrupted, "But that's not the ride we're interested in." She tapped on the train's coupler with her cane. "Take me up to Dire."

"Love to, Miss Adele, but you know I can't do that. Company rules."

Throwing her head back, Addie led a friendly glare with her chin. "Tell you what, Aulis." She pointed to a split railroad tie leaning nearly upright on a crop of large rocks. "I'll take that knife you're wearing, and I'll bet you that from here I can hit the bird doo at the top of that wood. If I do it, I get a ride." She knew it was a bet he wouldn't refuse, and she also knew she hadn't thrown a knife in years and wouldn't likely win. But she already had a plan. She winked at Buckley, who turned toward the tie and squinted.

Aulis ran a hand over his unshaven face, the other taking out the knife from the leather case at his waist as if it were one step ahead of his brain. "All right, Miss Addie," he said, presenting her with the knife. "You hit any part of that bird shit, and you win. But you got to stick."

Heavy in her hand, the knife had a thick deer antler handle finished with brass rivets. She looked at her target, which was small but clear as could be, even at twenty-five feet. Vision was not her problem. She could still see the eye of a needle, but getting her hands to cooperate with the threading was more and more of a chore. Gripping the handle, she made a couple slow practice moves. There wasn't any wind to speak of, and the only sound came from the general sigh of the engine. Then, without a word, the throw, which flew truer than she expected and struck the wood near the top. Close.

Aulis had said "any part," and it was possible she'd made it. "Hell," he said with a chuckle, walking off to check the mark. "You might have done it."

Buckley was wide-eyed, but Addie wasn't interested in admiration or finding out if she won the bet. She tossed him her cane and walked fast as she could down the side of the engine, scrambled up its side to the brass handhold, and pulled herself into the cab.

Aulis had run back, but he was too late. "You just missed," he said. "But I don't suppose you're coming down out of there?"

"Are you going to drag an old woman off your train?"

"I expect not, though you don't act like an old woman."

She looked at Buckley and reached out her hand without speaking. He tossed her the cane, which she caught practically without looking.

Aulis climbed into the cab, though Mix delayed himself. "It's going to get hotter up here in the engine," Aulis warned. Addie nodded. "You up here just for the Chinaman's sendoff?"

She might have upbraided him for the disrespect. Ah Cheong had a name. But she knew the history. It's why the trouble started and why the bad feelings never quite went away. There were men who never got their jobs back in the mines after Rock Springs. "He was kind to me," was all she said, and then, after a pause, "and I'm going to pay a visit to Muuk." She touched her throat, realizing they were raising their voices over the idling train.

Aulis turned from what he was doing. "Atso Muukkonen?" Clearly he didn't recall that Muuk had been her husband. He wiped his brow with a rag so wet and greasy it seemed to smudge his face more than remove any sweat or grime.

"I'm told he's still around."

Dipping his head out of the cab, Aulis pointed, raising his voice even higher. "The steeple." Though it was tucked beyond a roll in the hillside, she could make out the white spire of a church that hadn't been there in her day. Aulis ran his finger up the hillside and flicked his finger at the area where Addie was to look.

"I see it," she called after a bit, spotting a small dark cube nestled into the slope.

Aulis popped his head back inside. "That's where the old buzzard lives."

If Muuk had any self-respect, any decency, he'd meet her in Dire. He had to know she was coming. And if he didn't show, she knew where he lived, and though it was too late in coming, she intended to hold him accountable before she left Dire.

M uuk would return soon. Addie and he had married that afternoon, just as Tommy wanted. There was no pretending it was love. They both understood Muuk's offer was protective and practical as much as anything else. She'd seen the winter almost all the way through, and now it was the tail end of March. Addie lay in the dark on Muuk's small bed, a narrow straw mattress resting on a shelf cut out of the dirt. Dirt. Everything smelled of it. She still wasn't sure how people lived like this, was even less sure if *she* could.

At the moment her new living conditions were the least of her worries. She ran her hands along the cotton nightgown given to her by Muuk as a wedding present. It wasn't the kind of thing she'd choose for herself, but at least it was something soft in a very hard world. Strange music made its way from Little San Fran. She was told they'd been playing the same tune almost since the mine collapse, but Wing would say nothing more than they were preparing for a celebration. She guessed it had something to do with the building of the new joss house. The one she'd seen that first time she rode into Little San Fran wasn't big as half a box car, and they'd brought in forty more Chinese since then. She'd always been afraid to ask what kind of gods or devils they were praying to, but she understood one thing, prayer takes elbow room.

Tommy had been gone for months, and Addie was just then coming out of the daze of it all. When her father died, she wasn't saddened for herself, but for the man in his last year who made an honest effort to set himself right. But Tommy was another matter. Loss felt like a carpetbagger had set up shop in her heart, and she wasn't in charge of it anymore.

W here was Muuk all this time? Addie wondered. Light sifted through the roof, and with her head at just the right angle, Addie saw the half-moon, a delicate, speckled thing, permeable even, like a dandelion partially blown away. The light that reached inside the dugout gave her nightgown the dull glow of midnight. She looked down the length of her nervous body, almost not recognizing it; her knees not her own, but snow-covered hillocks. Is this what brides did, lie in bed thinking of their grandmothers and mothers waiting for their new husband to stumble home drunk? Was it part of some Finnish ritual? Is this what her mother warned her about?

Addie was still a child that day they had been stacking wood. "Adele," her mother said sternly as she tossed a last chunk of maple onto the pile. "Adele, baby, I got something for you to hear, and I don't want to say it twice." Addie followed her mother to the cabin door, where they sat side by side. "I been watching," her mother began, "and it seems pretty certain that it won't be long until men start looking at you different." Her mother's face was red and sweaty from work, her hair a frizzy brown pile.

Addie looked at her dress to see if there was anything changed. Except for sap stains and wood dust, she found nothing.

"I don't remember your grandma ever telling me this, so I don't want you walking through life with a sack over your head like I did." She put her hand on Addie's shoulder and smiled. It wasn't a pretty smile, but she had all her teeth, uneven as they were. Such gestures were few and far between, so Addie knew there was something important about to be said. "Do everything you can to avoid it until you're married. Men is going to try to take it before then, but you hold 'em off." She wiped her brow with a forearm and looked into the treetops.

Addie wondered what "it" was. She didn't think she had anything a man might want. Their whole family put together didn't have anything anyone would want.

"Men will hurt you, Adele. That's why I'm telling you this. They will throw you to the ground and hurt you." Now her mother's voice took on a different tone, like it was coming from another part of her. "It ain't just strangers I'm talking about. Your grandpa come after me in the woods one time. And he took what he wanted. Don't ever let that happen to you." She looked straight at Addie, fiercely now. "He come at me another time and dragged me down to the ground, and just as he was about to get what he come for I scooped at leaves and dirt and pushed them all up inside me. He was mad, but he didn't want none anymore. Took me three days before I got it all out, but it was worth it. That's what you got to do, fight them any which way."

Addie still didn't understand what was being said, but she saw that whatever it was had brought angry tears. Behind her mother, a male cardinal fluttered into a pokeberry, a gash of red in the green clutter.

"So all I'm saying is that you don't trust any man, not even your husband."

"What about Pa? You trust him."

"No, Adele, I don't. A husband is just as like to hurt you too. Your pa and I come to an understanding some years back that I won't go into. But there was a time. I should of straightened him out from the start. That's what you got to do, too. On your wedding night your husband is going to take it from you. There ain't no getting around that. And it's going to hurt. Men don't have no sense, so you just got to be brave that first time and remember it don't last long."

Wedding night? What was her mother talking about? She was all of nine. But if that's what getting married was like, why did women do it in the first place? She asked her mother the same question.

"That," her mother said, holding up her hand with its partially missing index finger, "that is something I wish I'd asked a long time ago."

It was too bad, Addie thought now, that only as a woman could she see the sadness in her mother's face, hear it in her voice; now that she had lived enough to understand it. If it were right then, she'd open her arms and take her mother in, hold her, let her soak her shoulder with warm tears if that's what it took. Had she done it back then, maybe her mother wouldn't have run. There had to be more to a woman's life than fearing men.

Addie was still thinking about her mother and her warning

when she heard Muuk at the door. It swung open, the rectangle of evening light behind him offering her new husband as a dark form with a mushroom cap. Addie didn't stir but listened to Muuk's surprisingly quiet movement in the small space. The same moonlight that illuminated her nightgown now filtered across Muuk's shoulders, a dim cheek, the parsnip-white fingers of his left hand. Then the flash of a match and the lamp was lit, his hat removed. He was clean as when they married earlier that day, shirt buttoned up to his neck, suspenders perfectly vertical across each side of his torso, his formerly long hair cut and parted neatly, the color reminding her of the spun gold she'd heard of in her grandmother's bedtime stories.

As Muuk approached, holding the brim of his hat with the fingers of both hands, Addie sat up and pulled her legs close in. Was he going to hurt her now? She closed her eyes and felt the heaviness of this new husband sitting on the thin mattress of straw. She waited, for what she didn't know, a slap, pulled hair, but after a few seconds when nothing happened she cracked open her eyes. Muuk sat at the edge of the bed, head down, staring into his lap. His cheek was wet, and when he turned to look at her, so was the other. He'd been crying outside the mine the day of Tommy's accident too, and in all her life she couldn't remember seeing the same man come to tears twice. With the coal dust wiped off Muuk's face and in the yellow lamplight, his general aspect was brighter, though his blue eyes dimmed without the contrast. He was younger than she thought all along, couldn't be more than ten years older than she. What happened to folks? she wondered. In ten more years they'd look like her mother and father, tired, broke, broke-down, and leathery. It happened to everyone.

"Kiss now?" he asked.

It wasn't a request that Addie expected, but it was preferable to being hurt. He leaned forward, and she met him halfway, realizing on the journey she had no idea how to kiss a man. She stopped and waited, closed her eyes, felt his lips press against her own. They were tight and closed, like a pair of fence rails stacked on one another. She felt the weight of him leaning forward. Is this what her mother had talked about, she wondered, how it was supposed to hurt? When he was fully above her, she stretched her legs out between his, and there was room and ease, as if he had no weight. His lips did not move but stayed pressed against hers. He began to make little noises, intermittent mouselike squeaks. She felt one of his tears run down the side of her face to her ear. "Oh," Muuk said quietly. Then he sat up abruptly. "I cannot," he said. "Cannot." Now he was crying full force as he stood up and replaced his hat on the top of his head. "You go to sleep, Addie," he said, and with that, he left the dugout shack without closing the door behind him.

There were two things about Maye that Addie liked most, the thatch of grassy yellow hair that looked done with sheep shears, and the motto she lived by. They were sitting in the kitchen having sassafras tea when Maye offered it up once more. "Don't take nothing from no one that you ain't willing to give to others when you got the means, but don't take food out of your own mouth." They were talking about Muuk. Addie had done her best. On their wedding night he'd left and not come home until morning, and now it had been a week and he'd been sleeping on the floor or in the chair. Not that she particularly wanted him to lie with her, but even after their worst drunken fights, her mother and father bowed to the reality that there was just one narrow bed for the two of them. And Addie had gone out of her way to be kind, fixed him johnnycakes to take to the mine, and managed dumplings boiled in broth made from the leavings of two sage grouse. But no matter what, Muuk treated Addie like she had the fever. "He's not unkind particularly," she told Maye. "He's just, well, he just ain't . . . nothing. What am I doing wrong?"

Maye scratched her head, then dug under her thumbnail with a fork. "That first night, did he smell of liquor?"

"Not a bit."

"The thing you got to know is that Finns is crazy." She sipped from her cup, following her statement with a simple "Hmm."

"I laid there that night and waited for him to hurt me. I didn't even say a word."

"Hurt you? Why were you waiting for that?" She placed both her hands on the table, as if bracing herself.

Addie was confused. Certainly by now Maye knew what her mother did, and she said as much.

"Sometimes that's true, honey," Maye said. "But it don't have to be. If you get the right man by your side it's the opposite of hurt." She told Addie about a time when she and her husband had been in bed and spent half the night laughing at themselves and what they were doing. "That's where you got to head, to the point of laughing at what you're doing with no clothes on."

Maye wasn't making sense. "Laughing? Then why would my mother lie?" She sipped her tea, but it had gone cold.

"Your mother was telling the truth for her, I expect. But what a terrible thing to go all numb." Maye shook her head over Addie's situation. "Give it some time. Remember, he's been cooped up in that dugout with only mud for company. He might not know what to do with you any more than if someone offered him a fancy new chest of drawers. In lots of ways a wife takes up more room in a man's life than an iron stove."

Addie hadn't thought of it that way. What, after all, had Muuk's mother told him about *his* wedding night? Certainly she hadn't instructed him to hurt women. Was that a father's job? If it was, she didn't think her own had gotten around to instructing Tommy. She also hadn't considered that Muuk's place, awful as it was, had been his alone until Tommy. She wasn't so fond of comparing herself to a piece of furniture or her brother, but what Maye meant by it seemed right. Addie had even told Wing she wasn't sure how she and Muuk would get along living together in such a small space. "You can not," was all Wing said, but it sounded more like speculation than prediction.

"I seen some of the folks in Rock Springs have proper houses," Addie said to Maye. "And Orner and Ah Joe aren't walking on dirt floors. Maybe we'll be in something like that not too far off." But even as she said it, Addie didn't like hearing herself talk about the size of the place that would hem her in, no matter how big it was. She threw up her arms. "To be honest, I just now been realizing I got myself stuck for the first time in my life. Real stuck."

"Yep," Maye said. "That's what that ring on your finger means all right." She drank to the bottom of her cup. "Miss Addie," she continued. "Good *will* come of it someday. Like me. When I was a girl like you I wouldn't have guessed it, but I got a husband, such as he is, and little Aulis. I'm a mother." She touched her belly. "And one more on the way."

It was fresh news to Addie, the announcement lightening the moment. The pair hugged. "Oh, Miss Addie," Maye said sweetly, placing her hands on Addie's cheeks, "someday you'll know exactly what this feels like. We got Aulis, and this new one on the way. There's nothing like growing a family."

Maye's expression was bright and showed that the feeling she talked about was alive inside her. But it was also something Addie couldn't imagine for herself. She'd lost so much, and the addition of Muuk didn't fill the hole in her heart. "Family," Addie said. "Seems like mine is always paring down the opposite direction of yours."

"Now, Miss Addie, you're going through a rough patch sure, but you'll come out the other side." She put her arm around Addie's waist and walked her to the open door, where they paused and looked out over the ranch with its small but sturdy barn, where inside Maye's husband was hammering away at something. "This ranch took a lot of work," Maye said, "and if we'd once stopped and thought on the times when life seemed against us, none of this would be here." She squeezed Addie close to her. "You can't focus on the hardships. There's just no time for it in this life. These things we can discuss in heaven."

It was true, what Maye was saying. It was wasted energy feeling sorry for oneself, but awful hard not to do it anyway. "You're a gift to me, Maye Grood," Addie said. In such a short period she'd become like a combination of an older sister and soldier who'd been through the war and lived to tell about it.

"Likewise, Miss Addie," Maye said. "And look, you're a new bride, and all of this is confusing, but it'll pass. If you remember anything I said today, know that a married woman has a right to feel."

It all sounded reasonable, but with Tommy gone and Muuk turned to stone, Addie wasn't sure if it was a right she could take advantage of. The truth was, more and more, what she wanted to do was hunt up that small bag she'd arrived with hardly a year earlier, fill it with what would get her by, and leave without saying a word, leave Muuk, leave everything. She could picture the solitary ride down the draw on Racer. There'd be no looking back. What her mother had done made sense, seemed a wholly plausible option, the only option. *Run.* But when her thoughts brought her that far, she recalled that morning when she discovered she no longer had a mother, saw the quivering astonishment and loss in the face of the child she had been. She thought of Wing, even as the thought continued to echo in her mind. *Run.*

EPISODE EIGHTEEN

Six weeks had passed since she'd gotten married. Though she was still thinking of her brother, Addie's life settled into a new if awkward routine with Muuk. She kept what she thought useful from her brother's homestead, a fry pan, a coffeepot, the rigging she made to stand over the fire for roasting game. The rest she gave away, because it wasn't practical to fill up Muuk's shanty, and not necessary. She did not look back once when she got on her hinny and left the odd little shack built by her brother. She wanted nothing to do with any of it any longer. It was that unworkable land, after all, that drove Tommy into the mine.

It was early in the morning when Addie woke and saw Muuk's dark form slumped over their narrow table, his eyes catching what little light there was. He was in his mining clothes, and his cap sat in front of him between his hands. "Are you all right?" she asked. When he didn't reply or even stir, Addie stood and walked to his side. "Muuk?"

He looked up, his eyes a pair of dim stars. "I am too broken," he said. "Nothing fixes me."

Unsure of how to respond, or if she should, Addie placed her hand on Muuk's back and waited.

"Your brother was good. I thought we would partner in the mine very long."

"Yes, he was," Addie said, unsure of why, after all these months, Tommy's death had pushed forward in Muuk's mind.

Taking Addie's hand, Muuk cleared his throat. "We are not so different, Addie. Our families. All we love are gone."

She rubbed Muuk's wide back. What he said was true, but Addie was trying to live up to Maye's advice, to not wallow in regret. She hadn't gotten there yet, but she was trying. She spoke this to Muuk, told him that their job was to find happiness, that it did no good to weigh themselves down with sadness.

Standing, Muuk looked at Addie, unconvinced. "I cannot even like when others are happy." He walked to the door and turned. "I am broken," he repeated.

You must smile again," Wing said. It was early on the same morning. She was walking with Wing along the track through Dire Draw, talking easily, which was not something they did much of anymore. For the time being Addie was done selling game, but she hoped to get a rabbit for herself. Wing was along for the company. Now that she wasn't selling game, was married, there was no natural reason for them to be together, a fact Ah Joe had made clear to Wing, and which he had sadly reported to Addie.

Wing tapped her on the shoulder, and when she turned, he

presented her with a round, rust-colored object. It was an orange. She'd never tried one, but she'd seen the Chinese eating them now and then.

"For you, Miss Addie," Wing said.

The fruit was surprisingly heavy, the skin leathery, and it didn't smell like anything. It wasn't the kind of thing a person would think to eat, but she was happy to try. "Should we cut it open and have a bite?"

Wing waved her off. "This is for your home. For a happy marriage."

She wondered what if any complaint had showed on her face. She hadn't said anything about Muuk that she could think of. "It's a real sweet thing of you to do," she said, placing the fruit in her bag. "Real sweet." She touched his cheek, and he cowed.

It was something she liked, these blushes of shyness that came over Wing, which seemed even more frequent lately.

"Some day," he said, pointing to the fruit, "I would like an entire farm of these."

Another dreamer, she thought. What was it about men? "One piece of advice," she said. "Before you buy any land, make sure you can grow oranges on it." Tommy came to mind, but it broke her heart to think of him, so she let it go.

"I think I will go to California and try, before going back to China." His tone was so sincere that she believed he might make a go of it. "And another surprise." He raised a finger to emphasize the importance of his statement.

"What's that?"

"Tomorrow night you will smile."

"How's tomorrow night going to be different than any other night?" When Wing didn't answer, she tried again. "Why?"

He nodded. "Because you will smile tomorrow night." Then he stopped and pointed into the brush. Addie raised her shotgun and found her target almost immediately.

"Ought to call you bird dog," she said after the shot. "Or rabbit dog, or something." But as they walked toward the dead animal she realized she didn't like the sound of any of it. Innocent as it was, Wing was a man, she thought, not an animal of any kind.

He held the rabbit by its hind legs as Addie slit the gut and pulled the contents out, holding the bloody mess to the light to check for worms. It wasn't something to really talk about, but she liked this feeling, the heat in her hand. "Looks good," she said.

"Handsome," Wing offered.

Addie laughed at this new word. "I suppose it is," she said. It was the first time since her brother died that she'd even come close to laughing, and it felt good. She took the rabbit from Wing and gave a light punch to his sleeveless shoulder. "Thank you."

Wing was caught off guard, but he fell into a smile when he saw the fist-sized blood-stamp she'd left behind. "Soon you will feel good," he said, putting a finger to his lips to indicate he was holding a secret.

"What are you up to?"

Wing gave her a look as if he didn't understand the question. She was suspicious, wondering if this was just a momentary convenience.

"Ah Cheong will ask for you," Wing stated, now pinching his lips shut with his fingers.

The following evening the air was crisp, but not intolerable. She followed Ah Cheong toward Little San Fran, his queue whipping back and forth in time to a frantic stride. A crowd of white miners gathered along the gulley, though she couldn't immediately tell the reason. But as Ah Cheong led Addie through the men, she saw that something quite strange was happening. Across the bridge, and about forty feet beyond, stood what she guessed was the unfinished joss house. In front of that was a large area marked off by a line of burning candles, and on either side of the joss house was what looked like the entire population of Little San Fran. Ah Cheong delivered Addie to a single chair draped in silk in a shade of brilliant red she'd never seen, and couldn't begin to imagine if it wasn't in front of her. "Please sit," Ah Cheong said. Addie complied, wholly in wonder. When he had knocked on her door just a half hour earlier and said "Please come with me," she'd put aside Wing's cheery warning from the day before, thought perhaps he was in some sort of trouble. Even without the candles, it was an unusually bright evening. A near full moon hung low and shone clear as a silver dollar in a rain barrel. Behind her, Addie heard the white miners talking. They were as baffled as she.

Ah Cheong shook Addie's hand and darted off into the incomplete joss house, the curtained entrance of which she faced directly. The structure was roofless and built of what looked like fairly new lumber, its doorway concealed by a length of black cloth split in the center. She knew that they were building a larger joss house, but it was odd to see the structure moved to this spot, sitting on the half dozen wooden crossbars used to carry it.

Suddenly there was a clamor of drums and cymbals from behind the building, and then a burst of yellow light as six Chinese men rushed out with blazing torches, aligning themselves, three on each side, in front of the Chinese miners, creating second and third walls for what she understood to be a stage. The cymbals abruptly stopped and a stringed instrument began, each of its notes played in a way that made Addie think of plucking petals from a flower.

A woman emerged from behind the black curtain, her face painted white, her lips a mere suggestion like a small red butterfly on a field of snow. She wore trousers, a leather vest, a hat like the one Addie wore, and she carried a rifle. It's me, Addie thought. She looked over her shoulder. All of white Dire was behind her, taking in the curiosity. How had they managed to drag a Chinese woman all the way out to Dire? She began to sing in a style Addie didn't recognize, high and nasal, and anyway, in Chinese. But it was clear she was narrating her actions as she raised her rifle grandly, taking aim at an invisible target offstage. When she took her silent shot, a cymbal clash punctuated the deed.

As the woman exited to retrieve her game, the percussion and strings steadied into a staccato thrum, and a male voice took over. Seven Chinese men with lit miner's caps on their heads and tools in their hands walked in a deliberate line from behind the building, moved in sync with the music up to the line of candles past Addie's chair, then turned toward the curtained entrance, the music heightening a little as each went inside. Maybe it was the rhythm, Addie thought, but she had a sense the men were being swallowed. "Guess they're going into a mine," someone from behind said, and just then, the line of men reemerged with two additions, a pair of men dressed in denim and near-white shirts. The actors were miners, all of them Chinese but playing both Chinese and white, and when they began to mime their work onstage, the sounds of the drums and cymbals elevated again.

The singing narrator was Ah Cheong, the only one not engaged in the mining. He was small, but seemed inflated in this role, stomping to one side of the stage where the white miners labored, planting his feet and leaning toward them, arms stretched forward as he sang their condition, a gesture he repeated for the Chinese workers on the other side.

"You understand any of this?" an unwelcome voice said at Addie's ear. It was Orner.

Though she was surprised he'd crossed the bridge to be here, she didn't turn away from the action. "Not the words. But I got eyes." He grunted and she felt him leave.

A pair of Chinese emerged from behind the black curtain and unfurled a length of dark cloth four feet wide and almost twenty feet long. Each man stood at opposite sides of the stage holding the four corners of the cloth parallel to the ground, arms fully extended upward. Ah Cheong's voice lowered as he pointed to the cloth that loomed not two feet above the miners' heads. He stopped abruptly and the miners froze in position, the cloth moving slowly in Addie's direction. She couldn't recall if ever in her life something as thin and harmless as a bolt of fabric had ever held so much menace. When the cloth was fully stretched in front of the stilled miners as a narrow ribbon, drums began a growing rumble, and the men turned the face of the cloth toward her, unraveling it. The ribbon became a descending curtain of rock, the ceiling of the mine. Drum vibrations coursed through Addie's body.

The miners were silhouettes, activating at the height of the drums an exaggerated scramble, some tumbling and regaining their footing, all of them eventually becoming lighter and smaller until they were no more. Now the cloth dropped, and the torches on one side of the stage were carried away. What remained were three fallen miners, two white and one Chinese, each animated only by shifting torchlight and the squirming flames from the caps at their sides. The music altered into pure strings, which sounded plaintive to Addie—voices, maybe, that the injured men could not make themselves. Two men at the rear of the stage, one white, one Chinese, were on their backs, limbs akimbo. The man nearest Addie lay facedown, a pile of brown cloth covering his legs. It was Tommy, she knew, and she wiped away tears with her sleeve. She had been in the mine, sure, but there were those long minutes between the collapse and when he'd first heard her voice when his thoughts must have been just like the music, which sounded like more than the pain itself; the terror of thinking maybe that's how your life would end, no second chances, no good-byes, reduced to inhaling dirt and the revelation of helplessness.

The day before, Wing told her she would smile soon, but their play was having the opposite effect. What was he thinking? And where was he? He wasn't among the actors or stagehands, not among the audience, and though she couldn't see the musicians, he never displayed any talent in that way. What was it Ah Joe had said about his musical ability?

Percussion joined the strings as if from a distance, like an incoming train, Addie thought, then no, not a train, something more solitary, like a rider and horse in urgent approach. Addie recognized the music as it changed once again into the theme that began the program, and just at the moment of this understanding, the woman playing Addie dashed from behind the curtains. With half the torchlight as before, her whitened face was less dramatic, appeared more like the autumn yellow of a harvest moon. Her clothes were blackened with soot as Addie's had been, and her voice was urgent, almost desperate, as she searched the stage. Finally the woman discovered the first miner, her voice becoming promissory as he stirred for the first time. With the second, she was incantatory, and he too began to show life. It was as if she was bringing these men back from death.

The music stopped abruptly, and the woman fell silent.

Addie's first sight of Tommy flashed in her mind. She wasn't sure if this was an event she wanted to relive, but something about seeing it play out in this form made it possible to hope for a different outcome. Her brother didn't have to die this time. The white-faced woman could be powerful enough to pull him from the rubble. She didn't have to fail Tommy. Things could be set right.

When the woman reached her brother, she knelt and sang a cappella. He was still at first, then sang his reply, but it was song in guttural form, as if thick clots of soul escaped with each syllable. The woman removed her hat and placed it next to her brother's flickering cap. Her voice became reed thin as she stroked his hair, and he calmed. He was nodding, gesturing softly for her to go. When she stood, Addie wanted to call out. She wanted to say, Don't leave, you will never see him again. She saw that the woman was not only wearing Addie's clothes. She had donned her heart, too, Addie could see it in the woman's eyes, which glowed with tears that did not fall.

Then the woman did something remarkable, running to the other two miners, rousing them to their feet, each one slung over her shoulder. A cheer went up from behind Addie. It was not how it had happened, but Addie didn't mind because it made clear the dilemma. There were three men, just two shoulders, and fate laid bare.

The woman reached the back of the stage, still carrying the two miners, and the bolt of cloth that had been the mine collapse raised between them and Tommy. Behind it two of the remaining three torches extinguished. It was the second collapse that sealed Tommy away. When the cloth fell entirely, only her brother remained, his head now resting on a block of wood, Tommy barely lit except for the single torch on the opposite side of the stage and the thinning flame of his miner's cap, the light from which fell on his hair as a kind of outline, and suggested too, the woman's hat left behind. Again there were strings, soft and precise. The brother looked up and directly at Addie, singing to her, and his voice rushed forward like a prayer, but not for himself. His expression was perfectly calm. Be at peace, he seemed to be saying. "All right, Tommy," Addie said to herself. "I love you. Good-bye." And almost as if she'd been heard, the music faded and her brother extinguished the small flame next to him as he laid his head on the wood block. It was done.

At first there was silence. Addie knew the men behind her had never seen anything like this. Certainly she hadn't. But then came tentative applause, not from lack of appreciation, Addie felt, but perhaps out of respect for her. So she stood and applauded too, and the sound behind her grew. It was only when the players and musicians filled the stage that the Chinese audience bordering it began to applaud as well. The players did not bow, only stood. When Addie put her hands down, the players continued standing. Nearly a minute passed before she understood. There she was standing between these two groups of miners, and they were clapping for her. She nodded to the white miners, then to the Chinese, and as she performed this latter act, the woman who played her part smiled. "How do you feel?" the actress said. It was Wing.

EPISODE NINETEEN

The torches had been relit, and now came the surprise of applause. There was Addie in front of a wall of white men across the bridge, she in tears, but all of them clapping. Standing before them was her husband, Muuk, his face stoic, arms at his side. During the performance Wing was sure things were going badly. The music seemed off cue, and none of them except him had ever been onstage. They had rehearsed when they could, but rarely had every musician and every actor been there at the same time. It was a coal camp after all, hard work, and even though it was a unanimous decision to offer this gesture of appreciation, Fatigue and Hunger would always be more powerful masters than Gratitude.

For his own part, Wing had not worried the audience would see him as a man, but as best he could, he kept an eye on Addie as he performed. Tried to discern from her expressions if the play was doing its intended work, or if it was merely wounding her heart once more. There was little he could give her outright, but she had lamented she had not had the chance to say good-bye to her brother. As he sang his part, saw her cry, inside he was praying she would make it through to the end, where he had directed his actor to look directly at Addie when he sang Tommy's dying words. They would come from a Chinese face, but if it was successful, they would channel his soul, and the brother and sister could say their good-byes.

Wing thought of the night in San Francisco when Sing Ten was counting receipts and shooed him away. Maybe this wasn't 1,500 people in the Lung Look. Maybe it wasn't even the kind of play that could sell tickets, but judging from Addie's face, he had a full house. There was yet another act, an encore of sorts. Wing waited, and just as the applause diminished and the white men began to turn, he raised his arms. In response, his makeshift troupe raised their arms in unison. "Ho!" they cried together, clapping their hands above their heads. The crowd grew silent as Wing approached Addie. When he drew closer, he saw that the men behind her took on surprised expressions, only then fully understanding that a man had played the stage role of Addie. The sight of a woman was so much like a mirage in Dire, it wasn't surprising.

"How do you feel?" Wing asked.

Addie extended her hand. "Thank you." She had stopped crying, but her cheeks still shone with flags of light.

Wing accepted her rough hand in both of his and shook it once before letting go. "Please sit," he said. "We have more." He stood behind her as she complied. Then he again scanned the crowd for her husband. This time he found Muuk's stony stare in the back of the gathering and waved for him to come. As if it was possible Wing meant someone else, Muuk looked to either side of him.

When he finally complied with the silent request, Wing discovered a twinge of regret in his heart.

The trio—Wing, Addie, and Muuk—faced the troupe. Wing simply nodded, and again they cried "Ho!" clapping their hands, this time leaving their places on the stage to stations on either side of what they'd been calling their new joss house. Orner had reluctantly gotten them the materials through the UP, rough as it was, and not enough for a roof, but still, four sturdy walls, twelve by fourteen, one empty window, and doorways front and back.

Ah Cheong was in charge now. The buttons on his shirt gleamed like a vertical set of bright eyes as he stood in front of the joss house and called out to the men. They bent at the knees and took hold of the poles supported by wood blocks. The men, two abreast at the ends of each pole, twelve in all, responded to Ah Cheong's second call, heaving the structure to waist level, then immediately on the third call to their chests. It was a heavy undertaking, but the lack of materials for a roof turned out to be a kind of blessing. Ah Cheong pivoted, and on his command the joss house moved forward toward Addie, Muuk, and Wing.

"What's happening?" Addie said, looking up at Wing. In the approaching torchlight, her freckles looked like a braid of flowers across her nose and cheekbones.

"A gift," Wing said. He looked at Muuk to see if he understood, if he even noticed that Wing had uttered a word in English.

"Kyllä," Muuk said, placing his hand firmly on Addie's shoulder.

Wing allowed his own hand to drop to his side so that it only just grazed Addie's arm. If she noticed, she did not let on. The structure approached steadily as the men carrying it walked in near unison. It was a simple box ready for a pitched roof, but Wing felt as if they were delivering a castle. If they'd told the UP and

Orner what they planned, the answer would have come back no. So they built their "joss house" knowing all along it would be Addie's house—Addie and Muuk's. It would have to be moved again, certainly, but that was a detail to be worried about later.

When the men and their load were just a few feet from reaching their destination, Wing hunched down so that he was no higher than Addie's head. Muuk followed, bringing one knee to the ground as if he were genuflecting. The black curtain used for the production had been removed from the front door. The structure floated above them, Addie, Wing, and Muuk, the support poles clearing their heads by several inches, and then, when it was centered, Wing called out, and it creaked as it lowered around them.

At rest, open-aired as it was, no roof, no doors, the house took on a distinct silence. Wing watched to see if Addie understood. She looked around the space slowly, took in, surely, the strange combination of light, torches outside creating the yellowish hues of sunrise at the windows, the stunning moon positioned as if it were sitting at the top of the wall looking in. It had not been planned, but Wing liked the effect of an entire day compressed in one moment. It was a favorable sign. A happy life could be lived in this house.

Muuk stood and shook his head as if he couldn't believe they'd gone to all this trouble. Wing hadn't expected to see any appreciation from Addie's husband. He knew Muuk was content with the two of them living in a bachelor shack, but Addie deserved better, Wing thought, and he meant it in more than one way.

"I can't find the right words," Addie finally said, standing. Muuk took his place next to her, but the pairing was brief as she stepped forward and hugged Wing tightly, which Wing took to be acceptable given that they were in Muuk's presence. Her body was warm, and he was certain he felt the beat of her heart. When she stepped back, a white streak from his makeup ran across the side of her face. He touched his own cheek to let her know, and they laughed as she smudged it away with her palm. Muuk did not join their laughter. He said something Wing could not understand, but it was clipped, and his brow was lowered. Had the embrace been acceptable, but the laughter too intimate? Was this a man with no joy, with no interest in his wife's happiness?

It was clear the evening was over. Ah Joe had promised to speak with Orner about a permanent location for the house, something he would certainly have to accommodate given Addie's confirmed status as the bravest person in Dire. Less certain was where the lumber for the roof would come from, but they would get it somehow. Wing remembered a saying of his grandfather's: "A toothless ox is a gift to no one." Certainly none of these details could be discussed right then anyway, Wing understood, not in Chinese, Finnish, or English.

Muuk snatched Addie's hand and offered a nominal nod of his hat to Wing. The pair exited their new dwelling, but Wing stayed behind, watching as they left. He listened as the men outside offered their appreciation, but Muuk never stopped to speak to anyone, seemed to be warding off as much happiness as he could. When they were out of sight, Wing sat in the silk-draped chair from which Addie watched his play and received her house. Certainly Muuk didn't understand the honor he would have in sharing these walls with her. The moon seemed to agree. Only its top half was visible, looking to Wing like a punished child resting its chin on a wall, planning to run away from home.

Muuk gave in. They were sleeping in the same bed, though not soundly. Wing's play had an odd effect on him. He'd practically dragged Addie home afterward, sat her down in their shack, and paced the small distance of their floor. "This is not right. People will ask why her husband doesn't give the house. I am her husband." Addie had never seen him this angry, though he wasn't yelling. It was almost as if he was talking to himself, and she just happened to be there. "They must see that I am the husband."

"Muuk," Addie said, "the entire camp knows we're married."

He turned and held a finger close to her face. "No."

She didn't understand what he was trying to say, or perhaps understood that, as usual, there were things he would not say. It was true, Wing and all of Little San Fran had provided a spectacular gift, but it had been lifted around both of them. "It's a house given to a husband and wife, Muuk," she said. "It was a kindness for both of us."

He sat on their bed and buried his hands in his face, spoke Finnish words into his palms. As he moved, the lamplight played on his hair like full sun on wind-blown wheat. "My grandfather," Muuk said, looking up, "he was in his mind very sick. My grandmother was dead, but he thought no, my mother was his wife. He tried, and my father beat him till he slept."

"Muuk," Addie began, but he held her off.

"I have told you my father died, my family, after my mother. A man cannot live long without a wife. He must be a husband."

The words struck Addie as she hadn't expected. At first, it was merely Muuk's sad history, but she thought of her own father dying without a wife even though he tried to live a better life. So this was part of it, Addie thought—she was a kind of charm toward a longer life. At least now they both knew their separate reasons for this union. It was like the story of the cat and dog that went their separate ways all day but at night in the barn slept in the same bed of hay, where their fleas and ticks more or less divided their number between them.

The next morning it was Muuk who made the effort, though awkwardly. "Teach me?" he asked, holding out Addie's rifle. "I want to shoot." She hated to waste the ammunition, but then again, since Tommy died, she'd quit bringing game into Dire, so with a sack full of cans she walked Muuk out to the shadowed base of White Mountain and taught him as best she could. His hands knew drills and stone, his eyes dark walls; she only had to teach him trigger and touch, beaded aim. He was clumsy at first, barely spoke when she gave direction, but he listened with squinted eyes, one ear leaned in her direction. "Hyvä," he said when he understood what she wanted. By midday most of the time he could hit the can.

Now that they were sleeping in the same bed, Addie thought

perhaps it meant they were officially married, though Muuk would only lie down after Addie drifted off, or pretended to, and was gone before she woke. She had her own reasons to be up early a few days after Muuk's bitter reaction to Wing's play, but she kept her eyes closed, waiting for Muuk to go. Wing had promised to ride out to Tommy's homestead with her. She thought she might make use of some of the wood from the upturned wagon that was the shack's roof. She needed it for what was going to be her and Muuk's new home.

As Muuk dressed in the dark, he spoke to himself in Finnish, which made him more of a haunt than a man, she thought. She was beginning to think that maybe this was normal behavior between husbands and wives in Finland, and she felt sorry for their women. Maye was right, she thought, Finns are crazy.

The point had been made just days earlier, when Dire was nearly blown off the map. Jacob Narinen had gotten paid and had gotten drunk, which wasn't unusual for him. But he'd come into possession of a pistol too, and for some reason thought it a good idea to jump on a mule and take a shot at the powder house, which was built of sheet iron on a rock foundation. The sound of the explosion left ears ringing for days. Most of the mule's head landed in front of Addie and Muuk's shack. One of Narinen's bloody ears and part of his skull splatted against the cheek of Ah Cheong, and Emrys Clough, the man who'd told Addie how Dire got its name, was killed when the mule's torso came down and broke his neck. In the spot where the powder house had been was a hole three feet deep, and the tracks alongside it were bent out of shape as if they'd never been made for trains in the first place. Narinen's casket was more like a market basket than a box built for a man, the pieces of him gathered up and laid as best as could be made out, in their former order.

When Addie heard Muuk leave that morning, she got up and poked her head out the door. It wasn't only him headed to the mine. Except for starlight, the landscape was black, interrupted by the individual flames of lit caps that were scattered until they joined together at a distant point. They looked strung out like yellow-white beads—or no, Addie thought, like a wavy line of fireflies. But there was no joy in the vision. Every lamp represented a silent man, and Addie couldn't help but feel like it was one of the loneliest things she'd ever seen.

It was time to get herself ready to gather lumber for her new roof. Wing would be expecting her at sunrise. As she got dressed, she found herself being a little more tidy than usual. Even though it was paid work for Wing, she was looking forward to his company, had felt more so since the death of her brother, and whatever this was she was doing with Muuk. Marriage, people called it. With Wing, it was just easy, and maybe that was because she put a few coins in his pocket, but she doubted it. He'd given her a house, after all. Four walls, anyway.

It wasn't that long ago she'd given a man, a boy, money and got nothing to show for it but a robbed heart. Denny. She remembered it like it was happening right then, even the quality of the fall air, the way each day the sun slid lower and lower across the sky.

Denny was seventeen, big shouldered, with a man's chest and a boy's shock of straw-white hair. She met him when she was in town and sometimes made up excuses to go into Orgull in the hopes he'd be around. It was a new feeling for her, something inside like a concentrated warmth she carried around in her chest, a warmth stoked every time she saw him, when he placed his wide palm on her head to tousle her hair, or when he picked her up from behind and said she wasn't any heavier than a melon. That's what he called her, Melon.

Then the news. He wasn't getting along with his father and he was headed out, maybe to Cincinnati, maybe all the way up to Pittsburgh. His story was Addie's story. A father who drank too much. Mother gone, though his died in childbirth when he was six.

"Take me with you," Addie blurted.

They were standing on the street, and Denny shushed her, looking around as if it were a secret. "Can't."

Addie pretended not to hear, but she lowered her voice. "I'm a real good cook, and I can chop wood like I got four arms."

Denny smiled. "It ain't that, Melon. You're sweet and all that, and for a girl, I know better than anybody you can fend for yourself. But I just can't take you."

Now Denny wasn't smiling, and Addie wasn't either. Behind them, an empty wagon clacked by on the rutted street. "I promise I won't be no trouble."

"Trouble? I got no plan other than leaving, Melon. That's the trouble." He pointed to the river. "I got just enough saved up to get on a boat in Louisville and maybe to eat for a couple days. I can't take you because I don't have the money."

Addie considered this. Maybe he didn't *want* to take her. Maybe he was just trying not to hurt her feelings. "I have money," she said quietly.

Denny turned, eyebrows slightly raised.

"I have some money we could use," she repeated.

"How much?"

"Around nine dollars. I pinch some from Pa every now and then when he's drunk. I learned it from Ma. That's how we get by. I got it on me right now." Addie lifted her pant leg and extracted a leather pouch from her boot.

Denny shook his head, but she could tell it wasn't disapproval. She searched his face as he thought about it.

"Okay," he said quietly. It wasn't the ecstatic reaction she hoped for, but it would do. They made a plan. He would take the money from her and maybe buy a bit of hard tack for the trip. She had to go home and act like nothing was going on. They would meet that afternoon under the big dogwood where she'd come across Denny napping the first time she saw him.

Addie rushed home and prepared her bundle. It wasn't difficult, as she didn't own much more than what she was wearing, denim overalls, her brother's shirt that sometimes still offered up the light scent of him. When she was done, she looked around the small cabin. At one time not long before it had held four people, a family. There was the slim bed where her father slept with her mother, and the even narrower one where she and Tommy fell asleep every night whispering about their lives. Four people, a family. Now Addie was leaving too. She wondered when her father would notice she was gone. What would trigger it? That there was no wood brought in for the stove, that midday had come and she hadn't woken him up from his drunk? And would he care?

She didn't have the words to put in a note that would explain why she left, and anyway, he'd have to go through the indignity of finding someone to read it to him. Addie thought of the morning she woke to discover her mother had left. Even with Tommy still there and her father asleep, the room and her heart had felt empty. She couldn't do that to her father. So she did put wood on the stove and set a tin plate and fork on the table with a chunk of cornbread. At least he would know she thought of him before she walked out the door for good.

Addie arrived at the dogwood early. It was the beginning of fall, the time when the woods perform their second act. Spring is about flowers and bright green leaves. Fall is all fiery blush. Addie placed her bundle against the tree trunk and lay on her back looking up through the branches. The sky was overcast, and though she couldn't see them, she heard the squonking of passing geese. It was a time to be on the move. In a few hours Denny would meet her and their adventure could begin. Maybe he would be as eager as she and show up early.

She waited and waited. No Denny. He hadn't come for her; would not. Full daylight was slow in coming, felt delayed. A thick fog had settled into the woods, an opaqueness that made lines of small birds look like thread being drawn through gray cloth. Above her the dogwood leaves were turning pinkish red. In a couple weeks, they'd be on the ground. Another fall, and then another cold winter. Was this her life?

Noisy crows cawed somewhere not far, and the woods clicked with dew dropping leaf to leaf. If it could all stay just like this, cool, damp, and calm, yes, she thought, that was a life she could live. But then there were men who her mother had warned her about. They will hurt you, she'd been told, and Addie hadn't been given any evidence to the contrary. Only she was beginning to understand that hurt comes in more than one size.

No smoke rose from the cabin, which was a good sign. Addie slowly pushed open the door so as not to wake her father. Both light and her shadow wedged into the room. The table setting was as she left it, and her father's bed was empty. She hadn't known it until then, but she was counting on his presence, needed it. Tossing her bundle onto her bed, Addie plunged herself alongside it, facedown. Denny had not shown up. She would have given him the nine dollars even if he didn't take her with him, but he had tricked her. As she thought this, she felt the heat in her heart intensify, become molten, and then, like hot iron dipped in water, it cooled and hardened.

Denny's betrayal wasn't so long ago that Addie forgot its lesson, though at every turn Wing contradicted what she'd been taught about men, had learned on her own. Now Addie and he were within sight of Tommy's homestead. Maye loaned the wagon without a question, but got a curious look on her face when Wing sat on the buckboard next to Addie instead of in the tray. Addie had to be careful about that, she guessed, couldn't look too familiar, so she tapped on Wing's shoulder and pointed to the tray as if bothering with English would be futile. Wing complied, and she appreciated that he didn't make a fuss about it.

Not since she married Muuk had Addie seen Tommy's place, and the sad part of it was, it didn't look much more abandoned than when she'd lived there.

"I hate to be out here, Wing," she said, pulling up next to her brother's dusty, makeshift shack, which looked to her now like a large, fossilized clam. The height of their ride put them about even with the roof, which itself had once been a wagon tray. The lumber was salvageable.

"We will not be here long," Wing said, hopping off the wagon. She loved his optimism. Even though they'd gotten an early start, by the time they'd gotten to Maye's ranch and hitched the hinny, they were running behind schedule. The air was starting to warm and smell like honey, a scent that she remembered lasted just so long and didn't come from a single plant but from the entirety of the plain.

Wing and Addie weren't minutes into the work before he tapped her on the shoulder. "Look," he said. It was a bachelor pronghorn, the animal she'd seen from a train and confused for a Chinaman. "Would you take your gun?" Wing's voice was restrained but excited, and she knew why. Their meat business ended when she married Muuk.

"The only thing I want from here is a roof," Addie said, but it wasn't too long before she knew she needed to take a shot, though she didn't say anything, didn't have to, because Wing knew it too, held the rifle out to her as if it had been requested. She accepted it because she understood in that moment she couldn't say no to him, couldn't say no to herself. She was back in business.

EPISODE TWENTY-ONE

The first time Addie saw the dunes, she thought they were snowdrifts, which didn't make sense because it was summer and there hadn't even been rain for a week. But there they were, a few miles off running along the base of the hills, the sight of them looking like a skirt caught in a breeze.

A year later she was sitting on the top of one of those dunes with Wing, trying to be careful with him. She didn't know exactly the feelings she was having, but it was nothing like back then with Denny. There was something to be cautious about, but she couldn't put her finger on it. Maybe it'd be different if Muuk ever said more than three words to her.

Addie had killed three rabbits and a small pronghorn, a good day's work. That's all it was between her and Wing, she told herself, work. The fact they could talk to each other was just something extra. Behind them were the side-by-side divots of their footprints in the dune. The sand itself was cool, wet, and cold when she pushed her toes into it. Even though it wasn't snow, the dune did seem to hold the months-ago winter, water pooling at the base that made a temporary marsh. That first time, she'd seen elk and antelope drinking from one of these. Wing was standing, looking out over the rare shade of cool green bordering the white dunes. The bare sun glazed his arms and face, set him in bronze. If they had courthouse squares in China, Addie thought, he could be a statue.

"You should have a beautiful silk dress," Wing said. "Yellow."

The statement surprised her, but Wing's tone was so sincere she didn't trouble him for thinking out loud. To her way of thinking, a dress was about as useful as braiding a horse's mane. And silk? Impractical. "Why yellow?" she asked.

He sat next to her in the sand, obviously pleased to take up the subject. "Yellow for good luck. It should be yellow with red . . ." He paused, searching for the word, pulled at his collar to get Addie's help.

"Trim," she said.

"Yes, red trim!" He beamed at the thought, was clearly searching her face for approval. She handed him a johnnycake and a piece of smoked pork. The cuticles of his nails held bits of blackish red, blood from gutting the animals.

"It's a beautiful idea, Wing. But to tell you the truth there's not much occasion out here for me to be wearing fancy silk dresses."

"No. No. Not here. Maybe San Francisco. We could walk down the streets there and everyone would see how beautiful." He reached into his pocket and pulled out a swatch of bright yellow silk. "Like this," he said.

The way it caught the sun reminded her of a shiny yellow perch. It was a beautiful color, too beautiful for her, she thought. She bit into her johnnycake and pushed her toes into the sand again. The last time she'd walked down any street in a dress she was what, maybe six, seven years old? A man had come to Orgull, and for fifty cents would draw your portrait in color. For another fifty cents he'd affix it to a frame. Her grandmother paid for both, borrowed a dress for Addie from the undertaker. It was light blue, she remembered, with shiny white bows on the shoulders and around the waist, hung nearly to her ankles. Her grandmother stood over the man, watching him work on the paper in front of him. "Be still, Adele," her grandmother repeated several times. Which was hard to do with the dress holding so tight around the neck and wrists. They'd posed her next to a stuffed parrot in a wood cage, and even with its empty eye sockets, it glared down at her.

"San Francisco," Wing repeated. "You would like it there." He told her about the buildings that seemed to have crawled out of the ocean and planted themselves on the slopes like crabs, and then he explained what crabs were. It was a city of fog, according to Wing, and constant, cool wind. It surprised her to hear that it was not so unlike Dire in that the Chinese lived in their own section.

"Are there many Chinese women there? Can you grow oranges?" Addie asked. She'd never seen a Chinese woman, and she thought she should change the subject because she was beginning to imagine herself walking next to Wing in that yellow dress.

Wing wrinkled his nose. "Some women, and no." He did not elaborate. He brought his queue over his shoulder and lay back in the sand, hands behind his head. "Yellow," he repeated.

Addie joined him, and when their elbows touched, neither of them pulled away. The sky seemed a flung blanket, a suspended blue cloth that might billow softly down and cover them both. "How do you say my name in Chinese?" she asked. When there was no reply, she turned her head. Wing had one eye squinting as if he were thinking hard on her question.

"I do not," he said.

"Do not what?"

"Say your name in Chinese."

Now she was up on her elbow. "But if you did. What is it?"

"Your names, Miss Addie, Miss Ah Dee, Miss Adele," he began, propping himself up to meet her eye to eye, "they are not in Chinese."

The news disappointed her. She called *him* Wing, after all, could spell it in four letters. Certainly Addie meant something. It even sounded Chinese if you thought about it. She sat up. "If I was Chinese, what do you think my name might be?"

He thought for a moment. "Maybe Yuen Sai?" He laughed. Was he making fun of her? she asked. "It means Far West," he said. He jumped up and ran to the summit of the dune, disappearing on the other side. She followed, and when she got to the top, he was using a finger to score the fresh face of the firm dune with broad strokes. "This is what it looks like in Chinese." Standing next to him, she saw what he'd drawn, two separate jumbles of lines that looked to her like piled sticks. How did he make sense of it?

Wing backed off from his work, which sat in front of them as if at the slant of an easel. "And what English name would you give me?" he asked her.

"You already have one."

"No. Wing Lee is a Chinese name." It hadn't occurred to her that she'd been speaking a Chinese word all along, that it was even possible. She'd heard them talking with one another in Dire, and it sounded exactly like what Wing had just scratched out in the sand. But when you reduced it to a single word, a sound, it suddenly wasn't so bad. *Wing*. He wasn't a William or Zachary or Benjamin, or any kind of usual name like that, but she remembered a dockworker in Orgull about Wing's size, and as strong and quick, who hoisted crates on his back and met himself coming and going.

Spede McCallum. Never was a man with a more appropriate name, Addie thought, saying it out loud. "Spede."

She spelled it in the sand the way she'd seen it on his grave marker after he got crushed between two boats, decided maybe she wouldn't tell Wing about the one time McCallum hadn't been speedy enough.

Wing nodded. "I like these names," he said. "But I like Addie and Wing better."

She looked at the Chinese name Wing had scrawled on the sand, and the one she wrote. The lines were already breaking down, as if they agreed with Wing's preference for the names they used every day. "They're going away," she said, and it came out in an unexpected way, as if there were some sad consequence about it. Wing stood side by side with Addie, watching with her as the figures softened by fractions. The truth was, they were Addie and Wing. She liked the sound of the pairing, imagined it painted on a board above the door of some business they might run.

Then she felt the warmth of Wing's hand in hers, as easy as if it were a breeze.

They were covered by the sky, only now it wasn't a blanket, it was a lake in which they swam. Wing held Addie tight in his arms as they kissed. They were minutes into the embrace before Addie thought for a fraction of a second to stop. Wing wanted to feel her return his affection, and she did. She was another man's wife, to be sure, but marriage is not consummated by grunts of in-difference. Addie's heart spoke. *Run*, it said, *only not away*.

Addie thought of Muuk briefly, and only as the image of a man walking in the dark, becoming the flicker of lamplight. She knew now what Maye had meant. A woman has a right to feel. Wing would not hurt her, he would help, was already doing so. His lips were invitation, his breath sweet. She felt sand in her hair, riding under her shirt and at her waistline.

Wing sensed that she encouraged his embrace. Then he thought she murmured something, the word "Once," but he was unsure. He asked what she'd said, whispered his question softly in her ear. She did not reply, knew if they began to speak, the moment would peel from him, the magician's cape pulled away too soon.

Wing rose to his knees. The tip of his queue was frosted white. He removed his shirt, but made no attempt at Addie's clothing. He wanted only to feel the double warmth of the sun on his back and Addie beneath him. Her cheek was patched white with sand, which he gently brushed away, as she moved herself to lie on the shirt he spread beneath her. He wanted nothing more than just this moment, to give the affection and respect Muuk refused her. There was a pressure now, though Addie couldn't tell from which of them it advanced. She reached up, took his queue in her hand, pulled its length through her fingers, appreciated its dense core and the contrast of lightness.

Wing recognized a form of panic in Addie's eyes, knew his own projected the same. But it wasn't just that; this was remorse and urgency poured forth, funneled together as passion. Spede, Addie thought, and what had he called her, Yun Sigh? Just this once, she told herself as she pulled him toward her.

EPISODE TWENTY-TWO

Addie was right. He couldn't stay in Dire, but there were some things he needed to say to her. Perhaps he wouldn't be leaving alone, which is why he packed and found himself approaching the small home he had arranged for her. It had a roof now, an assemblage of scavenged lumber and other pieces that caught the morning light like the mottled feathers of a rooster. Wing paused and considered the effect. It seemed appropriate. It was the year of the Wood Rooster, after all, and even if it wasn't Addie herself, the image made sense. A rooster is outspoken and the center of attention, attracts suitors, and, as Wing knew, is fiercely protective of those close to him. He knocked.

In a split second the door swung open as if Addie were expecting him. Her face was clean and bright and her hair tied back. "I figured you might come," she said, and though she wasn't smiling, Wing heard that she was pleased.

"Ah Joe is traveling me to Rock Springs today." He took off his cap. "I do not want to go."

Addie stepped outside and walked a few paces beyond the house, facing the downward slope of Dire Draw as she spoke. "I wish you didn't have to, but it's best." She'd put him in a terrible spot, she knew, but this was the only way. And there was no doubt it would be difficult. At first she might see him from time to time when she called on Rock Springs, but this period they enjoyed together needed to be over. She was certain his life depended on it.

Her back was to him, which he didn't like, not because he couldn't see Addie's face, which he knew better than his own, but because it forced him to see past her and toward the very direction he'd be leaving Dire. "Come with me," he said so suddenly his own words caught him off guard. Addie didn't face him. "I've saved my money. We can go anywhere."

There was something about the tone in his voice that reminded her of her brother, of the letter she'd gotten asking her to join him in Wyoming Territory. It was Tommy, in a way, who'd brought her and Wing together, and now as she turned, the pair seemed to be standing side by side, dreamers both. She hadn't been able to save her brother, but she wasn't going to allow a similar fate for Wing. She looked at him, this man with pleading eyes standing in front of the house he'd presented her. His hat was in his hands, and she noticed that he wore new clothes, blue as usual, but with sleeves down to his forearms. What she was about to say is not what she wanted. "Some things are best to just let be. If I tell you I can't go with you, it's because it's the best way we can take care of ourselves."

She felt cowardly saying it, hated to see Wing's increasingly solemn expression. He couldn't have been more solitary standing in front of her shack, in front of the very doorway he'd burst through when he performed his play. Only now, without a costume, he seemed stripped down, vulnerable.

"It doesn't seem the right decision," Wing said. "I have enough money we can go to California. Grow oranges." It was true. He had a small chest stuffed with all the money he managed to save. "We can go anywhere."

If she thought they couldn't be seen, if it wouldn't have made things worse, Addie would have hugged Wing just then. He was a good man; it was a shame more folks didn't know it, but they didn't and those were the facts. She approached him, as his head was lowered. "For us, Wing, there's no such thing as anywhere."

He looked in her eyes. They were sharp but sympathetic. "I would spend my life looking," he said. He did not want to kiss her one more time, or even hold her. They had done that, and it felt important, but that's not why he needed her. In all his life she was the first person who listened to him—to the important things, and the unimportant things as well. He was saying good-bye to the only true friend he had in the world and to the child he might never meet.

"That's just it," Addie sighed. "You'd *have* to spend your life looking. There's nowhere for us. They want every last one of you out of this country. I hear it. Even Tommy, rest his soul, even my own brother would have put you all back on a boat to China." She hated to say it, but it was true. In a strange way this territory with its anonymity of open space had opened this brief window for the two of them, and now it was closing tight.

"Sometimes I think we are already picking oranges," Wing said softly. He reached into his pocket and pulled out the one thing he wished to give Addie until he saw her again, a small brass locket. He handed it to her.

"What's this?"

"It is so we can never be apart."

The piece barely had weight in her palm, as if he'd handed her a bubble. She opened it. Behind a thumbnail-size glass oval was a lock of black hair. "Is this yours?"

"My brother cut it from me for bad luck, but it didn't work because my mother saved it like this."

"I can't take your luck, Wing."

"You're not taking it," he said. "You're sharing it."

She wished she'd thought to give him something, but perhaps this new start was just that. And too, she had just a few months to figure out what she was going to do, a few months where the weight of a baby inside her would keep her from pulling up stakes herself. It certainly wasn't possible for her to produce a child with Wing's face, a baby with hair the same color as in the locket she held. But these things she didn't tell him, or he would want to go with her.

Addie clutched the locket in her hand and extended the other, which Wing accepted. It was how they'd first met that day when she simply wanted to hire someone to work for her and Ah Joe mediated the deal. This was a new contract, a sadder one, and Addie watched their firmly gripped hands closely. The truth was, there was a time not too far off when it was certain they'd never see each other again. She felt unsteady, as if she were walking across a log over a creek, and as they released their hands from each other, she felt as if she was falling. "Wait," she said, her determination defeated. "I'll take you."

EPISODE TWENTY-THREE

She did it, delivered Wing to Ah Say and Ah Koon in Rock Springs. There were several times on the ride back when she reconsidered, almost turned Racer around and returned. But it would be selfish, she reminded herself, to return to Dire with Wing. How long could he possibly stay before they were found out? It would be all she could do to figure out how she was going to get by after the baby was born, a child that would look nothing like Muuk.

It would be dark before she could get home, but instead of riding back to Dire, she decided to use the remaining light to get to Maye, whose voice was what she needed most. And maybe it was time to tell Maye that Wing was the father of her unborn child. When she'd ridden to Rock Springs earlier that day, Wing's arms had been around her waist, and she felt his absence now. That, and the renewed sensation of smallness from riding on the plain. On that count, it was easier to keep her eyes on Racer's brindle mane, or on the not dissimilarly colored ground that passed beneath them, patches of brown and black and white, the earth's dried-out, crackling hide.

She was a few miles beyond Dire Draw when she pulled Racer up. Maybe twenty yards beyond and to their right was a gleaming domelike stone with two large spots that seemed to glare at her with dark soulless eyes. She focused, stilled Racer, then knew what she was looking at as she jumped off her ride, excited. When she was upon it, she knew she was right; it was a skull, and near it two long, narrow bones, but nothing else. Could it be an Eckonen, Brother Two? she asked herself as she walked a small perimeter. There was nothing else, no mule-like rib cage, no long jaw filled with ragged teeth. This person had died on his own.

She didn't lift the skull, but crouched to its level, the lower half buried. It was an odd thing, the human form stripped to the point where she couldn't make out if it was a man or a woman, a white or Chinese, or an Indian for that matter. The elements didn't make that distinction, had treated these bones indifferently, had baked and blown, rained on, and encased them as if they were no different than anything else that found its way to the plain floor. That was the truth, after all, Addie thought, though folks spent a lot of time trying to believe otherwise.

The thing to do, she decided, was to at least cover this poor soul with rock, not gawk at it as if something might be done to help. She placed the two longer bones on either side of the skull, then gathered enough stones to create a mound sufficient to cover it all, sturdy and thick enough to withstand the worst of each season. When she was done, she looked at her work, which had come out arrowhead-shaped. Maybe that was a sign. Or maybe it was Brother Two, and that story about his bones being found under a mule was just that, a story. If the latter were true, it was a shame, she thought. A person's history was worth more than the temporary pleasure of a good yarn. She said the same in a prayer, though she realized as she spoke, it was an easier thing to think than say out loud. When she was finished and still deciding if she'd done right by whomever she'd buried, she paused, had her only moment of real sadness over the discovery. It hadn't bothered her at all to come upon a person's bones. That was the Territory, she guessed, seeping in.

Back on Racer, Addie tipped her hat to the little grave and continued on to Maye's. But as she rode, she couldn't help wondering, if the hinny gave out beneath her just then, perhaps rolled and cracked Addie's back, what would they say if they found her bones and knew by her hat and rifle who it was? What story might they conjure that made folks lean in but wasn't altogether true? And what if there was no one living who knew her that might correct the record, and given her present circumstances, would she want them to?

"Yes," she said out loud. "Yes," then laughed at the vehement response to her own interrogation.

When she arrived near the Grood ranch she saw something new. Maye and her son Aulis were sitting outside at a makeshift table covered in a white cloth that fluttered near the ground as if it were swaying to music. Her belly large with a child that could come at any time, Maye sat across from Aulis, who wore a surprisingly clean blue shirt haphazardly tucked into his pants. Maye waved but did not stand as Addie approached on Racer. "Come have a piece of sugar pie," Maye called. "The husband's gone to Cheyenne."

It was unusual for a rancher. It seemed as if, fairly often, her husband wasn't around. At the table, Addie saw they were drinking coffee and eating slices of a thin pie with a dark filling. "What are you celebrating?"

"Pa found some coal," Aulis said brightly. It'd been two weeks since Addie had given the boy a riding lesson, and she felt guilty for the lapse.

"Aulis, shush," Maye said. "We're not to talk about it until Pa brings the man back." She looked at Addie, rolling her eyes. "Won't trust a soul about it except this man he knows in Cheyenne."

Sliding off Racer, Addie stood next to the table, Maye holding out a slice of pie. Addie waved it off and turned to Aulis, whose upper lip was covered in a mustache of crust. She thought to tell the two of them about the skull she'd found, knew it was the kind of story boys liked to hear. But she'd set that soul to proper rest with her prayer, however awkward, and it would be disrespectful to mention it. Instead, she offered Aulis Racer's reins. "Want to take him out for a bit?" In seconds, he was in Addie's hands, lifted into the saddle. When he trotted off, Addie sat in his place. Maye had one hand resting on her abdomen. Addie guessed the baby was kicking, and she wondered just when she might feel her own do the same. "What's all this about?" she said, looking at the outdoor spread of pie and coffee.

"Aulis' pa told him to take good care of me while he was away, so he got it into his mind to use up our sugar and molasses to make a pie."

"And the crust?"

"Said he knew how by watching me. So I let him at it just for the sport of watching." Maye looked like the happiest person in the world, plump and shiny skinned. She'd forgone a bonnet and let her hair fall wild. She loved being a mother, it was clear, loved being a wife. What would she think of Addie when she heard the truth about Wing?

Addie delayed, picked up a fork and nipped a bite-size piece from the pie, which didn't want to give way in her mouth, and seemed to fight her tongue. It was grainy, and tasted strong. Black-strap molasses, she guessed.

Before Addie rendered judgment, Maye laughed. "Trust me," Maye said, "the only reason I made coffee was to melt that pie down my throat." Addie hadn't come to talk about pie, and she guessed it showed on her face. "What brings you out, Miss Addie?"

"I took Wing into Rock Springs today. And . . ." It was something she needed to say, but as well as she knew Maye, she wasn't sure how it would go over. She took a deep breath and looked into what was left of the sugar pie. "You told me once I had a right to feel, and for a bit I followed your advice." She brought her eyes up to meet Maye's. "Muuk isn't the father. It's Wing."

Maye gasped, bringing her hands to her cheeks. "The China-man? Dear God." She looked out at the plain where Aulis was gal-loping Racer. "If he comes back, you can't let on what you just told me. You can't tell a soul."

"I'm telling the only soul I trust." It was true. In her life there was Maye and Wing, and he already knew what she'd just revealed. When she told Wing, his reaction was wide-eyed and impossibly bright. She'd not meant it as good news, but he took it that way, pulled her close and thanked her. "I thought I would die without leaving a future," he'd said. When Addie argued the pregnancy wasn't a good thing, he scoffed. "How can the child from an angel be bad?"

Maye looked agitated but controlled, thrumming her fingers on the table. "Miss Addie," she said directly, "don't doubt I love you like a little sister. But what you done ain't right. Not for you or Muuk, or whatever type child'll come out of this. Folks'll go to hell for less." She seemed to grow angry. "We're not to mix, the Celestials and white. It ain't in the order of things. What you done is wrong, and I can't get my head around it just now."

It was painful to hear Maye's vehemence, but it wasn't entirely unexpected. "I can't get my head around it either, which is why I'm here asking for advice. Like I said, it was you told me I had a right to feel, and I listened. So if I'm hell-bound, it was you put me on the path."

Maye looked like a rabbit in lamplight, frightened and cautious, but on the precipice of decision. She tapped her nose, took several breaths, for a full minute stared down at her own pregnant belly. Addie waited. Finally, Maye spoke. "First thing is, I'm here." She caught Addie's eyes and held them. "Second thing is pure truth. There's no telling what that child will look like. But you can be sure it ain't going to look any kin to your husband."

"I seen mixed come out beautiful in Kentucky," Addie said.

"But were they accepted by folks?"

On that point, Addie had to concede. Those she'd known with white fathers were thought of just the same, colored, niggers. Certainly there was a name for the child she would bear soon, though she had no idea what word would be used.

"One thing's sure," Maye said sternly. "You can't be seeing that Chinaman again, or it'll just make it worse on yourself."

Addie nodded. "I already told him that. It's done with, but it ain't right because he was a good friend." She lowered her head and began to cry.

"Oh, Miss Addie," Maye said, "you didn't fall in love with that Chinaman?"

She shook her head, blotted her eyes with the tablecloth. "It's love," she said, "but not the kind you're thinking. It ain't like anything I known. And what got me in this condition ain't anything to do with it either. We quit that. He told me once I made him feel good because he had someone besides himself to care for. I suppose I felt the same."

Maye offered a strange sigh, like a person locked out of the house and suddenly let in. "That part I understand. Aulis and I are that way, though his father is another story. Like with this baby of ours. He ought to be here." She struggled to her feet and came around the table behind Addie, putting her hands on her crying friend's shoulders. "Best thing for you, Miss Addie, is to go where there's Chinamen might help you. California. Maybe this child can have a chance there. But the Territory? Even if you leave Muuk, I can't think of a safe corner for you out here."

Maye's grip on Addie's shoulders was strong and comforting, and what she said made sense. "I'm sorry I disappointed you," Addie said.

"You have, and then some," Maye said, softly patting Addie on the back. "But that don't mean I don't understand or want harm to come to you. It don't mean you won't be first in my prayers."

She'd gotten a taste of it. Maye's first reaction was enough to confirm that it would be impossible for her to stay in the Territory. She looked at Aulis and Racer way off, the pair struck golden by the lowering sun, wondered if someday he'd be out on the plain, or anyone for that matter, and find the stone grave she'd made, maybe kick it over to reveal the skull that might revive the Eckonen story, or start a new one altogether. These were things out of her control.

Once Aulis got his own horse, there wasn't a place he couldn't ride if he had a mind to. It was a kind of freedom unique to men and boys, certain men and boys, and she envied them. But there was a territory no man could enter, she knew. She raised a hand to Maye's, held it tight, and said, "I want to be a mother."

EPISODE TWENTY-FOUR

He'd written down the date like he had every day in the month since Addie left him in Rock Springs and rode alone back to Dire: September 2, 1885. He could have run, fled to the hills in the east like many of the others, but Wing was convinced the trouble would pass. The white miners would calm. In any case, it was too late to leave. He had barricaded himself in his barrack and gone into the narrow underground space dug below. The light from three dim lamps threw cramped shadows in multiples, as if the burrowed room was populated by more than just one man.

Even from his concealed space he heard terrible things, gun-shots, men screaming for their lives, other men, white men, calling for blood. It was difficult enough for these men, Chinese and white, to get along. How could they look each other in the eyes after this?

Earlier that day there'd been more than a hint of trouble, but Rock Springs was larger than Dire, and he'd been there such a short time he wasn't sure if the tension was normal, especially because the other Chinese didn't seem particularly concerned. Around noon one of the mine superintendents rode through Chinatown. Wing didn't know him personally, but he seemed sympathetic to the Chinese, warned them about a fight that had broken out in one of the mines. "Ain't ever seen it get this hot," the man said to Ah Koon from atop his horse.

Ah Koon helped the UP keep the Chinese in order, wore an oversize fur coat, and generally acted more important than Wing thought he had the right. "I tell all the China boys," Ah Koon said.

Worry still showed in the superintendent's bearded face, and he didn't appear to listen to Ah Koon, or perhaps didn't believe him. "Best tell your men to be on guard." But no angry mob descended, and Chinatown was far enough away from the main part of Rock Springs that the warning soon seemed unfounded. Even the air, which was cool and drizzly, boded the unlikelihood of an attack.

Wing was mincing pork when he heard the first shots around two o'clock. It sounded like hammering at first, then the random multiples gave it away for what it was. Five or six Chinese men ran into Chinatown, and behind them, a horde of white men and a few women with raised arms, the ones at the rear listing and stumbling. There were too many to count, maybe a hundred, two hundred? Most carried guns. Their movement was slow, and they walked in an odd formation, thin columns at either end with the bulk of them in the center, reminding Wing of a snake after it's swallowed a rat. He understood the ones speaking in English, screaming, "Take back our territory! Take back our jobs."

Wing found his heart beating faster as he checked the expressions of the other Chinese who had come to face the trouble. All of them seemed perplexed, with some calling back with their own taunts. Wing knew better, understood they would have no recourse if the mob's guns came into play, and that couldn't happen. Couldn't. Addie was in Dire, but he was sure when she found out what was happening, she'd ride into Rock Springs, and then there was no telling what kind of danger she'd be in if she found him dead and tried to take matters into her own hands.

And besides, he'd already decided it was not right for them to be apart, no matter how much she feared her husband might go after Wing. There was a way for the friendship, he was sure. He thought he had time to figure out how, but now the approaching crowd threatened his plans. He gripped his cleaver tightly and fixed his gaze solidly as the mob of angry miners stopped at the edge of Bitter Creek, milled in angry pods. Three men crossed the wood bridge into Chinatown, where they stood and waited. A light drizzle had darkened their clothes and laid down their beards, glossed their angry faces. One of them called out, "You yellow devils got one hour to pack up and get out of town." They stood their ground, surveying for a response, which came in the form of a red flag that went up over the joss house. The three men turned, and then all of Chinatown became a scramble.

Wing stood above the pork he'd been preparing. He'd not been told what the red flag meant, but the way it rolled in the slight breeze didn't convey the urgency that was evident below. He scanned the mob to see if they looked to keep their word, and what he found was Muuk's angry blue eyes and hard stare. Muuk stepped to the side of the crowd, never taking his eyes off Wing, spitting on the ground in front of him. It was just more proof that Addie needed Wing. An hour, Wing thought. It was enough time to gather what he could and head back to Dire. He would find Addie and show her the money he'd saved. He hadn't wanted to leave her in the first place, but now she couldn't deny the urgency. And if she did, he would stand his ground. It would not be a proposal of marriage, but a proposal of service. If she said no, he would repeat it.

The pork lay in a minced heap in front of him, and Wing popped the blade of his cleaver into its center. Ah Leo ran to his side and grabbed Wing's elbow. "What are you waiting for?" Ah Leo said in English. "Get to your quarters until they calm down."

Wing kept to his resolve not to let on to anyone but Addie that he spoke English, remained silent until Ah Leo repeated himself in Chinese.

"They will not calm," Wing said.

Ah Leo was older, had gray in his brows, and muscles around his eyes that punctuated every word he spoke. "The UP will hold them off. And remember, we are more than them."

It was true, there were many more Chinese than whites, but the latter had the advantage of firearms. When Wing told Ah Leo of needing to get back to his former employer, Addie, the man laughed. "If you try to leave alone, you will be beaten or shot or both. And then what good will your money do this woman?"

Wing listened, understood that Ah Leo's was the more rational approach, though his heart pulled him the other way. He would stay, he decided, but he would not let this event pass without utility. It had confirmed where his heart was. After things calmed down, he told himself, he would not stay in Rock Springs another day. "If something happens to me," Wing said, "go to Dire and give my things to Miss Addie through Ah Cheong."

Ah Leo agreed, though he expressed confusion about why Wing felt so obligated to this woman who had merely been Wing's boss.

When he returned to his barracks, he was surprised to find it nearly emptied. His bunk mates had bundled their belongings and were carrying them to another building where their gathered numbers might give them a chance against the mob. Wing decided the opposite, that a barrack which appeared empty was a less inviting target. He closed the door and shoved what little there was against it. The air was starting to cool beyond comfort, and he wanted to heat the stove, but thought perhaps the smoke would draw attention if the mob attacked. No, he would sit in the dim, windowless room and wait, prop open the trapdoor in case he needed to get below quickly. Positioning himself in the corner opposite the door, Wing leaned his head against a wall, listened as Chinatown fell into a silence even more deep than at night.

Closing his eyes, he thought of Addie, saw her on Racer, smiled at that hair of hers, the reddish color that had so intrigued him when he first saw her coming up the draw with Tommy. That had been just a little more than a year earlier, but it felt to Wing as if he'd known her all his life, and maybe that was because his life seemed to have really begun when they met. Why was it an impossible dream to imagine making a home with her? Hadn't they already had a successful partnership?

It was almost precisely an hour when another round of gunfire announced that the mob was going to keep its promise. He heard them scatter to all corners of Chinatown with furious volleys of gunfire. Pursued men ran by his barrack, yelling for their lives. Wing had one thing on his mind; he had to safeguard the small chest of money he saved, not out of greed, but for Addie. He would keep it buried until Rock Springs calmed down.

Before he could get below, the pounding started, not at his door, but across the alley. Then came a great crack of wood, and Ah Leo's cries for help as he was pulled from the building. Wing didn't know what to do. He looked at the open trapdoor, but Ah Leo's pleas and the thud of struck flesh outside pulled at him, made him thrust aside his barricade and fling open the door. Two men stood above Ah Leo, who lay on the sloppy ground, bloodied. Both of the attackers were filthy, their clothes smeared with mud. They were kicking Ah Leo in the sides, spitting and yelling. "Told you bastards to get out. Told you," one of them said as he bent down and sliced off Ah Leo's queue.

The one with the knife looked prepared to do more than cut hair. Wing ran out the door, caught the man's arm on the backswing, and startled the weapon from his grip. He picked up the knife and stood directly above Ah Leo, thrust the blade at the pair, lunged at them and struck one of them in the hand. For a split second time seemed to freeze as all four men watched the shiny blood seep from the gash, as if an invisible brush had made a thick stroke of red paint. The man looked at Wing, astonished. Wing thrust again as a warning, and the pair fled.

"Get inside," Wing said, looking around. He could hear other rioters around them, but they were out of sight. "Inside," Wing repeated, helping Ah Leo struggle to his feet. His face was an almost unrecognizable canvas of smeared earth, and blood drooled from his nose.

"No," Ah Leo groaned. "We must leave. Take nothing. They are killing." He was in no shape to run, Wing thought, but that's what he did, surprised Wing with a limping trot. "Now," Ah Leo called over his shoulder back to Wing. "Now." He was almost run over as a man, his wife, and his daughter ran out from behind one of the buildings and headed in the same direction as Ah Leo. They were one of the few Chinese families in Rock Springs, and they seemed so out of place with events around them, the blank-faced girl in pink silk looking directly at Wing as her terrified parents ran out of Chinatown.

That's when Wing saw it, the hills beyond studded with dozens and dozens of his fleeing cohort, like blue beads defying gravity, rolling uphill. His heart thudded in his chest and he felt his grip on the knife pulse as well. He would have to join those running away, but he was not leaving without the money he planned for Addie. He was halfway through the trapdoor when he heard them, the two men he'd fought, plus a few other voices. Hurrying down, he pulled the door over him, crawling across the low-ceilinged room to the corner where he'd stashed his small chest of savings. The dirt space where he crouched was covered with a thin straw mat, and its earthen walls muffled the sounds from outside. The men had reached his barrack, one of them stepping just inside, the sound of his boots on the wood floor ominous as thunder. Wing froze, waited for more footsteps. He still held the knife. "Musta run with the other devils," a man said, stepping away. The voices of those he was with peaked, then moved away as if carried by a current.

What was his next move—climb out and make a run for it? If he did that, carrying with him the money he intended for Addie, and if he was caught, she would get nothing. No, he would wait until night at least, escape under cover of darkness. The mob would certainly exhaust themselves, or the UP would surely step in. When he'd first met Ah Say and his assistant Ah Koon upon arriving in the Territory, they'd made a point to emphasize how the Railroad protected its Chinese. It was something he already knew, but now he understood why they belabored the point, and also that they were wrong.

EPISODE TWENTY-FIVE

Earlier that day none of this seemed possible to Addie. It was late afternoon, cool, flat September clouds patterning the sky in frayed strips like white rags. Muuk was working his room at the mine, while Addie spent the day chinking alkali mud and straw into the seams of their cabin. She wanted to be prepared. Soon enough little bits of winter would nip at them, darting in like a clever jay stealing at a windowsill pie. It would come slow at first, but not too far off it would be all winter. You can afford to share the crust of a pie with a bird, but you can't give in to winter one inch, or you're lost.

These days she kept her mind on such tasks because it was necessary, and because it kept her from thinking about Wing. It had been just over a month since she sent him away for his own good. Addie stepped back from the cabin to inspect her work. That Muuk would be free of draft all winter, she was certain. That she would not be with him, she was equally confident.

She climbed to the roof, which was makeshift shingling of her own design. Wing had helped her gather the materials, odd bits of tin, smashed-flat cans, scraps of wood, and here and there, thin flats of stone. From a distance it looked calico, but standing directly above it, Addie didn't think it was pretty as all that, though it was good and tight and certainly better than what most of Dire was sleeping under. Only the Beckwith Quinn & Company store, she ventured, might have it better. Her roof wouldn't rain in, or fall in. Muuk could sit in his own gloom all winter without fear of that, a fact that didn't erase the guilt she felt for what she was really doing. It wasn't right, leaving her husband, but it was what was best for the two of them. Maybe that was the reasoning her mother had used when she left their family all those years back. Addie wasn't yet sure where she was going or how she would get there, except she'd go without a word. She wouldn't even leave a note—not to be cruel, but because Muuk couldn't read English.

Addie looked out at the camp, though some were starting to call it a town. It was all too familiar and close to the bone: the treeless, flowerless hills, clumps of bachelor huts and dugouts along the gully walls, the wooden tipple that brought to mind a long-legged circus giraffe she'd once seen in a book. She reminded herself that it wasn't the kind of place people would live if it weren't for the fact that the ground beneath them was pregnant with coal.

The familiar clatter of Maye's wagon played behind her. It was a surprise visit, especially given that Maye was expecting her baby in short order. But there she was atop the buckboard, larger, but that same proud woman Addie met out on the sage plain. She wore a yellow dress Addie hadn't seen before, with a bonnet to match. When she was fully alongside the cabin, Maye looked up at Addie on the roof and smiled. "Not sure how much longer I can make it over this way," she said. "Thought I'd check on you."

"Pretty dress."

Maye inspected herself. "The husband saved up some money and sent away for it. Had to let it out, of course, but by God, can you believe he did something nice?" She patted her belly. "Not sure if he's caring for me or his new little ranch hand, but I'll take the kindness anyhow."

"Always in short supply," Addie said, and then she fell silent because it hadn't felt that way when Wing was in Dire.

"Miss Addie?" Maye was looking directly in her eyes. "You holding up?"

"Sure," Addie said. "Thinking things through." She paused and took a breath and looked around to be sure they weren't in earshot of anyone. "Truth is, I don't guess I'll be in Dire much longer."

Maye didn't look surprised. "You and Muuk headed out?" When no answer came, Maye closed her eyes and nodded. Addie wondered what she was picturing. "The husband brought the preacher by the other day," Maye said, opening her eyes. She pointed out at the draw. "For some reason they got to talking about how all this must have been just like what Moses walked through during his trials. Don't know what got into me, but I reminded them what he put his wife through, and it was that same poor old Zipporah saved his life when God got angry."

It wasn't clear to Addie what meaning Maye was trying to say. "Not sure me leaving is any comparison."

"Miss Addie," Maye said in a tone like what she was about to offer was something she wouldn't say to another soul, "if ever there was a woman to take matters into her own hands, it's you. Do what it takes to be happy."

There was no time to take in Maye's advice. A man's voice came from below and behind the cabin. "Miss Addie!" It was Ah Cheong, a firecracker of a man who spoke and moved as if everything he said or did must be completed with a sense of urgency. It was he, in fact, who had waved her down outside Dire not long after she'd arrived. He heard her talking to her brother and took exception to the way they referred to the Chinese miners. "We are not any of those things you call us," he said without introduction. Looking at him from atop her brother's hinny back then, she didn't bother to introduce herself nor ask for his name. What did it matter? To her they all looked the same. "And what do you think you ought to be called?" He set his hands at his waist and shook his head as if there were no good options. "Chinese. But you will say Chinamen."

Now she knew Ah Cheong by name, and he was yelling to her from the back side of the cabin. "Miss Addie! Something bad in Rock Springs."

Though Ah Cheong was agitated and shining with nervous sweat, Addie was not immediately concerned. She looked at Maye and shrugged. Perhaps it was another mine cave-in or some such, she thought as she climbed down from the roof. She'd been through so much during the previous year, it was pretty certain whatever it was wouldn't be as urgent as Ah Cheong made it out to be. And if it was, Wyoming Territory was the kind of place that would pick-pocket your heart if you didn't keep your head about you. She knew from experience. "What's wrong?" she asked calmly.

"A big fight in the mine between us and the white men."

Addie paused, stuck on the word "us." Ah Cheong, she understood, was not just speaking about the Chinese; he had included her, and she knew why. "Oh," she said with a clipped gasp, looking again at Maye. "Wing's in trouble."

"Go," Maye said.

Addie didn't wait for an elaboration from Ah Cheong, got off the roof and ran for the corral, down through the grit of Dire, where Racer stood in the company of a bony white goat that kept the draft animals calm. Something was brewing for sure, as the horse and four mules that usually stood with Racer were gone. Red-nosed and drunk, Dolphus Bend called to her from beneath the eaves of the slim barn next door. "Where you headed? Going for Muuk, or that Chinaman of yours?"

Addie ran over and grabbed him by the shirt. "Muuk went to Rock Springs?"

"With a coupl'a the others." Dolphus offered a peppery smile.

In no time Addie had Racer saddled and was coursing down Dire Draw toward Rock Springs as fast as the willing hinny would go. She wasn't sure exactly what the men would do in Rock Springs, but she had an idea. Just two nights earlier a member of the Knights of Labor from Rock Springs held a meeting for the white miners in Dire. He'd parked his wagon on the road running through camp, lit two torches on either side of him, and after he gathered a crowd, started in about how the coolies were taking away the white man's God-given right to make a living. Half his all-white audience didn't speak English, but it didn't seem to matter.

He was a thin man with a loud, reasonable-sounding voice that came from behind a mustache that nearly covered his entire mouth. "The railroad brings in these coolies to drive down wages and force you all out," he said. There had been a general nodding all along, but this last part encouraged shouts of agreement. "I'm telling you what the KoL won't. Ain't one man here alone can stand against capital and these heathen Celestials taking food out of your mouths. But together we can stand up against anyone or anything." The cheers grew louder, just as loudly from the men who didn't even understand a word of what was being said. Taking off his hat and holding it in front of him in a way that looked almost humble, the man's voice grew louder. "Three years ago our congress told

China, 'Stop sending your rats to our shores.' Three years, and yet you all are still suffering. Action's what's needed, and the Knights of Labor won't quit until we get fair wages, even if it means driving every last coolie out of every last mine." Now the crowd was cheering fiercely and thrusting fists into the air. If he'd told them to, they would have taken off right then and burned down Little San Fran.

Addie didn't like it one bit. She'd watched Muuk take part in the frenzy, grow pinched-faced even for the things being said she was sure he didn't comprehend. She saw the anger in him rise even when Aatami Ukkola didn't lean over and translate in Muuk's ear. These were hard times for the white miners to be sure, but the man from the Knights of Labor was turning every one of them into cornered rattlesnakes. The Chinamen were no saints, she understood, but what man was? As far as she was concerned, it was the Union Pacific that wasn't doing right by anyone, and that was the problem. You can't shoot a railroad.

It was a too-long ride to Rock Springs, delayed by the dazed and injured Chinese man she'd come across a mile outside town. She tried to help, but he refused, though he at least stumbled off toward the railroad tracks as she'd urged. When she finally arrived in Rock Springs, she barely recognized the town, backlit by fire, smelling of smoke. A man in a black apron stood with a rifle in the doorway of a saloon, while dozens were gathered in the street, some clustered in conspiratorial groups, others standing alone, yelling at the top of their lungs in a chorus that included languages she didn't understand. What did come to her ears, clear as hawks calling over a corn field, was "Kill the coolies," and "The Chinese must go!" One of this screaming mob was a hatchet-nosed woman who looked to be in her late twenties. She wore a brown bonnet and an oversize dress of the same color. In one arm she cradled an infant in a wool blanket, the other arm raised and punctuated in a fist as she goaded the men on the street to take up arms. Her face was flushed red, the fierce shine in her eyes like bullets on end, and though her baby cried, she did nothing to calm it. "You going to let a bunch of yellow-faces take what's yours?" she yelled at a man crossing near her, but he was so involved in his own anger, he didn't respond.

Addie turned Racer in front of the woman, snapping her out of her rant, at least for the moment. "What's happened?" Addie asked, hoping for more information than she'd learned from the wounded Chinaman.

"Finally got their comeuppance," the woman growled. "Them damn coolies was up to the mine stealing rooms again, and for once our men stood up to 'em."

The woman's voice was too gravelly and angry for someone so young, Addie thought, and she didn't like being included in the phrase "our men." From somewhere beyond came the repeated crack of struck lumber, soon replaced by horrific cheers and a single gunshot. Her heart racing, Addie slid off Racer, holding him close with the reins. The street was muddy, which surprised her. She'd been so anxious to ride in she hadn't paid attention to the chilled and spitty weather, the wetness adding to the town's fiery sheen. "How many was it?" Addie asked the woman. Behind them the crowd grew louder, and the woman kept looking over Addie's shoulder as if she feared missing something.

"From what I hear, pretty much everyone in the mine joined in," the woman said, pulling the edge of the blanket over her baby's face. "At first it was three damned coolies stoled a room that was just ready to work, and when our men showed up, the coolies told them to get out. So they commenced to fight, and then some other coolies come up from behind and attacked. Then some more of our men came in."

The light was dimming, and the smoky air carried a sourness like rancid meat. Down the street a few men were throwing whatever they could get their hands on at the Beckwith Quinn & Company store. All of Rock Springs was raw as a lanced blister, a brawl of shifting targets. She'd never felt so unsteady in her life, so unsure if there was a living soul left to trust. "It don't make sense," Addie said almost to herself, but not quite.

"It sure do," the woman said. "And we ran 'em all out of town, though you know there's still a few rats hiding in their opium dens." Then the woman offered a proud brown smile and looked at the swaddled child in her arms. "I'll tell you what. I wasn't about to let the Partridge name go to shame. I beat one myself. I caught that little coolie by his hair right here in the street and I thrashed him. Set Patrick here down on the ground and used my fist and my feet both." The woman walked a step closer to Addie. "It was like punching a pillow. They ain't got no bones inside."

Addie wanted to put her boot in the woman's face. She was surely close enough. But she didn't. She wanted to tell her she knew for a fact that Chinamen were just like them. She'd seen the fractured end of a leg bone sticking out of a Chinaman's skin, felt his ribs pressing her shoulder as she carried him to safety. She knew even more than that, but didn't speak it. She couldn't. Her fists trembled at her sides.

The woman began to elaborate on her feat just as another flare of orange went up beyond the edge of town, then another. The crowd knew what it was, more fire in Chinatown, and they rushed in that direction. The woman ran without saying another word, and Addie hitched Racer to a post, taking off toward the fire as well.

She didn't get far. Running past a stack of crates, she saw the zip of a queue as it slid into the fray of wood. She stopped and looked around, then peered into the stack, hoping Wing's eyes would meet her own. What she found was fear in a different Chinese face smudged with dirt. She put a finger to her lips, then whispered, "Stay here. I'll come back for you." The man nodded, but she found suspicion in his expression. "Trust me," she said. "I'm a friend of Wing Lee. Do you know him?" She looked around again to make sure she wasn't attracting attention. Most everyone had run toward the fires.

"I do know," the man replied.

Addie's heart jumped in her chest. "Can you tell me where he is?"

"He run," the man offered uncertainly, his statement punctuated by a distant gunshot.

"I hope he did," Addie said. She wished this man could do the same, but if he made a break for it, she guessed he'd be set upon. She needed to find Wing, was already delayed by helping the man she met right outside of town, but it wasn't in her to leave this man on his own either. "Wait here," she said, not knowing exactly what she was about to do. When she turned, she saw Racer where he was tethered, and a man in a suit trying to mount, a man who clearly had no experience with horses. She ran back and grabbed him by the collar. He had one foot caught in the stirrup, was red-faced and puffy, sweating, and a shock of his bright silver hair swung over one eye. She guessed he was drunk. "This is my ride," Addie said.

"They're going to skin me alive if I don't get out of town." He had a raspy voice, was so out of breath he could barely produce enough air to form words, and he didn't smell of alcohol after all.

She helped his foot out of the stirrup. "No," Addie said, "they're after the Chinese."

"Young lady," the man panted, "some of them got the idea I'm mixed up with bringing in the Chinamen. I just come in from Evanston on the wrong day, and they about strung me up. It was luck called them off. They found some Chinaman to pounce on instead. But one of them looked me up and down and said I better not be around when they come back."

She'd sent Wing into a powder keg. "Why didn't the UP do something?"

"If you don't mind," the man said, "I don't have time to be telling bedtime stories. But I'll say this. Don't know what the UP could've done. I was standing right here on the street this morning when some men came marching down the street yelling, 'White men, fall in.' There was a meeting at the Knights of Labor hall, where I guess all sorts of grievances were laid out against the Chinese. Then half the town got so drunk they closed the saloons. Wasn't long before a Chinaman got rousted out of the pumphouse, and they shot him in the back. Hell, there was women shooting at the Chinamen scrambling up the creek bank. Fish in a barrel." The man reached into his coat pocket and pulled out a thin leather billfold. "Given my situation, I'll take this animal off your hands for a fifty-dollar banknote," he said, pulling out one corner of the bill for proof. "Been more blood spilled here today then a person ought to see in a lifetime, an' I don't wish to add mine to it."

She'd come for Wing, but Addie knew what she had to do first. Since her first day in Wyoming it seemed as if nearly every moment was a detour from the thing she meant to do, to the point she figured that's just what folks in the Territory called living. "Won't take your money," she said. "But I'll saddle you up if you take some-one with you."

"Who?"

"Fella in a spot same as you."

It was like cutting off a limb to give up one's horse, but it had to be done. With no little effort she helped the bulky man onto Racer's back, then realized the reins were tethered just as she'd left them. If this man had managed to mount before Addie returned, he wouldn't have gone anywhere. "You've never been on a horse."

The man pushed away the silver hair covering his eye. "I've seen folks ride."

Maybe it wasn't going to work like she wanted. She quickly led Racer to where she had discovered the man hiding among the crates. Her new charge cupped his hands around his face, an action Addie chose not to point out made him no less conspicuous. Damp with perspiration in the cool weather, Addie's face stung as she pulled Racer as fast as she could. At their destination she whispered to the Chinese man. "You know how to ride a horse?"

"I very yes," he said.

She removed her hat and coat and explained he was to wear them and ride Racer and his silver-haired companion out of town. When things calmed down, he could return Racer in Dire. "Wait," the man on the hinny said. "You expect me to grab hold of a Chinaman and ride off with him to who knows where? He'll do me in sure."

Addie threw her coat and hat into the crates, then approached the man on Racer, got so close beneath him she felt the heat coming off his fat thigh. "I don't expect nothing of the sort," Addie said. "You just slide down, and I'll let him ride off on his own." The man furrowed his brow but didn't speak. "That's what I thought," Addie said.

The man crossed his arms and looked to the end of town, where the fires were going strong, the sound of it like hundreds of flags whipping in an angry wind. "It ain't right," the man mustered, "you putting my life in the hands of a Chinaman."

Addie stepped back and gave him a hard look. "Best be careful," she said, "before I agree with you and put you off my ride." She turned and told the Chinese man to hurry, and he scrambled out of the crates wearing Addie's coat and hat, both of which were slightly too big, almost like a boy wearing his father's clothes, but the more of him that was concealed the better, she figured. She locked her fingers and hoisted him up in front of his scowling companion, who merely pinched at the coat on each side, reluctant to take hold. She knew that would change once they got up to a full trot. The Chinese man clicked Racer to a start, and in a few feet had a pair of arms wrapped tight around his waist.

Addie watched as Racer took the two men away. He could ride a horse all right, she thought, steeling herself against what she felt as she saw the last of what she had left of her brother head out of town. It was two lives saved at quite a price, but none too soon. There was blood in the air. She could feel its heat, as if all of hell were caravanning right through the center of town. Which is what it would take, she thought, Satan himself, to keep her from finding Wing and keeping him safe. The image of him, the urgency of the moment, inflated inside her once again, and she was off toward the fires.

Most of the crowd had stopped at the edge of Bitter Creek, and it looked as if the entire town had shown up. Addie pushed her way through the mob, her ears filling with cries of "Burn 'em!" When she got to the front, nearly all of Chinatown was ablaze, the early evening sky pluming with smoke made yellow by the flames and the half moon looking like a face turning away from the men setting fires. Would she have been on time if she hadn't helped those others? It was clear that all the Chinese here were gone, dead, maybe Wing too, and as this latter thought took hold in her mind, Addie's own anger grew. A jeering man next to her held a rifle under his arm. "Smell that?" he asked. "Figure we got a passel of 'em trapped in their burrows. That there is the sweet smell of roasted Chinamen." On rage-driven impulse Addie snatched the rifle and ran toward the bridge. A collective whoop exploded at the sight of a woman taking up arms. There had been another moment, in Dire, when she heard a similar sound from behind her, when white miners were actually cheering *for* Chinamen, but now that moment was stolen away in columns of smoke.

Addie started across the bridge without a plan or thought of what she might prevent. But as far as she was concerned, aside from her brother, Wing was the only man in the Territory worth saving. She was rushing headlong toward a field of flame, where some of the buildings had already been reduced to cinderous rectangles flat to the ground. A little more than halfway over the bridge, a single voice behind her cut its way through the angry choir. "Get your coolie, Miss Addie." It was Aatami, and that meant Muuk was not far off for sure. Certainly only the three of them knew what he meant. Addie turned to find their faces but saw only Aatami standing in front at the edge of the crowd, glaring out of his stubbly face. The entire mob looked just like the way her grandmother had described hell, the light from the fire seeming to both sustain them and tie them to the spot. Addie's own shadow jittered in front of her, and suddenly she felt the weight of a weapon in her hand. Behind her, heat from the fire pressed at her back. The sound of flames and calls from the angry crowd felt like two train engines pushing at Addie from opposite sides. She was too late this time, and she knew it. She took one step forward, away from the burning mass of Chinatown, and the crowd jeered their disapproval. She wondered what they would do if she raised the rifle right then and scanned it along their ranks. Would they be more startled by the black eye of the barrel, or the fact that one of their own was facing them down?

That's when she felt it, the punch to the gut that dropped her to her knees. The part of the crowd that saw what happened grew silent, and two men ran across the bridge to Addie, got under her arms, and pulled her back, her boots futtering over the planks the entire way. She could hardly breathe for the shock of heat blistering her insides, and she felt it palpably, being pulled in the wrong direction, away from Wing. It was like the tearing of flesh. Addie's vision began to fuzz and darken as the crowd parted to let her through. Images flashed in her mind, a white-faced woman with red lips and a house being lowered around her, small flames like starlight in a collapsed mine, her husband's sad blue eyes on their wedding night.

She felt someone lift her legs. She was floating parallel to the ground, her head rolling to one side. The storefronts were liquid darkness swirled with orange. That's when she caught a glimpse of him, standing behind a wagon, watching her being carried away. It was the last thing she saw that night.

EPISODE TWENTY-SIX

Time passed slowly. It was the silent intervals that frightened Wing most because it meant that anything might happen next, gave no clue as to whether it was all right to come out early from his hiding place. From his position, the light escaping through the trapdoor leading up to the ground floor of the barracks looked like a sliver of moon, made him smile despite the chaos above. It made him remember one of his great disappointments as a child, during the Moon Festival when much of their family had come to stay with them. As they enjoyed mooncakes, Wing proudly announced that he had cataloged every moon he saw in the sky. "Is that so?" his father said with a raised eyebrow. His father wore a bright new outfit of black silk acquired just for that year's festival. "And how many are there?" Wing produced a scroll from behind his back, on which he'd drawn all the moons he observed over many weeks' time.

The family continued with their tea and mooncakes as Wing's

father opened the scroll and studied it. There were twenty-four separate objects, beginning with the thinnest curve, gradually thickening to a full moon, then back again to a curve. Wing bit into his pastry, waiting for his father's evaluation. He squished the lotus seed paste between his tongue and the roof of his mouth, savoring his mother's inclusion of salted duck egg. "This is quite impressive," his father said, showing the images to the rest of the table, the family applauding.

"But, Father, I have just one question," Wing said. "On which moon does Chang Er dance?" He had heard the story many times, about the woman whose husband shot down all the suns but one, and she drank an elixir that allowed her to fly to the moon.

"How do you mean, son?" his father asked.

"If there are twenty-four moons revolving around the earth," Wing repeated, "which one did Chang Er fly to?" The table erupted in laughter, his father once again holding up Wing's scroll of a hand-drawn moon cycle. When his father explained that there was just one such celestial object, and Wing realized that the family's laughter was directed at him, he snatched the scroll and bolted from the table, swearing to himself he would never forgive them for the humiliation.

Lying now beneath his barrack in Rock Springs with his fate unknown, he thought of that young version of himself, how children can find tragedy in even the smallest slight. His father's good-natured correction had been humiliating enough. Wing swore then he would never speak another word to any family member. If only that Wing could see his adult form in his present danger.

These thoughts, the comparison, reinforced the urgency of his current situation, and he returned to the necessity of safeguarding the wood chest meant for Addie and their child. Instead of fleeing with it, he would bury it in the wall, and if he could define his life by one desire, it was that he would see Addie's face again and find that burying the chest was an unnecessary precaution. He clenched his teeth, willing these things to come true, but as he stashed the chest in a narrow hole dug into the wall, backfilling it with dirt, pounding started above, on the walls. He had lit three small lamps and now blew two of them out, upbraiding himself for not thinking about any light they might give off above. But if anyone detected it, surely they would have discovered him by now.

He could tell that it was almost dark outside. Again gunshots, and more pounding, then a strange halt to the barrage before a new sound emerged. At first he wasn't sure, but it sounded as if they were prying through the wood. That couldn't be right, though, the cracking was too timid. He thought to peek above, but it wasn't necessary by the time the smoke came to him, serpentlike.

Sinking farther back in his underground room, Wing understood it was over, stilled his fast-beating heart. He faced the lone shadow cast by the remaining lamp, a silhouette surrounded by a sepia moon. In this dark form, instead of his own, he placed Addie's face, made her Chang Er, saw her as clearly as if she were right next to him, the auburn hair and freckles, the confident green eyes. If there was balance to be found in the universe, Ah Cheong would locate the chest and get it to Addie. Just days earlier Wing had met with Ah Cheong and asked him to order yellow silk, and though it wouldn't be a dress, he imagined Addie unwrapping a brown paper package tied with string, the chrysalis for a bolt of shining cloth.

And then there was her unborn child. It would not be easy, this life she was about to live, and he was sorry he wouldn't be there to see her through it. It was impossible to think of Muuk being a father to the child. Perhaps she and Wing would meet in some other life under better circumstances. He closed his eyes to the rushing heat and pictured Addie once again, Addie standing tall and resolute somewhere beyond Wyoming. And if she needed and their child needed, there were the contents of the chest. She would feel him at her side. He would be her shield after all.

When the fire started snatching at his flesh, Wing screamed in pain, swore to himself he would scream even louder until his last tortured breath, so that the sound of a man burning alive would haunt the dreams of everyone who heard it.

After she was shot, they'd taken Addie to Green River, then all the way to Evanston. It had been nearly two weeks of recovery. She hadn't intended on staying in Evanston a moment longer, and she told the doctor just that, but then the bleeding started, and he explained to her that in short order she'd have cramps and considerable pain. It wasn't something to take lightly. She agreed to one more day, and then she was going to get on the train to Rock Springs to find Wing, to get him away from Wyoming, away from Muuk. She was thinking more and more about California, only south, where she heard the weather was warmer. He could have his orange groves there, perhaps. And if she couldn't find Wing in Rock Springs . . . She discarded the thought, recognized the urgent feeling inside her, that same ache of not being able to help Tommy, and she wouldn't let it happen again. She would find Wing and take him away.

It was a decision she understood would upend her life. There were few Maye Groods, folks that would even try to understand. Even Maye had suggested Addie might go to hell. But Addie gritted her teeth against the possibility, because she was never surer in her life about what was right. It wasn't *Run* she heard now, it was *Rescue*.

The doctor was right. The next day it was as if an invisible hand was strangling her insides, letting go, then having at it again. All the while they were rolling her over to place fresh linens beneath her and between her legs. She didn't have to ask, and she wasn't told. The baby was gone, going. It had happened to her mother twice, once in the dead of winter during an ice storm. All night her mother moaned in bed, and outside the trees sounded as if they were exploding as huge limbs cracked off under the weight of ice. Each time, she queried her father's face as if to ask if he thought the next branch or an entire tree might come down on the cabin. But his face was not available to Addie. He was fully focused on her mother, a display of care she rarely saw and wouldn't see again.

The only face available to Addie now was the black-vested doctor, a dark-haired man, gray at the temples, with skin so white Addie doubted if he even crossed the street in daylight. He held his hands behind his back and leaned slightly forward, which gave him the odd angle of a woodpecker. He had a teacherly look, she thought, held his mouth open like there was a lesson at the tip of his tongue, and he smelled like saddle soap. At that moment he was either about to console her, or run through the alphabet. "These things," he said, "are quite natural. Still, for a young lady such as yourself, it doesn't give one much repose to hear it, I suppose. There are great mysteries in life that we shall never comprehend. Think of all those young men lost in the war." He paused, bogged down in his own thought. Addie was listening, but had no idea what he was talking about. "So it is, young lady, sometimes God gives us the gift of a child, and no greater gift there is. And sometimes, as you are experiencing, He has other plans. But you shouldn't despair. Imagine our great Creator's benevolent hands reaching into the cradle of your womb, bringing your child gently to his chest and to the comforting thrum of his beating heart, which is the sound of all of time and human experience. We cannot know God's plans, but they are great and good, and that thought lifts us." With that, he stood upright, tilted his head to see if Addie had received the word.

Just then, she wasn't sure what she was supposed to be feeling. The child had only caused worry since she learned she was pregnant. How could she bring it into the world, and where? She tried to imagine God's hands lifting the baby out of her. Maybe the doctor didn't know why, but Addie did. God had done her a favor, and he left behind the pain in her gut as a reminder.

The doctor handed her a newspaper. "I thought you might want to see this, young lady."

It was immediately obvious what he wanted her to read. "Victim of Celestial Savagery Recovering," read the headline. The article itself was more of the same.

> News has reached this paper of another casualty as a result of the riots at Rock Springs. Mrs. Adele Muukkonen is recovering in Evanston from grave wounds received at the site of the riots. It is believed she is the only white injured in the incident. If ever there were cause to send the Celestial devils back to where they came, surely all rational men will agree this is it.

*Mrs. Muukkonen, who resides at the Dire Draw coal camp, was
in Rock Springs for unspecified business when the conflict erupted.
Witnesses say that Mrs. Muukkonen was standing at the edge of Bitter
Creek among the hostile crowd when a shot came from the Chinese
camp and struck her in the abdomen, nearly making a widower of her
husband, Atso Muukkonen, a miner at Dire. Mr. Muukkonen reports
that the couple was expecting their first child. That happy event is,
however, believed to have been concluded by the gunshot.*

*Representatives of the U.P. state that Mrs. Muukkonen is being
cared for at their expense.*

*If there is any justice in this world, the assassin Chinaman
was one of those burned alive in the riot. Certainly no man would
begrudge Mr. Muukkonen a wholesale hatred of the Celestial for the
harm brought to his fair wife and the abridgment of his family.*

Addie stared at the slim column, overcome. They were writing
what they wanted. She touched her abdomen. The child had only
been an idea, really, had not yet announced itself inside her, but
now she felt a distinct absence at her core. She spoke but didn't
bother to look at the doctor. "Do they have a list of the men killed
at Rock Springs?"

"There weren't any men killed," the doctor said, "only some
Chinese."

She knew better than to meet the remark.

"I am surprised your husband is not at your side," the doctor
said.

"I ain't," she managed, at the heel of a cramp. And she wasn't
surprised for more than one reason. It was as if Muuk's own boot
was grinding into her gut, only it wasn't new pain that shot through
her, but an absolute final clarity. Muuk was the one who shot her.

It wasn't right, she knew, but it was a fact, and she'd been brave enough to tell him a few days before the riot direct as she could, everything except who the father was. She had positioned herself between him and the door in case he went to strike her.

"Good," Muuk said at first, which surprised her. Maye told her how a woman gets pregnant, and Muuk had never been with her that way. "The child is mine," he continued. It may have been the most confident sentence she ever heard him utter. They were sitting at the table in the newly roofed house. The added height and space made Muuk seem smaller to Addie. He'd washed his hair, parted it, looked about as fresh as their wedding day, and she noticed he'd gotten a new hat, which rested in front of him like a curled-up cat.

"No, Muuk," Addie said. "It isn't." She was looking directly into the same blue eyes she'd first seen when Tommy introduced him, the last eyes she saw before she ran into the mine to save her brother. Only now, with his face wiped clean of coal dust, they shone in a different way. Maybe she was seeing it wrong, but there was a calmness to them that led the rest of his expression. He seemed oddly relieved. She began again, but he raised a thick-knuckled finger.

"No, Miss Addie," he said. "This child *is* mine." He stood, placed the hat on his head, and left. It was not the conversation she imagined, but it gave her time to think about what she was going to do. The first thing was to get Wing out of Dire, though she wasn't sorry for anything. There had been that day on the sand dune, then again, and a final time that was simply a kiss followed by laughter. What were they doing? They understood it simultaneously. They were friends who talked and gutted game, closer than this other thing that brought them both a sense of freedom but seemed less. It wasn't love between Addie and Wing, could not be in any case, but it was something akin and just as important.

If there was going to be any comeuppance, she didn't want him to be part of it. A white man might only get a thrashing and be run out of town for carrying on with another man's wife. There was no telling what might happen to a Chinaman who did the same thing. Ah Joe was amenable to finding work for Wing in Rock Springs, did not ask questions except for who would pay his fee.

Then Addie understood what made Muuk content with her condition, as she received congratulations from everyone in Dire. Her husband was spreading the word that he was going to be a father. Addie's child would be proof of the thing he did not do with her. She assumed Muuk would suspect Wing, but what was she thinking? What white man could bring himself to believe a white woman, his wife, would be with a Chinaman? And that is where she knew she'd made a crucial mistake. She sent Wing away, an absence Muuk took notice of after several days. "Who?" he'd said, storming into the room on a day he should have been in the mine. Addie wheeled around, surprised. "The Chinaman?" He'd brought his voice down.

She was frightened but knew better than to get small, so she straightened her spine and said, simply, "Yes. But he's gone now, and I will be too."

Muuk looked surprised at the second piece of news. "You cannot be with him." He was dark as a bear, standing in front of her, had brought the sulfurish odor of the mine in with him.

"Maybe not," Addie said. "But I can't be with you either."

Before she knew it, Muuk sent a chair flying into the pitched ceiling, opening a stream of light filled with dust. He had not thrown the chair at Addie, but it was close enough that she burst by him and out the door. After that were the days of brooding silence leading up to the massacre, when he shot her. So what did she need now, then? Before she took Wing away and headed west with him, she had to stare into Muuk's eyes and tell him how her unborn child had been murdered, force him to say he'd done it. The law would let him alone, it was clear, but it wouldn't look the other way if she took her own revenge. Addie understood she'd know no peace until she stood her ground with Muuk toe to toe and heard the words.

Ah Joe brought the news. It had been three days since the cramping began, but now the pain was subsiding. "Miss Addie," he said, standing above her bed, "as you have witnessed, there has been a great deal of trouble in Rock Springs." He was somber, dressed in his usual suit, and looked tired. In his hands he held a dark wooden tea-kettle-size chest with a latch and hinges of black metal. "I am here against the wishes of the Railroad. There are many Chinese dead, and it is not generally safe for me. But the Seventh Infantry has arrived, and now I take my chances coming here." He extended the box, and she accepted it, the surprising weight collapsing toward her like a found child.

"This was Wing Lee's. He directed you should have it."

Addie's heart lunged, and she was short of breath. Ah Joe hadn't said it. He didn't have to. She was stunned enough that tears would not come. She couldn't even bring herself to ask how Wing had died, but she knew it was her fault. If he hadn't gotten mixed up with her, he wouldn't have been in Rock Springs. How could she have been so foolish to think this place would allow even a friendship between them? It wasn't the way of things here. Wasn't the way of things anywhere she could think of. The wood chest sat in her lap, still and quiet as a stone. It smelled slightly of smoke, and now Addie noticed Chinese writing carved into the bowed lid. "What's this say?" she said, pointing.

Ah Joe's eyes moved to the chest, though his head remained entirely motionless. "Wing Lee."

Beneath her fingers Wing's name brought to mind late autumn trees with leafless limbs. She did not want to look in the box, because if she kept it closed, there would always be one more thing to expect from Wing, like a new conversation to be had. She looked at Ah Joe. "I won't see him again, will I?"

He wiped his brow with a handkerchief and confirmed what she already knew. "Miss Addie, he was one of those killed."

Yes, she'd known it, but to hear it out loud struck her. Now her vision felt tunneled, black except for Ah Joe's face. She'd known this feeling all too recently, but it would not be like losing Tommy, because Wing had given her a play to say good-bye to her brother. There would be no plays performed on Wing's behalf, she knew. Death was taking away everyone she loved, it seemed, as if her life was a stick for whittling. "How did he go?"

"This is not something to discuss."

"Tell me, Ah Joe."

His face was grim, but after a breath he spoke. "It is not proper to describe the death of any one man," he said. Then he told her some things she knew, some things she witnessed. The lucky men had merely been chased and shot in the first wave of the mob attack. In the second wave, the mob had run out of targets. There was the old Chinese launderer who barricaded himself in his shack, and when the crowd couldn't get to him, they broke through his roof and shot him in the back of the head. They did the same to Chinatown too, setting fire to everything. The chest Addie held in her lap had been buried. It was the only thing of Wing's that hadn't been incinerated. Ah Joe took a deep breath and exhaled slowly. He explained that because Wing had originally been one of his men in Dire, they asked him to send the box to his relatives in China.

"Then why didn't you?"

"When he left Dire Draw, Miss Addie, he told me about this chest and said that it was to be given to you if harm came to him. They found it buried."

She didn't think she deserved it, this final gesture of kindness from Wing. But then, too, it was all Addie had left of him.

"It is complete," Ah Joe said, pointing to the box.

She reminded herself to breathe. "Wing was burned alive?"

"Miss Addie . . ." He looked at her sadly. "Yes." The silence that followed became a physical thing, something dark and still as a lake at midnight, its depths folding around her. It had been for different reasons, but her brother had warned about her hiring Wing. But she'd gone ahead, ignored the plain truth that announced itself the moment she arrived in Wyoming. She could beat back any trouble, she had convinced herself. And now what? The fire that killed Wing was started the day she hired him. She'd struck that match herself.

Wing was dead, his child too, and she was responsible. She'd hoped to get him away, and now, her plan defeated, she tried not to think of Muuk. She'd wanted the peace of mind of telling him to his face he'd failed. But now what was left except giving him the satisfaction of her misery? No, she would go herself, leave Muuk and the Territory behind. When she tried to think otherwise, and imagined Muuk's smug grin, it made her ill. She'd regret for the rest of her life not having a final word, most likely, but perhaps that was her punishment for thinking she could make everything work in a place that did nothing but give signs to the contrary. One thing was for sure: she was defeated, reduced.

Her hands trembled, caressed the small chest resting on her lap. She couldn't guess what mementos he'd saved important enough to keep for her. Perhaps it was the chest itself. Addie flipped the latch, finding its lid snug but movable. "Oh, Wing," she whispered. "Wing." She was alone.

Racing ahead in the Maibohm, Buckley looked glad to be rid of Addie for a while, she thought. The train engine was loud, the men busy, so there wasn't much talking. Aulis's partner clearly wasn't happy with Addie's presence, kept his head low and back bent to the shovel. She didn't mind. She'd boarded for the ride up to Dire and, after all these years, to prove Emrys Clough wrong. When her brother first brought her to Dire, Clough had suggested the impossibility of what she was now doing, though he was right in one respect. Maybe it was 1927, but there was a woman on a UP train to Dire over Clive Orner's dead body.

The sensation of heading upslope in the draw caught Addie off guard. The last time she'd been here she was on horseback, headed in the opposite direction and running, as it turned out, toward a bullet that drew her down near death. She felt Aulis tap her elbow as he pointed up the hill. They'd passed the white church and come even with Muuk's shack, the worn path leading to it looking thin and useless as a collapsed vein. Addie shook her head. He was living in the old way, it looked like, in a half house, half cave. And why down here, where the town had disintegrated? It certainly couldn't be the church he wanted to be close to.

The ride was brief, maybe ten minutes total, but Addie was satisfied as they pulled through New Dire and beneath the tipple labeled No. 6. It was a young town of shiny plate-glass windows with paved streets, though she recognized that same dense smell of mining. Buckley and the Maibohm had gathered a sooty-looking crowd, but they weren't half the attraction of Addie when she climbed out of the locomotive. None of the faces were familiar to her, but in a general sort of way, she knew each coal-stained expression. Some things don't change, she thought. She scanned the crowd. No sign of Muuk. They'd likely invited him to the luncheon.

"This is Miss Addie," Aulis called from the train's cab. Eyes widened. Caps came off. In Los Angeles, she grew oranges. She hadn't thought that in coming back, she was also reviving her old self, the Addie that lived among men like these, held her own and then some. She was one of them, even scrubbed clean. She thanked Aulis, shook his hand, and walked through the gathered crowd. There were two things on her mind, Ah Cheong's luncheon and settling things with Muuk. As a young woman, she'd run from him, let him off the hook. Now, she'd make him say he'd done it.

These forty years since they first met, Addie had a favor to ask of Ah Cheong. The room smelled of cigars and overcooked chicken. Addie didn't recognize most of the faces when she stepped into the restaurant. Certainly Muuk wasn't there, and if they were hiding him away as some sort of surprise, they'd get a surprise of their own when she called him out in front of the entire luncheon. In the back, a boy sat next to a Victrola whining a song she didn't recognize. It was 1927, but there was a time not too long before without radio or music on records, and it seemed to Addie as if people had forgotten what the world sounded like when it was left on its own.

Two long tables stood side by side, each readied for what passed for a formal luncheon in New Dire: celery stalks standing on end in water glasses; two spoons, two knives, and a fork for each setting. On the left were men in Sunday suits and high-collared shirts, the women in avian-inspired hats, each diner with skin as puffy and gray as oyster meat. Some of these she thought she knew from younger days, and she nodded as they stood in recognition. The room was full, but felt empty at the same time. On the right was a table of Chinese, too young for Addie to have known, all but one— the elderly man at the head of the table who was now standing as straight as he could, Ah Cheong.

It had been over forty years since they last saw each other, but there was no mistaking him. Addie approached her old friend, who was slightly bent and wearing a suit a size too big for him. She felt the eyes of the room on her as she extended a hand. "Miss Addie," he said, wrapping both his hands around hers. His grip was strong and warm, as if this elderly man in front of her was merely a costume worn by the younger man she once knew. He gestured to the seat nearest his, shooing a Chinese boy from his place.

When she sat, those who had stood when she entered took their seats as well, and a general whispering ear-to-ear began as those unfamiliar with Addie were filled in. But her interest was solely in Ah Cheong. He'd been the only man other than Wing who knew about them, and he cared.

"You're really going back to China after all these years?" she began.

Ah Cheong was expressionless, but he nodded. "It has been too long."

"So you have family there?" Though the table was full of Chinese faces, Addie supposed none of them were related to him.

"My brother's children. I will live with them." Ah Cheong placed his palms on the table and looked directly at Addie with a little sadness. "But dead are my mother, father, sister, and other brother." He paused, then put his hand on Addie's shoulder. "And Wing."

Addie leaned in toward Ah Cheong and smiled softly, surprised at how good it was to hear Wing's name out loud; even she had not spoken it in decades, and now it felt as if he'd been called back to them in just one syllable. The room blossomed into loud conversation. Soon, Addie expected, men on the other side of the room whom she recognized would come over and talk to her. They would not sit, but they were old horses from a dwindling herd, and she was one of them, so they would come with little to say but with too much time to say it. She needed to finish her business with Ah Cheong.

"Old friend," Addie said, "I have something for you to take back to China with you." She reached into her pocket and felt the locket Wing gave her. Between her fingers it had its own warmth. She held it out to Ah Cheong, a simple unadorned brass oval that she placed in his palm, so deeply crisscrossed with lines it looked like a road map. He cupped it as Addie gently and briefly revealed its contents, a simple lock of black hair. Ah Cheong nodded. "I want you to take Wing home with you. Bury this someplace special." As she said this, she understood she was also sending part of herself, that girl, that Addie from long ago. But Wing had walked with her in the orange groves long enough. Now he belonged in China.

Ah Cheong shook his head. "You should keep it," he said, though he did not resist when Addie curled his fingers over the locket until he held it into a fist. He called to the young boy he'd shooed from the seat Addie now occupied. As Ah Cheong whispered into his ear, the boy looked confused, until finally a smile worked across his face, a smile that looked like a miniature piano keyboard. When Ah Cheong finished, the boy looked at Addie directly, pinching his shoulders up to his ears, pleased he was in on some sort of secret, and then ran out of the restaurant. Ah Cheong had a smile of his own.

"I want to ask you about Muuk," Addie said. "Why isn't he here?"

"No good," Ah Cheong said. "I think he is no good." Addie didn't understand, and he clarified. "Not well," he said, emphasizing the last word.

"Guess I'll have to go to him."

Ah Cheong shook his head. "Maybe this not a good idea. Muuk is bad now."

"You mean not well?"

"Bad," Ah Cheong said, waving his hands as if there wasn't a more appropriate word. She didn't press the issue, since it wasn't about to keep her away.

Across the room at the other table, the faces were so similar to Addie's. Had she stayed in Wyoming, had Wing lived to get such a send-off, at which table would she be expected to sit, white or Chinese? Would they enter the room together, Wing veering right and she veering left? Had their child lived, would it have been stranded in the middle in the glare of the electric chandelier, a light that reminded her of the insistent noonday in California, the sun above her citrus groves, trees that needed nurturing like children and responded with their vocabulary of fruit?

A man at the other table whom she did not recognize tapped his water glass with a spoon and stood to give a toast. Addie had come to say good-bye to her friend, and to hand him the locket. She had no interest in reconnecting, really, with any of those other solemn gray faces she vaguely recognized. As the man spoke, Addie looked at Ah Cheong, who seemed ambivalent about the attention. When the toast was over, Addie kissed Ah Cheong on the cheek. "Thank you," she said, and then, recalling a phrase Wing once taught her, she offered her clumsy attempt. Ah Cheong smiled and raised a finger, repeating the phrase. "Yes," he said, "yutgo yee yuen hy ngau." One language is never enough.

After the various and brief speeches praising Ah Cheong's years of service, Addie applauded along with the rest of the room. At the end Ah Cheong did not smile but stood, giving appreciative nods, then raised a single hand toward the crowd, as if he were a saint about to bless them. "Thank you," he began. "Too many years, but not too many friends." He turned. "Like Miss Addie. A friend to all Chinese."

Addie was not one to blush, but when the eyes of the room turned in her direction she felt awkward. It was, after all, Ah Cheong's occasion. He spoke for just a few minutes more, and when he was done, he asked Addie to speak.

At first she declined, but the gathered tapped their glasses with tableware until she stood, not knowing what she would say. What was the use of telling them some of her wounds had never healed even after forty years? And really, mainly it had been the rioters down in Rock Springs who had upended her life. "There's only a few of us left," she began, "remember what it was like back in those days when we rode horses instead of cars. When from day to day it wasn't a sure thing if you would get a square meal, or make your water last until the next train come in from Green River. You relied on yourself, and if you were lucky, there were some kind folks around you. My brother Tommy was one. Killed in the mine. He was a good man. Maye Grood was one. Died giving birth. She was a good woman. Wing Lee was one. Killed in the riot." She paused, swallowed the emotion she felt rising. "He was the best man." She looked around the room, at the mostly blank expressions. She bit her lip and nodded. They didn't understand. All except Ah Cheong, who was teary-eyed. "I was shot in that riot," she said. "I can only hope it's wore a hole in the heart of the man who done it." She thought to say Muuk's name aloud, shame him right then, but thought better of it; word might get to him that somehow she knew, allow him to tuck himself away until she was gone.

Ah Cheong stood. "And Miss Addie is the best woman."

They hugged, and the applause came fast, sounding to Addie wholly genuine. Most of those clapping didn't live through the troubles of forty years earlier, and she wondered if they grasped that the sight of her and Ah Cheong embracing wasn't at all how it was. It certainly wasn't something she cared to explain, because she knew she'd just be some old fossil rattling off a tale from those good old western days.

When the applause died down and the meal was being served, Addie leaned over to Ah Cheong with a confession. "I'm so happy for you. But I don't feel comfortable staying." She pressed her hands against the table as if to leave, but Ah Cheong grabbed her wrist softly and held up a crooked finger. "Stay until the boy return?" His tone was earnest, and though she thought better of it, she did not go.

Then, what Addie feared realized itself. Those whom she recognized, and some she didn't, approached the table. They wanted to talk about old times. Some wanted to hear what it was like "back then." She had declined the chicken dinner, and so had no distraction to diffuse these queries. What was she to tell them about a time when a couple dozen Chinese were killed, when she herself was shot? She guessed that Ah Cheong understood. "They don't know," he said, shaking his head.

There was a young man, hair black and slick as an olive, who was the last to approach. He wore a button-up gray cotton shirt that had seen better days, but it was clean and tucked into faded jeans of about the same vintage as the shirt. But that perfectly black hair was parted to the left, a razor-sharp white line traveling over his scalp. He extended his hand. "I'm Pal Yurksen," he said, shaking hers. "Wondering, ma'am. Is it true one time you saved some men from a cave-in?"

Addie looked into the young man's face, already too full of worry for someone his age. "I suppose that's true," she said.

"My grandfather died in Number Three. I wish you'd been around then."

Taking the young man's hand, Addie offered a sympathetic smile. "I'm sorry. But I want to tell you one thing I've learned." She gestured toward the room. "I don't know how many of these folks might be kin to you, or friends, but every time you say a kind word to them, every day you show them that you care, well, that's just the same as pulling them from a cave-in."

He looked around the room, then returned to Addie. "Um, thank you," he said, excusing himself. She could tell he was just being polite, but a time would come, she knew, when he'd understand exactly what he meant, though like for most folks it would probably be too late to matter.

The boy reappeared at Ah Cheong's side, handing over a brown envelope. Ah Cheong patted him on the head and took the envelope. "This is for you, Miss Addie."

The envelope lingered between them for a moment before Addie took it. There were no markings on the outside, and it had weight. If it was a letter, there were a number of pages. When Addie opened the flap, she didn't need to remove the contents to know what it was. A thin line of yellow silk peeked from the opening. She took a breath, then looked at Ah Cheong, who smiled in reassurance. Addie gently pulled the cloth from the envelope, perfect and shining as the only other time she'd seen it.

"Wing said he wanted to buy you material. I kept for the day if I see you again."

She remembered when Wing dreamed of an entire silk dress. She never expected to see the swatch again, never really expected a silk dress. She wasn't the kind of woman who wore pretty things, but she loved that Wing saw her that way. "Thank you, Ah Cheong," she said, standing. "You've been a fine friend. Safe journey." As Addie crossed to the entrance, the room grew quiet, and just as she got to the door, a light applause and tapping of glasses began. She could not turn around, she thought. But she paused, placing both hands on either side of the doorjamb, and nodded, facing away from the praise. That would have to do. She and Buckley had another stop to make. It was time to reckon with the man who was still her husband.

"Muuk," Addie called, her voice cracking with anger. The shack was about like she suspected, half built into the hill, the wood so dry she could practically hear it splinter. No answer. "Muuk!" If he was home, maybe he didn't want to answer an unfamiliar voice.

But she didn't see him check from the one cracked window. She'd have to do something she wasn't too anxious to do. At the door, she knocked, pounded, but still no answer, though she thought she heard something stir inside. She went to the window and looked in, felt her fast-beating pulse in her fingertips. At the dim back of the single room, she made out a man on a cot, facing away. He was snoring. On the floor in front of him and distributed across the entire room were opened food cans and empty liquor bottles. When she returned to the door and stepped inside, she caught the sourness of what smelled like long-spoiled fruit, though she knew better.

"Atso," she finally said, thinking maybe nobody called him Muuk anymore. He stirred weakly, managing to face her but saying nothing. His face was thin, not even filled out by his sparse gray beard, his eyes glassy. Addie didn't approach. If he was drunk, she didn't know what he might do when he figured out who she was. Still, he said nothing, just stared blankly. "Don't you recognize me, Atso?"

He raised his head slightly, which seemed all the effort he had inside him. "Kyllä," he said, *Yes.* "You're Venla." Addie was caught off guard. His sister had been dead since he was a boy. Before she could say anything, the explanation became clear. "And Äiti?" Muuk asked.

She recognized the word. He was asking for his mother. "Yes," Addie sighed, "she'll be here soon. She wants you to get clean for dinner." It didn't look to Addie like he was eating regularly, or much at all, as he struggled to sit up. She looked to the empty shelves near the small cookstove, empty except for one can of sardines. Sitting up, head sagging between bony shoulders, Muuk looked skeletal beneath his soiled clothes. The front of his denim shirt was stained with food and drool, the crotch of his pants browned from urine.

He was vulnerable, a remnant, but that didn't mean Addie wasn't going to get the answer she came for. She went to work. At the edge of the small room was a galvanized tub leaning against a table with the bits and pieces of some distant meal, a fork, a darkly caked tin plate, and an overturned ceramic cup. Holding the heavy tub to the light of the door, Addie saw the bottom was sound. "Muuk," she said, then catching herself, "Atso, Äiti wants you to take a bath." Muuk raised his head and nodded, offering an expression indicating he knew he had no choice but to comply with his mother's wishes. Addie set the tub in the middle of the floor, grabbed a tipped-over bucket, and stepped outside to the rain barrel. Muuk had enough water for a bath, and about half again as much. She dipped the bucket into the barrel, pulled it out half full and swished away the dirt, waving for Buckley to join her.

By the time Buckley reached the door, Addie had drawn three buckets of water for Muuk's bath and gotten him down to his filthy long underwear. His toenails were a dingy yellow, long and curled clawlike over his toes. His fingernails weren't much better. Adele caught Buckley's gaze as he stood at the door. Clearly, he didn't understand why she was preparing a bath for this reeking old man who stood between them, half undressed and obviously confused. "He was my husband," Addie said, pouring a fourth and final bucket of water into the tub. "But this is about as far as I care to go. Make sure he gets washed." She spoke as if Muuk couldn't hear her, as if he wasn't even there, and this was because she understood it was mainly the truth.

Buckley removed his hat and stepped into the room cautiously.

Addie's next instructions were direct and decisive. She handed him a knife. "Use a strip off your shirttail for a washcloth, be quick about it, and give him your pants. You can cover yourself with the blanket in the car." Buckley flinched on the last point and shook his head until Addie held up the blackened jeans Muuk had been wearing. She didn't need to say another word.

Keeping her back to Muuk and Buckley as best she could, Addie picked up the cans and bottles off the floor and tossed them outside. Aside from the sardines, there wasn't a speck of food in the shack. Maybe he was getting his meals in town, but she doubted it.

Near Muuk's washbasin she found a cracked soap bud, which she tossed to Buckley. Muuk's back was to her, a washboard with a spine. She shook her head. How does it happen? she wondered. How does a man come to this? Can he feel the disintegration bit by bit, or does he wake up one day and find everything fallen down around him? And then she thought, in Muuk's case he was most of the way toward not knowing the difference.

"This is Buckley," Addie said. "Your mother sent him to get you washed, so you mind him." Muuk didn't reply, but he was compliant, and that was all Addie cared about. She took a seat on one of two stools that comprised the remainder of the room's furniture, keeping Buckley between herself and a view of Muuk until Muuk got down in the tub, which was too small for him. His bony limbs poked upward like cypress knees.

Addie started in with some questions, though she doubted she'd get any results. "Atso, how's your wife?" Again Muuk held silent, not willfully, she could tell. "I thought you had a wife, Atso."

Buckley did his best to motivate Muuk's hands to clean himself, but the memory seemed gone there too. Then Muuk smiled. "Adele," he said, and for a moment Addie thought he recognized her. But no, the version of her he would remember was not in this room, it was behind his eyes, which now, even more than before, located him in some place other than the present.

"Yes, Adele," Addie said. She leaned forward on the stool, elbows on her knees to give him every opportunity to recognize her. "Whatever happened to her?"

"She left," Muuk said sharply. He scrubbed one shoulder with a wet, empty hand. Buckley looked helpless, overdressed for such work, for any work. "Adele left."

"That's not the way I heard it. The way I heard it is that she got shot." There it was, out in the open, and it gave her some relief just to say it directly to Muuk. But what was the utility of the rest of what she came for, his confession? And then it struck her, something she'd never thought of. It wasn't this brand of justice she sought for herself as much as it was for Wing's unborn baby. She had lived and thrived, after all. It was that child whose future was stripped away by the wreck of a man in front of her.

Both Buckley and Muuk were looking directly at Addie now, Buckley with a bit of astonishment at what she'd just said, Muuk with narrowed eyes as if he was trying to bring her into focus. "You know Panu Lankinen?" he asked her.

She'd heard this name before, but couldn't place it. "He the one that shot your wife?"

"Not Panu. He is my friend." At the repetition of this name Muuk drifted away again, stopped washing, his hands falling between his legs, but they weren't motionless.

Buckley stood bolt upright and turned his back to Muuk. "Miss Addie, I think you need to look away."

"Hell, Buckley, what's wrong?" The interruption irritated her.

He stammered an answer. "He's holding his private parts."

"For heaven's sake." Addie pushed Buckley aside and stood above Muuk. "Atso, Atso," she said sternly. "Let me see your hands."

He looked up at her with empty blue eyes, raising his hands out of the water, his erection just breaking the surface. She furrowed her brow and shot Buckley a look to indicate that they needed to go on. "He don't know what he's doing." In Muuk's state, she needed the momentum of what she understood to be a temporary thread of memory. She began again. "Did this Panu Lankinen shoot your wife?"

Muuk looked into the water, shaking his head slowly. "Not Panu," he said. "I did." Around his waist and knees, white lather mourned on the surface of the water as it expired into grayer depths.

There it was, a confession of sorts. A confession from a confused, deteriorating old man who'd taken Addie's unborn child—but, looking at the broken form in front of her, she thought he'd stolen more from his own life. And broken; it's what he called himself one early morning, said he couldn't be fixed. What was it that had done it to him? Something long before she met him had cast the die. He'd been her husband, but she'd never really known him. He hadn't wanted to be known. He was a dark form that slipped in and out of her days, and here in front of her, that darkness stripped away like a cloak revealed the human wreckage brought on by what she'd never know.

"Is that it?" Buckley asked.

She wanted to laugh, because it was what she was thinking herself. Her entire body trembled as if it had unmet expectations of its own. Both her arms hung at her sides, but her hands were balled into tight fists. Forty years earlier she'd lain in bed, forced to wonder if it was Muuk who shot her, a question she'd packed away as best she could when she left Wyoming. She'd done too good a job; refreshed just days earlier, the question was fresh as the first day she'd asked it. She stepped forward so that now the tips of her boots bumped up against the tub and she was looking directly into the crown of Muuk's gray thin head of hair, his scalp pink as a newborn's. Buckley stepped back as she raised a hand. But it was empty of riot, and she brought it down slowly, placed it on Muuk's wet, naked shoulder. "Your bath is over, Atso," she said. His skin was cool, and she sensed nothing but frailty beneath her palm. Whatever anger Addie had brought with her up the hill fell away like sand through a funnel. The oncoming lightness was palpable.

Muuk's ending wasn't something she would wish on any living soul. She couldn't cry for a man who'd done what he did, but she could pity him, this naked little skeleton half living in another time. "I guess you're clean as you'll ever get," she said.

As *the Maibohm approached*, the man stood with fists punched into his waist, a red handkerchief fluttering from one hand. He was short and round, his leather suspenders digging into the flesh of his shoulders beneath a startlingly white shirt. Addie couldn't tell by his impatient expression if he was a man with a big heart, or just a big appetite. But he was the preacher for sure. Behind him, the small church looked like a bright chunk of ice fallen from the sky, bright even so late in the day, tinted blue in its shadowed nooks and crannies. Addie told a pantsless Buckley to wait in the car.

When she introduced herself, the preacher brightened and dabbed his shiny forehead with the handkerchief. "I heard about you in town," he said. "Everyone was talking." He shook her hand and waited.

She told him about Muuk's condition. The preacher shook his

head. "Sad. Been here eleven years now, and I've seen the man . . . could count the times on one hand."

"So I'm wondering, if I leave you with some money and send a bit more later, if maybe somebody in the church can check on him, make sure he gets meals. He's in a bad way."

The preacher looked up the hill toward Muuk's shack. "I don't believe I could make it up there myself. My heart wouldn't take it. But it sounds like God's work, and I'll see that he gets looked after."

A few minutes later Addie was back in the Maibohm with Buckley, speeding out of the darkening draw. On the plain ahead the last of the setting sun threw its light nearly parallel to the land, every rock and bush streaming with shadow. The turn onto the highway toward Rock Springs headed them west and into what was left of the sun. Addie closed her eyes and felt the light on her face, not warm, really, but present. "You feeling all right, Miss Addie?" Buckley asked. "You going to tell the authorities who shot you?"

She kept her eyes closed. "I'm real fine," she said, as if she hadn't heard the second half of his question. She was thinking of Muuk, not the version they'd cleaned up and looked after. She was thinking of him sitting in that tub with his hands working between his legs. It was a strange thing. On their wedding night he'd been on top of her and said, "I cannot," but today, beneath the murkiness of his bathwater, she saw that he could, even years after everything else about who he was had melted away. He did it while thinking about someone named Panu Lankinen. It was something she couldn't figure. Maybe he was just more far gone than she understood.

"I don't get what happened back there. Don't you want justice, now you know who shot you?"

She shook her head, half wanting to simply remain silent, but she sighed and spoke, her eyes still shut. "Buckley, you didn't meet

the man who shot me. Those were the fingers that pulled the trigger all right, but that wasn't the man."

"Can't imagine letting something like that go."

It was a luxury, what young people assumed now, Addie thought.
"You ever had a real lady friend, Buckley?"

He was caught off guard by the question, stammered a response.
"Once, but she got cold feet and called things off. Didn't make
any sense."

"I'd place a bet it made sense to her," Addie said. And then it
came to her, what her mother had gotten wrong, or maybe what
was true for women now in a way it wasn't back then. There were
choices today. A woman could stand . . . must stand. One thing
remained the same, though. A person can run from her circumstances, she thought, but she can't escape them. Maybe her mother
had loosed herself from a drunkard husband, though Addie was
sure not a day could have gone by when she hadn't wondered what
had become of her children. Certainly it was a rare day when Addie
hadn't wondered about Muuk, hoped his conscience was doing the
work that should have been her own. He'd have heard she'd lost
Wing's baby, but she'd chosen to run rather than face him. How
long ago that seemed.

When she opened her eyes, the sun had vanished behind a yellowish blue band of light sweeping across the horizon. In a week,
Therese, Addie's young housekeeper, would greet her at the door
in California, and the comfortable working life Addie had built
would resume. "One last stop," she said to Buckley now. "Pull over
anywhere." She had one foot out of the car before it came to a
complete stop.

"Where are you headed, Miss Addie?" Buckley asked, sounding
exasperated.

It was a question she'd been asked more than once in her life, and just at that moment she felt as if she were coming close to an answer. She left Buckley in the Maibohm without a word and walked into the brush, feeling a raspy caress at her legs. She thought of that first evening on the plain with her brother in a twilight glow nearly like this. The failing light back then filled the landscape with suddenly ambiguous forms, and Tommy told her a story about the afterlife. It wasn't heaven, exactly, but maybe something better, she recalled. When a person crossed over, everyone you ever loved and who ever loved you was waiting. It's a comforting idea, she thought, if only because people leave this world so abruptly. One minute they're here, the next minute a person's left with all the things she wished she'd said. It's a powerful, empty feeling.

Once again, the clumps of sage stood in front of her like the friendly mob of her brother's story. She saw their faces. When it was her time, Tommy would be first in line for sure, her grandmother and parents. "I understand," she'd tell her mother. "I ran too." And then there was Wing. The breeze caught her face as she thought of him. No regrets clouded the image of his shining black hair and generous smile. When she was young, she thought they had not known each other long enough to call it love, and the world wouldn't have made a place for them anyway. Maybe she was wrong.

In the distance, she picked out the shadowed bushes she could think of as these people who, someday not far off, would cluster around her. It was a destination she could hold in her head when she returned to California. The slender stand of sage she selected for Wing seemed perfect, but took her breath when she looked at the bush more closely. In front of it was a smaller clump of sage that blended almost perfectly into the gray of its taller companion, almost like a child looking up into a parent's face. In her brother's story, was it possible for her to see her unborn child? She was tearing now, and closed her eyes to push it away. But there was Wing in front of her, holding the hands of a child, their child, whose face she could not see, could not imagine. What would it have looked like? She tried hard to see, but only children she'd known in the past came to mind, and a strange new loneliness pricked at her heart. Can't say what we were or might have been, she told herself, but it sure was some kind of something.

There was already one bright star in the dimming sky. She closed her eyes and imagined the Wyoming sky she remembered, that darkness populated with countless diamond pinpricks. The nights were so quiet then, and if she chose to remember only that detail, she could say those were serene times. It wasn't right to try to forget, and how could she? Wing's face came to her again, along with the chittering insects of the plain. He'd assured her once about someday knowing peace. That was a long time ago, and it sure felt like she was getting close.

HISTORICAL NOTE

The riot at Rock Springs on September 2, 1885, was an actual event and was soon followed by similar incidents across the Northwest. A grand jury was convened, and over a dozen white men were arrested for their participation in the massacre of the Chinese in Rock Springs. There were no convictions.

ACKNOWLEDGMENTS

Much gratitude to the University of Louisville, American Heritage Center, Carol Bowers, Dr. Thomas Alvarez, the University of Wyoming, Sweetwater County Museum, Ruth Lauritzen, Wyoming State Archive, Rock Springs Historical Museum, Bob Nelson, Union Pacific Railroad Museum, and my mother—Catherine DiTomaso; Alice Davis, Matthew Brim, Aaron Davis, PJ Mark, Sally Kim, and Brian Yost.

Brian Leung began his writing life in San Diego and Los Angeles. In 2006 he moved to Louisville, Kentucky, where he is an associate professor at the University of Louisville. His fiction, poetry, and creative nonfiction have appeared in numerous magazines and journals. *World Famous Love Acts*, a collection of short stories, won the Asian American Literary Award and the Mary McCarthy Award for short fiction. His novel, *Lost Men*, has been translated into French and Italian.